UNICORNS CAN BE DEADLY

A DISCOUNT DETECTIVE MYSTERY

UNICORNS CAN BE DEADLY

A DISCOUNT DETECTIVE MYSTERY

CHARLOTTE STUART

Walrus Publishing | Harrisonville, MO 64701

Walrus Publishing | Harrisonville, MO 64701
Copyright © 2024 Charlotte Stuart
All rights reserved.

For information, contact:
Walrus Publishing
An imprint of Amphorae Publishing Group
a woman- and veteran-owned business
amphoraepublishing.com

Publisher's Note: This is a work of fiction. Any real people or places are used in a purely fictional manner.

Manufactured in the United States of America
Set in Adobe Caslon Pro and Avenir
Interior designed by Kristina Blank Makansi
Cover designed by Kristina Blank Makansi
Cover image: Shutterstock

Library of Congress Control Number: 2024938690
ISBN: 9781940442518

To all those who struggle with the seemingly intractable problem of homelessness.

THE DISCOUNT DETECTIVE SERIES INCLUDES

Survival Can Be Deadly
Shopping Can Be Deadly
Campaigning Can Be Deadly
Moonlight Can Be Deadly
Unicorns Can Be Deadly

MAIN CAST OF CHARACTERS

Penny-wise Investigations: Discount Detective Agency

- **Cameron Chandler**: single mom and investigator who isn't afraid to make snap decisions
- **Yuri Webster**: obsessed with trivia and doing the right thing
- **P.W. Griffin**: owns Penny-wise; startling white hair, suspicious connections, and a secret past
- **W. Blaine Watkins**: agency's invaluable, blue-eyed Man Friday
- **Norm**: average in every way with the exception of his outstanding investigative skills
- **Grant**: with the agency since the beginning; dependable and calm
- **Will**: wears trench coat; always willing to help out
- **Adele**: the go-to research expert for the team
- **Jenny**: farmer and part-time investigator who dresses like a 1960s hippie
- **Penny-wise mascot**: stuffed bear dressed like Sherlock Holmes

Cameron's supportive and close-knit family

- **Stella**: Cameron's live-in mother who watches out for the kids when Cameron is away
- **Mara**: confident teenager entering her freshman year in high school
- **Jason**: Mara's younger brother, obsessed with TikTok and a news junkie
- **No-name**: the family dog, determined to destroy stuffed endangered species

Clients

- **Cole White**: young boy who witnesses a crime and becomes a target of some very bad guys
- **Councilwoman Amanda Smythe**: concerned with homeless issues; has a homeless cousin who has disappeared
- **Broderick Kendall**: had an affair that resulted in an unwanted child that goes missing
- **Elinor Easton**: has homeless sister who is missing

Homeless People Related to Clients

- **Bess**: woman kidnapped from her tent; Elinor's twin sister
- **Luke**: cousin of councilwoman who doesn't always take his meds to control his schizophrenia; family has given up on him
- **Siana**: drug-addicted woman living in her car with her three-month-old baby

Major Crimes

- **Detective Connolly**: Detective who shows concern for Cameron's welfare while offering information and support for their investigations

Miscellaneous Characters

- **Gary Miles**: Mysterious and charming "consultant" with questionable skills
- **Elliot Walsh**: Doctor who treats the homeless and writes about drug addiction and depression

"We know only too well that what we are doing is no more than a drop in the ocean. But if that drop were not there, the ocean would be missing something."

—Mother Teresa

CHAPTER 1
OCCUPIED

THE BOY WAS RACING toward me down the narrow hallway in the shopping mall like he was being chased by demons, face flushed, arms pumping like frantic windmills. On impulse, I grabbed him by the arm, pulling him into the women's restroom with me. As the door closed behind us, I looked him in the eyes and asked: "Is someone after you?"

He stared at me, eyes wide, as if he couldn't believe what was happening.

We both turned toward the sound of heavy pounding of footsteps running in our direction. I dragged the boy into one of the stalls and said: "Get in. Stand on the toilet seat."

"What?" Confusion and fear fought for control of his facial expression.

"Now," I whispered, pushing him into the cubicle toward the open toilet. "Hurry," I said. "Climb up; get your feet out of sight." As soon as he did, I crowded in ahead of him and shut the door. "Stay quiet," I said.

Together we waited, him crouched on the toilet seat with me standing in front facing the stall door. I could sense he was trying hard to control his breathing. I wasn't feeling all that calm either, but it was too late to call for help. If my bluff didn't work, I wasn't certain what I would do.

It wasn't long before we heard the door to the restroom slammed open and several sets of footsteps rush into the outer area. "Check the toilets," a harsh, male voice said. "Quickly."

Moments later, someone rattled the handle of "our" stall, and I said, rather loudly in my distinctly female voice: "This stall is occupied."

There was no apology, but I heard steps moving away. Not long afterwards, there was the whoosh of the restroom door as it closed, and then … silence.

"Can I get down?" the boy murmured.

"Wait a minute."

I stood there for what seemed like forever, straining my ears for sounds of someone lingering near the toilets, waiting to attack. When I was fairly certain we were alone, I opened the stall door a crack and peeked out. Still being cautious, I quietly stepped out and bent over to look under the doors on the other stalls before motioning for the boy to get down off the toilet seat. "Stay here while I check the sink area," I said, keeping my voice low.

There was no one waiting in the anteroom with the sinks either, so I waved the boy out of the stall. "You in trouble?" I asked, even though it was obvious that he was.

For the first time I took a good look at him. He badly needed a haircut, his blond hair hung in clumps almost to his shoulders, and his rumpled clothes looked like they hadn't been washed in a while. I put his age as about that of my son, thirteen give or take. There was also a musty aroma unrelated to typical bathroom odors that I suspected were part of his aura. When he didn't respond, I asked, "Who were those men?"

"Thanks for your help," he said. He squared his shoulders and took a deep breath. "I'd better get going." He tried to move past me, but I held my ground.

"Who are they?" I repeated in my "tell me or else" voice. I sincerely hoped I hadn't helped him escape from the police.

He made another attempt to get me to move aside, but when it became clear that I wasn't about to budge, he caved, but only to tell me something I'd already guessed. "Bad guys. Really bad guys. Now let me go, okay? This isn't your problem." I took out my phone and started punching in a number.

"No, please, don't call the police," he pleaded, his eyes tearing slightly. "Please."

"Don't worry. I'm calling a colleague ..." Yuri answered on the second ring. "Yuri, I have a situation. I'm in the women's restroom across from Penny-wise with a young man who I think needs our help."

Yuri is not only a good investigator, he's great in an emergency. He didn't question what I was doing in the women's room with a young male but said, "I'll be right there."

"Come prepared and bring a jacket and a baseball cap," I said quickly before he hung up. "Come prepared" was my way of saying "bring a weapon," a slight variation on the Boy Scout motto for maintaining a state of readiness.

The boy was looking at me, obviously uncertain about what was happening and what he should do.

"I'm a private investigator," I explained. "Our office is on the other side of the mall across from here. Yuri is one of my colleagues. You'll be safe with us. We'll escort you to our office. Then you can tell me what this is about, and we'll help you figure out what to do next. Okay?"

I could see him struggling with whether to trust me.

"I can't force you to come with us, but given what just happened, it might be a good idea if you stayed out of sight for a while."

"How do I know you won't call the police?" In that moment he seemed very young and very scared. Under the layer of grime and mop of hair, he was a good-looking kid with brown expressive eyes and a dimple in his chin.

"Because I'm telling you we won't. If you've committed a crime, we may advise you to turn yourself in, but we aren't law enforcement."

"Cameron?" Yuri called from the doorway.

"Let's go," I said. I moved toward the entrance, half expecting the boy to take off the minute we were outside, but he didn't.

"I'm Yuri," Yuri said to the boy. Even though Yuri is my age, there's something youthful and reassuring about his demeanor. With his unruly black hair hanging low over his forehead, almost touching his thick black glasses, he's the geeky kid from high school all grown up.

"Cole," the boy automatically responded, then immediately looked like he wished he hadn't. Yuri held out the jacket and baseball cap I'd asked him to bring. Cole hesitated a few seconds before accepting them. The jacket was too big for his slight frame, but it made him look less disheveled. Yuri reached over and tucked the boy's hair into the hat.

"There are at least two men after him," I said to Yuri. "Keep your eyes out."

"Stay between us, Cole, okay?" Yuri said. "And if you see them, don't stare, just let us know. Got that?"

Cole nodded.

"Act like we're a family on a shopping trip," I said as we came out into the main concourse. "Smile. Look like you're having fun."

It was instantly clear that Cole was too afraid to be able to smile. "Pout, then," I said. "Like you'd rather be anyplace than here with us. That's what my kids would probably be doing."

Cole nodded. His expression didn't change.

The walk across the open square wasn't long, but time has a way of stretching out when you anticipate something bad could happen at any moment. Although I doubted anyone would attack us in front of so many witnesses, you couldn't count on it. Bad guys are often unpredictable. I didn't doubt for a moment that the two men after Cole were bad guys.

As we approached the office, I saw Cole peek at the display window with our Sherlock Holmes bear mascot in it. Under the circumstances, I wasn't sure if a frightened young boy would find it particularly reassuring to be protected by two investigators from an agency with a teddy bear next to a flier that said: "For the man or woman who has everything—give them the gift of vigilance. Special rates for gift certificate detection services." Whatever he thought of the toy sleuth and the flier, he stayed with us, and a few uneventful minutes later we entered the office of Penny-wise Investigations.

Blake, our agency's indispensable Man Friday and well-dressed receptionist, made a conscious effort not to stare as we walked through the waiting area, but I saw his nose quiver as he assessed the situation.

"We'll be in the conference room," I said. That was code for "ask questions later."

"I'll let PW know," he replied. That was code for "in case there's trouble." Blake is not only extremely competent but very intuitive.

Our boss P.W. Griffin has her own office, but all of the investigators share a large open space filled with standard office cubicles surrounded by what look like hand-me-downs from a 19th Century gentlemen's club. There are several floor-to-ceiling wood bookshelves, a couple of long oak tables, a dark brown leather couch with brass studs, and an assortment of overstuffed chairs. There are also the requisite battered filing cabinets as well as a kitchenette of sorts along one wall. The kitchen amenities include a sink, a coffee maker, a microwave, and a small refrigerator. We affectionately call the room the "pit," mainly because it's four steps down from the main reception area, but also because of the clutter.

Yuri's desk is a disaster, and mine could use some straightening, but the five other employees tend to be fairly neat. Today, two of the regulars—Will and Norm—were out in the field. Our bookkeeper works from home. Only Adele, Jenny, and Grant were at their desks. Adele is our incredible research specialist, Jenny is a parttime employee who works when she needs money to supplement her farm income and support her daughter and an assortment of animals, and Grant is our most experienced investigator. They looked up, quickly assessed the situation and simply nodded hello as we walked past.

"Would you like something to drink?" Yuri asked Cole. "We have Sprite, Coke or water in the fridge."

Cole's lips quivered. "Please," he said. "I'd love a Coke."

Yuri left us while I ushered Cole into the larger of our two conference rooms. There's a long table with four fairly comfortable black mesh office chairs in the middle of the room and six fold-up chairs stacked against the far wall. Nothing fancy, but the room is soundproofed for privacy and adequate for most of our needs.

"You're a real detective?" Cole asked as he took a seat.

"A licensed P.I.," I said.

"And you have kids?"

"Two, Mara and Jason. I think Jason is about your age."

Yuri joined us with a Coke for Cole and a half-full box of donuts. "Sorry, I don't have anything nutritious to offer." He raised his eyebrows at me to make sure it was okay if he let the kid have donuts and Coke.

"I have a protein bar in my desk, if you'd rather have that," I said to Cole who was hungrily eyeing the donuts.

"It's probably vintage," Yuri said. "She just pretends to eat healthy; always snags one or more of my donuts."

"Let's all have a donut," I said, trying to put Cole at ease. "You take your pick first; you're our guest."

He carefully considered the donuts, finally deciding on the largest, an apple fritter. Good, I thought, he will get a little fruit, albeit slathered in caramelized sugar and additives, healthy in name only, but what it lacked in nutrition it made up for in bulk. I took a glazed twist, and Yuri grabbed a chocolate sprinkle cake donut. Then we waited until Cole took a swig of Coke and several bites of fritter before asking him anything.

"Is there someone you want us to call?" I said.

He looked panicked. "No, please. No one," he mumbled with a full mouth. I gave him time to swallow before continuing.

"Let me tell you a little about our agency while you finish your fritter. Then let's talk about why those two men were chasing you and how we might be able to help, okay?"

"I don't need a detective," he said before taking another huge bite.

"But with two guys after you, you may need a friend," Yuri said.

"And we've dealt with our share of bad guys before," I added. I didn't want to sound patronizing, but we couldn't let him walk away without trying to find out what kind of a trouble he was in and seeing if there was anything we could do. He was, after all, just a kid. And there were at least two grown men after him for reasons I suspected weren't on the up-and-up.

"That's part of our job," Yuri said.

Before he could insist he didn't need a detective again, I started talking about our services. "As I mentioned, our agency is called Penny-wise Investigations. Our sign out front lists the kinds of jobs we do: accident investigation, recovery assistance, evidence gathering, domestic and other surveillance, missing persons, background reports, industrial investigation, investigative due diligence, child custody, photography, courier service, and private matters." I'd memorized the list when I first started working at Penny-wise. "Basically, we provide any services an ordinary person might need at prices they can afford."

My elevator speech of services was part of my usual spiel to prospective clients, but I knew he wasn't listening.

His need was more immediate. He'd devoured his fritter and was obviously more focused on the remaining donuts than on what I was saying. "Give the pastry a minute to settle. We can order some sandwiches for lunch if you'd like." I felt guilty using the promise of food as bait, but I didn't want him to run off, and we had no right to stop him if he did.

"Tell us about the guys who are after you," Yuri said.

Cole turned his attention to Yuri. For a moment, I thought he wasn't going to respond. Then, seemingly reluctant but resigned, he said, "They think I saw something I shouldn't have."

"And did you?" I asked.

Cole looked down. "Maybe."

"Was it something illegal?" I asked.

Cole was quiet for a long time. When he finally looked up, he was crying. "They hurt her."

"Who did they hurt?"

"We call her Bess."

"We?" I prompted.

"The people in the camp."

"You live in a camp?"

He nodded.

"Do you live with anyone?" I asked. I'd already guessed he might be homeless, but was now starting to get the bigger picture.

He shook his head no.

Yuri jumped in. "Do you live in a nearby camp?"

"No. I took the light rail here. I thought they would give up after I got away."

"But they managed to track you here," I said. "What do you think they will do to you if they catch you?"

"Beat me up." There was no hesitation.

"Do these men live in the same camp as you do?"

"No. I'm not sure, but I think I've seen them selling drugs in one of the other camps."

We waited.

"They kidnapped Bess."

"And that's what you saw?"

"She didn't want to go with them, but they hit her and tied her up. They thought there was no one around, but I'd been sleeping behind a shed next to her tent, and I woke up when I heard her trying to get away." The tears raced down his cheeks and his voice dropped to a raspy whisper. "I wanted to help."

"But there were two of them. Two adult males." Yuri's comment was intended to console, but it didn't seem to have much impact. Cole's tears continued to flow.

"I ran away. I should have tried to get help, but I ran away." His shoulders shook as he swiped at the tears with the back of his hand. "I thought I'd lost them, but they must have seen me get on the light rail. I waited five stops before getting off at Pioneer Square. When I saw one of the guys waiting at the entrance, I panicked. They must have guessed I'd head for a place with lots of homeless people. I wasn't sure if he saw me or not, but I raced down the stairs and managed to get on a car that was just leaving. I don't know how they figured out where I finally got off. I thought I'd lost them … then, there they were."

Yuri and I exchanged looks. We've been working together since I started at Penny-wise, and we've found that we usually respond similarly to people and their problems. Although he's a bit wacky at times and more of a risk taker than I am. As a single mom, I have to take fewer chances. But I knew without asking what Yuri was thinking, and I agreed.

"Okay," I said, "here's the deal, Cole. You can come home with me for a day or two, until we get this sorted out. My daughter is a good cook, and my son has lots of video games—if you're into that sort of thing. Meanwhile, Yuri and I will see what we can find out about Bess. How does that sound?"

Cole was thinking about my offer when Blake poked his head in. "P.W. wants to see the two of you in her office right away."

CHAPTER 2
GREEN LIGHT

WITHIN SECONDS after Blake exited, Jenny appeared in the doorway. "P.W. asked me to sit with your client while you're meeting with her," she said to us as she went over and extended her hand to Cole. "Hi, I'm Jenny."

Cole was looking her up and down as he shook her hand. Jenny is a free spirit and dresses like a throwback from the 60s. I couldn't tell if he approved of her peasant skirt and a homemade patchwork vest over a blousy beige shirt or just found it curious.

Jenny smiled at him and held up one foot with its high top, laced boots. "I always dress like this. I'm a farmer as well as a detective. Ever been on a farm?" She sat down next to Cole. The last thing we heard as we left was him saying "I'm not a client."

P.W.'s door was slightly open. I tapped gently and heard her husky voice say, "Come in." Yuri let me go first, not necessarily a gentlemanly act but more likely one of cowardice. It was very unusual for P.W. to interrupt us when we were talking to someone who might be a client or someone we might be interviewing for some related case. I had no idea what to expect, and I doubted Yuri did either.

It felt like he was putting me out there to test the waters, like a soldier in the trenches holding up a hat on a stick to see if someone shot at it.

My eyes were immediately drawn to the ornate clothes tree in the corner of her office. Hanging from one hook was a red fedora with a single white rose on the rim, a hat you might expect an actress from the 1940s or '50s to wear, a real eye catcher. P.W. was wearing a gray dress with red trim on the sleeves. A red silk scarf was artfully draped around her neck and fastened with a pin in the shape of a white rose. Her stylish outfit may have said "it's a happy day," but her face didn't.

"Blake says you have a young boy in the conference room. A rather scruffy looking young boy." P.W. is a striking woman, her white hair parted in the middle and brushed back from face, her dark eyes capable of seeing your inner thoughts.

"We rescued him from two men who were chasing him in the mall. He may have witnessed a kidnapping."

P.W.'s eyebrows went up. "You think he's in danger?"

"Yes, I do," I said.

"He isn't a paying client," Yuri added. "But I think we have a moral obligation to help him." Yuri could never pass up someone asking for a handout on the street without giving them money, so I wasn't surprised he was speaking up for a homeless kid, even though P.W.'s wary demeanor suggested she might not agree with our assessment of the situation.

"I thought it might be something like that. That's why I called you in here."

For a moment I feared that she was going to tell us to cut him loose and move on to a paying assignment. Business had been a bit slow lately, mainly because of the decline in the number of stores and foot traffic in the mall, although most of our clients came from word of mouth. And, no one had mentioned anything about the agency having financial problems.

"You may not know that I'm on the board of a consortium comprised of nonprofits and developers looking for sustainable ways to provide housing for the homeless." We both shook our heads "no." "My first thought when Blake described your young man was that he might be homeless."

"He is."

"And did this kidnapping take place in a homeless camp?"

"Yes. But we don't have many details yet."

"Find out what happened and follow up as if he were a paying client. Keep me up-to-date."

Yuri and I stood up, but I had one more thing I needed to say. "I know this is a bit unusual, but I'm going to take him home with me for now. It's a safe place for him to stay while we investigate."

After only a brief hesitation, P.W. smiled and said, "Good idea." Then she added, "It's sad to see kids on their own like that. Most adults have some story, some reason why they're living on the streets. Kids don't necessarily choose to be there, at least not in the sense of actually having a realistic choice. So, do whatever you can to help him. Let me know if you need anything."

"Will do," I said.

Blake nodded as we passed by his desk. When he informed P.W. about us bringing Cole in, he probably knew about P.W.'s commitment to helping the homeless.

The rest of us, on the other hand, only know bits and pieces about her current life and next to nothing about her past. We've tried to research her every way we can think of, at times even resorting to spying on her. Still, she remains an enigma. Over and over, we've asked ourselves, why would someone as remarkable as she is run a discount detective agency in a failing mall? We've spent hours speculating about whether the agency could be a front for something, but if so, we can't imagine for what. We've also wondered if she was in some sort of witness protection program or if she'd been part of some criminal enterprise and was laying low to avoid retribution. Maybe it didn't serve anyone's interests to probe too carefully into her past, but Yuri in particular was drawn to the mystery like a moth to flame—a saying I've found disturbing ever since I was a child.

Both Jenny and Cole were smiling when we returned. "Can you believe he's never ridden a horse?" she said.

"Jenny says I can visit her farm one of these days." He looked for an instant like the young boy he was. Then, his smile faded. I had no doubt he was remembering why he was here and wondering whether he would be around long enough to take her up on the offer.

"First we need to get you settled in with my family so Yuri and I can check out the camp."

"They're good," Jenny said reassuringly to Cole. "They'll get this sorted out and you'll be coming for a visit real soon." She stood up. "Just do what they say and you'll be fine."

I sincerely hoped she was right. The hard part was just beginning.

CHAPTER 3
THE ENCAMPMENT

I LEFT YURI with Cole while I went into the other conference room. It wasn't much bigger than a walk-in closet in a studio apartment, but it gave me the privacy I needed to call my mother with the news that we were about to have a guest.

My mother and I are both widowed and share a carriage house at the back of a large city lot. The main house, a turn-of-the-century Tudor, is divided into four spacious apartments with a winding, tree-lined path leading to our two-story home. Mom has the upstairs, and my two children and I occupy the bottom floor. It's a good arrangement for the most part. My job frequently involves long hours and occasional out-of-town work, so it's nice to have my mother as back-up.

However, there are a number of downsides about living in such close proximity to one's mother. For instance, Mom's fastidious and likes to stick to a routine. That's why I was fairly certain she would initially resist the idea of having a homeless boy stay with us. I was also confident that she would agree in the end. She wouldn't turn away someone in need, especially not a child.

Mom answered in her no-nonsense voice as if she anticipated I was about to ask a favor. She's intuitive like that.

"I'll be home in about twenty minutes," I said. "And I'll have someone with me."

"Someone? Does the 'someone' have a name?"

"Cole. He's about Jason's age. He'll be staying with us for a day or so. Until we can get his, ah, problem sorted out."

"And his problem is …?"

I had to tell her because she needed to know that his safety was an issue. "He may have witnessed a kidnapping. We need to keep him out of sight for now."

It wasn't the first time we'd harbored a fugitive, although the last one was a dog that some people were trying to find in order to track down his owner. Like following the money, but instead, following the dog.

Mom sighed. "Anything else I should know before you get here?"

"Well … he's been living on the streets, and he left the camp in a hurry. So, he doesn't have any of his belongings with him. He will need to shower and borrow some clothes from Jason, so we can wash what he's wearing."

"We?"

"I'll do it as soon as I get home. Just get him cleaned up, okay?"

"Is he dangerous?"

"I don't think so."

"Diseased? Like bedbugs or lice?"

"I haven't seen him scratching. He looks like he's made an effort to stay clean, but it isn't easy in an encampment."

"I'm not trying to be critical …"

"I understand, and I appreciate your concern. I just need you to keep an eye on him while Yuri and I see what we can find out about the person he believes was kidnapped."

"You can't leave him at the office, can you?"

"He's just a kid, mother."

She let out a long-suffering sigh. "You have to admit that if you'd managed to get a job as a professor you wouldn't be bringing home strays." I was tempted to argue, but we didn't need to go down that rabbit hole again. We've struggled to manage our differences, both in terms of personalities and her view of how I should be living my life. Currently, we have a truce in place—she no longer posts articles about the drawbacks of being a single mom on my refrigerator, and I make an effort to be more transparent about the details of my job, so she doesn't have to worry all the time. It's been a bumpy truce, but we're coping.

I took a deep breath and ignored the criticism, feeling proud for resisting the urge to defend myself. Being a PI was not what she'd wanted for me. Nor had it been my first choice after completing my PhD in an interdisciplinary liberal arts program. But I loved my work, and at this point I was glad I hadn't managed to find a job in academia.

It was getting close to the end of summer, so although my kids have been trying to squeeze as much pleasure out of their last days of freedom as possible, I knew my entire family would be home today. Mara, my soon-to-be a freshman in high school daughter, was busy doing a reading assignment she had put off all summer. Jason was supposed to be doing some chores that should have been done last week, but he was probably online doing something he wasn't supposed to be doing — like watching videos on TikTok or playing some time-wasting video game. Or, since there were some political hot topics in the news of late, and he's been a news junkie since he learned to read, there was also the possibility he was binge-watching experts, alleged experts, and attention grabbers discuss what was going on locally, nationally, and throughout the world. My mother thinks it's unhealthy for a kid his age to be obsessed with the news. On the other hand, at least it doesn't endanger him physically like some sport options. Who knew what it was doing to his psyche though?

The only other inhabitant of our tiny household is No-name, our dog, still unnamed after being part of the family for over two years—a surprise "gift" to Jason from Yuri. No-name is a medium-sized, black dog with a penchant for quickly destroying his stuffed animal toys. At this moment he was probably busily tearing apart his latest, an African wild dog that I'd purchased recently at a yard sale. It had been in perfect condition and incredibly cheap. With its orange and black mottled fur and tufts of fake hair sprouting out of its ears and cheeks, I'd wondered if it had originally been a white elephant gift. It was quite ugly by almost any standard.

No-name didn't seem to mind. His one requirement was that a plush toy represented an endangered species. We have no idea how he knows when a creature is threatened with extinction, but he turns up his moist black nose at ubiquitous, unthreatened stuffed animals, preferring to rip apart ones already destined for extinction. Maybe he thinks "why not"—they're not going to be around for long anyway.

Yuri came with me to drop Cole off with my family. At first, everyone except No-name hung back a little. No-name acted like Cole was a long-lost friend, his one floppy ear flipping back and forth as he did a welcome dance. Cole got down on one knee and rubbed him. That broke the ice. Jason knelt too and said, "We call him No-Name. I'm Jason."

"I'm Cole. He's a nice dog."

"Cole," I interrupted. "This is my daughter Mara and my mother …" I paused to let her determine how she wanted to be addressed by our guest.

"You can call me Stella," Mom said rather stiffly. "Now let's get you settled in while we let these two do their jobs." She motioned for us to leave. Turning to Cole, she asked, "Would you like something to eat? I could make you a sandwich." There was only a slight hesitation before she added, "As soon as we get you cleaned up."

"Could I have one too?" Jason asked.

Yuri and I slipped out without anyone saying goodbye.

"Your family is great," Yuri said as we headed back to my car.

"They have their moments. Living with two teenagers and a mother with strong opinions that she won't keep to herself does make life, ah, interesting."

"Speaking of what would make our lives better in the moment, how about we pick up a couple of coffees on the way. I doubt they have a food truck at the encampment."

"Good idea."

"And speaking of coffee … did you know they say that drinking 120 cups of coffee at one sitting can kill you?"

"I doubt that's going to be a problem for me. I couldn't afford it."

"What about 48 teaspoons of salt?"

"I could afford that, but … let me guess. You're on a 'common things that can kill you' trivia rant, right? If so, you can stop any time." Yuri just smiled.

"85 chocolate bars, 22 apples, 13 shots of alcohol in rapid succession …"

"Blah, blah, blah," I chanted until he stopped. It was a technique I'd learned from listening to my two children arguing. When they did it, I ordered them to stop acting rude.

As soon as I quit "blahing" at him, Yuri quickly added, "71 extra-strength Tylenol pills." He must have run out of examples because he fell silent of his own accord.

"Twenty-two apples? Seriously. Who ate 22 apples to make that list?"

"I admit, it makes you wonder how they figured all of this out."

"If you promise no more trivia, I will stop at the next Starbucks drive-through. I'll even buy."

Yuri made a show of zipping his lips and pointed to some Golden Arches half a block away. I obediently pulled into the MacDonald's drive-through and ordered two coffees and two orders of fries. "Any idea how many fries it takes to kill someone?" I asked.

"No, but what a way to go." Yuri loves fries. I usually don't order any for myself, but I have been known to snitch some of his. Okay, so maybe snitching fries from him is more like a habit, as addictive as bumming a cigarette after giving up smoking. But this time I needed more than a couple of grease-laden slivers of potatoes. I needed to consume enough trans fats to boost my feel-good serotonin levels to counter the stress of heading into the unknown of a homeless encampment. The people we were about to approach for information lived hand-to-mouth. It made me want to apologize for having a job and a comfortable place to call home.

Cole had described the location of the encampment. Still, without his warning that it was hidden in the trees, we might have driven on by without noticing it. But once you knew where it was, there was no mistaking that the area had been taken over by the homeless. A row of parked cars on a narrow side road with no visible houses was the main giveaway. There were so many vehicles lined up that there was barely room for one car at a time to get through. Below the road was what looked like an urban green space filled with a variety of trees planted in close rows. On the uphill side of the road, evergreens climbed the hillside to a community of 1950s houses at the top. It was an area that had not yet been gentrified, although a few modern houses and boxy condo buildings were starting to invade the aging neighborhood further up the hill.

We decided to park part-way up the slope on the residential side of the main street that transported traffic from the valley to the freeway. We ended up in front of a well-kept two-story house with a statue of a Buddha on a toilet in the front yard.

"There's a message there somewhere," Yuri said.

"And it's in poor taste."

"Well, flowers in toilets are no longer trendy …" I could almost hear his mind at work trying to figure out whether I was giving him a bad time or actually figured out something he hadn't.

"You didn't see the sign, did you?" I said, feeling a tickle of pleasure for getting the punch line before Yuri.

"No. What did I miss?"

"Holy crap." I laughed.

Yuri groaned.

We started walking towards the narrow side road that ran along the lower end of the encampment. The illegal encampment was tolerated by authorities but not sanctioned by authorities. Even so, it felt like *we* were the trespassers.

Cole had told us that there were a lot of long-term residents as well as people who came and went. He'd also warned us that once someone goes missing, their belongings are confiscated by those remaining. He was hoping no one had noticed that he and Bess were gone yet and that Bess's tent might still be there along with the backpack that he'd left behind the shed when he fled.

As we started down the road, we saw two men who looked to be in their mid-twenties, dressed in jeans and dark hoodies and wearing matching sneakers with yellow neon soles that could probably be seen from the Space Needle if it hadn't been for the trees and buildings in the way. They were leaning against an old station wagon about six vehicles down, not looking directly at us, but obviously aware of our presence.

"We going to look for her tent and his pack before talking to anyone?" I asked.

"It will be hard to walk past those two without saying anything," Yuri said. "How do you want to play it?"

"I think we should keep it simple. Say upfront that we're looking for Bess. A relative asked us to check on her."

"That works for me. Let's go for it."

The two men didn't change positions as we approached but followed us with their eyes. I was conscious of the fact that my black slacks and Houndstooth print blazer was as out of place in a homeless camp as a red dress at a funeral. At least, I'd left my knockoff Coach handbag in the car. Yuri was wearing jeans and a simple dark blue shirt, but even with his unruly hair, he looked more REI than Kmart.

"Hey," Yuri said in greeting, trying to sound friendly without overdoing the bonhomie. Neither of the men responded. Yuri continued talking anyway. "We're looking for someone. A woman named Bess. Maybe you could tell us where we can find her."

Still no response.

"Her sister is worried about her," I said. "We just want to make sure she's okay."

One of the men shifted his stance to face us directly. "What's it worth to you?"

"You know Bess?" Yuri asked.

"Might."

"Have you seen her today?"

The two men exchanged looks. Then they seemed to make a decision. "I'll tell you what I know for a dub."

"I can do that." Yuri got out a twenty and handed it to him.

"What about me?" the other guy said.

"I want to hear from your friend first."

"Haven't seen her today." He laughed. "But thanks for this." He made a show of putting the $20 in his pocket. His buddy laughed too.

Yuri looked neither surprised nor upset. I was fairly certain he would later claim the transaction went as he'd suspected it would—that the twenty had been a conversation starter. It still irritated me. Clearly, Yuri should have held onto his twenty until he got some information. On the other hand, we already had a pretty good idea as to where Bess's tent was.

Hoping to salvage a little of his twenty, I said, "Seriously, do you know Bess?"

"Might." They laughed again.

"Okay, I get it. You know her but aren't going to tell us anything." I held out two cards. "If you see her, tell her that her sister is worried, okay? Please let me know. There could be something in it for you." I paused for emphasis. "If what you tell me is helpful."

They took the cards and barely glanced at them. At least they didn't toss them on the ground right in front of us.

Yuri and I moved on, looking for the landmarks Cole had described. "That went well," I said when we were far enough away from the two men that I didn't think they could hear us.

"At least they didn't mug us."

"In broad daylight?"

"For all we know, they might be the two men who took Bess."

That hadn't crossed my mind. "You're right. We need to keep an eye out."

"Yeah, use the eyes in the back of your head and be ready to run."

"Think you can run faster than someone with neon-soled sneakers?"

"I sincerely hope we don't have to find out."

We hadn't gone far before Yuri pointed and said, "I think that's the big tree Cole mentioned—there's the broken limb hanging to one side."

"There's supposed to be a path just beyond it, right?" The words were no more out of my mouth than we spotted the path. It worked its way up the hill through blackberry vines and salal spread out under large evergreens, mostly Douglas fir. As we started up, I saw some makeshift shelters ahead and to our left.

"Based on Cole's description, the shed should be visible after the bend up ahead."

Sure enough, as soon as we turned the corner, I saw what I thought was Bess's blue tent nestled in the woods about twenty feet off the path to the left and the shed a few feet beyond. As we got closer, we saw that the shed roof was covered with moss and the entire structure was listing toward the downhill side.

"No wonder he slept behind it instead of in it," Yuri said.

We checked out the shed first, glancing through the doorless entrance to make certain there was no one inside. There were gaps in the walls where some boards had collapsed. It smelled like dead animals and human waste. There was no one inside.

Behind the shed we found a blanket spread out like someone had been laying on it. At the far end was a gray pack with a picture of a unicorn on it. "That must be his gray pack," I said. "But he didn't mention anything about a unicorn."

"Maybe he was embarrassed. Not what you'd expect a tough kid like Cole to be carrying."

"Just because rainbow colored, cutesy unicorns are popular with young girls doesn't mean unicorns are weak and feminine, does it?"

"Oh no, you aren't going to trap me with that."

I went over and picked up the pack. "Heavy."

"Everything he owns is in there."

"When you put it that way—he travels light."

We left the worn blanket where it was and headed for what we assumed was Bess's tent. The flap was down. I leaned over and said, "Bess, are you in there?" When no one answered, I pushed the flap aside and was about to enter when a loud female voice stopped me.

"What you think you're doing?"

I jerked upright and turned toward the woman standing about ten feet away. She had on a plaid flannel jacket that had definitely seen better days and a pair of jeans with a hole in one knee. I was pretty sure the shredded hole wasn't a fashion statement. Her long brown hair was pulled back in a ponytail. She sounded threatening, but she was keeping her distance, maybe because there were two of us. Or maybe she was waiting for reinforcements.

"Hi," I said, trying to sound friendly. "I'm looking for Bess. Have you seen her today?"

"What you want with her?"

"Her sister asked us to check on her to make sure she's okay. She hasn't heard from her for a week or so."

"She never mentioned any sister."

"Are you friends?" I asked. Yuri was standing back, letting me take the lead. Or maybe he was getting prepared in case the woman had a weapon … or hostile friends.

"We look out for each other."

"Do you mind if I look inside?"

"What for? She ain't there."

"How do you know? Did you see her leave?"

"She didn't answer when you called her name, did she?"

"What if she's sick and unable to respond?" I took several steps toward the woman and held out my hand. "I'm Cameron by the way. And you are?"

"None a your business." So much for the friendly approach.

"You can watch to make sure I don't take anything, but I'm going to look inside. I really do want to find her to see if she needs anything." I didn't wait for permission but flipped the flap back and went in. Yuri remained where he was. When I glanced back, I saw him trying to peer around me while keeping an eye on the woman.

There wasn't a lot to see—a couple of boxes stacked at the back of the tent and some blankets and clothes scattered across the piece of plastic covering the dirt floor, like a struggle had taken place. I went over to the boxes and glanced in them.

"Those boxes are Bess's," the woman screamed from a few feet outside the tent. "You have no right ..."

Yuri backed away as I stepped outside and was about to say something to her, but her shouted warning had apparently attracted some of the other residents. They appeared suddenly, apparitions from the woods, standing in a semicircle, watching. It felt a bit like a scene from a horror movie, but I told myself I was overreacting. These were simply people protecting one of their own against outsiders.

Yuri called out to them: "Anyone here know where we can find Bess? Her sister wants to get in touch."

A guy who could have passed for a mountain man from the 1800s with his long hair, bushy full beard, and baggy pants held up with suspenders stepped forward. "I don't think you're gunna find her."

CHAPTER 4
BESS

AS SUDDENLY as they'd appeared, the residents of the encampment faded back into the woods. Only one person remained, half hidden by the trees. She had a wrinkled face under straggly, dirty blond hair streaked with gray. There were jeans peeking out from beneath a long denim dress, a stretched-out sweater too large for her thin frame was buttoned crookedly, one side hanging lower than the other. As I walked over to her, I felt her eyes scrutinizing me as carefully as I was assessing her.

I stopped a few feet away. "I'm Cameron," I said, waiting to see if she would give me her name in return.

"Maddie," she said.

"Short for Madelaine?"

"Just Maddie."

"Do you know Bess, Maddie?"

"Knew her."

"Did something happen to her?"

"Once they're taken, they never come back."

"Do you know who takes them?"

"No."

"Have you seen anyone being 'taken'?"

"No."

"Then how do you know they didn't leave on their own."

"We hear things."

"How many have been 'taken'?"

"At this camp, one or two."

"The same thing happens at other camps?"

She nodded.

"Have you reported this?"

"You mean like to the police?" She snorted.

"What about a social worker? Or a city official?"

"All they want is for us to go to shelters. Or clean up the camp so neighbors don't complain."

"I'm sorry. I imagine it's not easy living here."

"Better than crowded in with a bunch of others. I like my space."

"These people that disappear. Are they all women?

"Men. Women. Children. Doesn't matter. No one is safe."

"Any idea what these people want with the people they take?"

"You'd have to ask them."

I paused, trying to digest what she was saying. "What about Bess? Can you tell me her last name or where she was from?"

"I thought you said you knew her sister? That she asked you to find Bess." She wasn't missing a beat. I sensed she was tensed for flight if I said the wrong thing.

"I want to make sure I have the right woman named Bess before I tell her sister she's 'missing,' That's why I need to verify her full name."

Maddie didn't say anything for a few moments, as if she was considering the logic of my explanation. Finally, she said, "We don't use last names here. But, one time she said she was from Oregon. Is that her?"

"Sounds like it could be," I said. I reached into my purse and took out a twenty, stepped a little closer, and handed it to Maddie. "Thank you," I said. Before she could leave, I added. "One more thing. Did you ever talk to the boy who was sleeping behind the shed?"

"Depends."

"Sandy hair, thin, about 13?"

"I heard he ran away. Don't you try finding him. If they put him back in foster care, he'll just run away again."

"Why?"

"Why do you think?" She turned and quickly walked away.

Yuri was waiting for me by Bess's tent. "Find anything?" I asked.

"These," he said, showing me a bottle of unmarked pills."

"What are they? Do you know?"

"No idea." He put them in his pocket. "I also found this." He handed me a picture of three women in their twenties and a teenage boy. Their names were written on the back: Darla, Jean, Kenny and … Bess.

"Nothing more specific to identify her?"

"Nothing. If she had any ID, it must have been with her."

"This place makes me so sad. Not the squaller, although I do find the living conditions hard to take, but the people. I know some of them have mental health problems, but not all of them. Like the woman I just talked to, she was sharp. I don't know her story, but I find it hard to believe she wouldn't rather be in one of the houses at the top of the hill with a bathroom, a kitchen and a comfy bed."

"Did she give you anything to go on?"

"Except for the fact that Bess may have been from Oregon, no. But she did say, indirectly, that Cole had a bad time in foster care."

"I figured as much."

"Let's go," I said. "I feel like no one wants us here, and I don't think we're going to learn too much more today anyway."

When we got back to the office it was almost time to call it quits for the day. Blake said Adele wanted to talk to us before we reported to P.W., so we headed for the pit.

"Learn something about our boy Cole?" Yuri asked as we approached Adele's desk.

"Yes, I managed to track him down. His full name is Cole White—I bet he took some ribbing about that in grade school. Anyway, DSHS reported him missing, and not for the first time. He has a history of running away. His mother has been in and out of drug programs, none of which apparently worked for her. His father is either dead or missing in action. No other known relatives."

"Whoever you talked to at DSHS must have asked why you were asking about Cole."

"Of course. But I didn't think you would want me to admit he was staying with you, so I simply said that his name came up in a case we're working. They accepted that."

"Thanks, Adele. That was perfect."

Adele shook her head. "Poor kid. Life hasn't been easy for him." Then she stared hard at me. "What are you going to do?"

"Are you asking whether I'm going to turn him in to DSHS? Of course not."

"What's the alternative?" Yuri asked. He'd been standing there listening to the conversation.

"I don't know. We'll figure that out once we get a handle on what's happening at these camps, okay?" I knew I sounded a bit snarky, and I've been told on more than one occasion that you can't save everyone who needs saving. Still, now that I was involved, I felt an obligation to make sure he ended up someplace better for him in the short-term than the encampment we'd just come from. He needed to be in school rather than making himself increasingly less able to become a functioning member of society by living on the street. If he'd been eighteen, that would have been different. Still a bit sad, but at this point I felt that he was too young to be making life-changing choices on his own.

"These kinds of decisions are never easy," Adele said, obviously sensing my frustration with the situation.

"No, and I'm afraid we have another challenge for you."

"Always up for a challenge," she said.

"That's what we love about you," Yuri said.

Adele was not only a whiz at doing research on topics, people, facts, whatever, but she has a ton of connections, including, I suspect, a hacker or two. Not that I would question where she gets her information. She prides herself on her professionalism and P.W. would not condone research that was not strictly legal. There were, however, a couple of times, I secretly wondered about Adele's sources.

Conservative on the outside, but a totally determined researcher on the inside. Sometimes when you feel you are on the side of truth and right, even the most righteous may find it hard not to step over the line, maybe just a teensy step.

We gave her the little we had found out about Bess, including the picture with the other names.

"It isn't much," Adele said, "... but if anyone has reported her as missing, it at least narrows the field. Although when someone lives off the grid, like the homeless usually do, it can be hard to find them." Then she looked directly at Yuri. "I almost forgot—I've got one for you: A sheep, two donuts and a snake walk into a bar." She paused just long enough for him to murmur "a sheep, two donuts and a snake" before delivering the dramatic punch line: "Bah-Dunk-Dunk-Sssss." She did a wonderful hissing noise, as if she had practiced. "When my ten-year-old neighbor told me that, I immediately thought of you," she said, smiling.

"Very funny," he replied with a hint of sarcasm.

"It is kinda," I said. "And it does sound like something you'd come up with, Yuri." Adele and I exchanged amused grins. Yuri is always telling corny jokes and teasing Adele. It tickled me to see her respond in kind.

"Bah-Dunk-Dunk-Sssss," I said as Yuri and I headed to P.W.'s office to give her an update on the situation with Bess. My kids wouldn't think it was funny, but I might share it with them anyway—it was fun making the sounds.

When we showed P.W. the bottle of pills, she said, "Leave them with me. I'll get someone to check them out. There could be a connection. And tomorrow, visit a couple of other camps. Find out if Bess's abduction is a one-off or if the woman you talked to is right—that it's a problem in other camps too. You may be onto something."

As we started to leave, she added, "And, Cameron …"

"Yes?"

"Don't get too emotionally attached to Cole. You can't save everyone."

That seemed to be the general opinion. I wasn't in the job of saving people, but once you get to know someone, even a little bit, it's hard not to try.

CHAPTER 5
COLE

WHEN I WALKED in the door at home, only No-name came to greet me, and he didn't hang around long. As soon as I asked "Where is everyone?" he took off upstairs. I wasn't sure if I was supposed to follow him like Lassie leading the way, or if he was already tired of my company. Then I heard laughter coming from above; it almost sounded like a party.

I set Cole's backpack down and headed upstairs.

My mother's compact kitchen was bursting with energy. Cole was wearing one of her floral aprons and was stirring something on the stove with a large wooden spoon while Jason was reading directions from a recipe book that was spread open on the dining room table. Mom and Mara were standing to one side, as if supervising the operation. They too were wearing aprons. Mom's apron had pictures of vibrant herbs and tiny red ladybugs against a light-yellow background; Mara's apron had colorful butterflies fluttering around equally colorful wildflowers. Together, they were a blaze of flora and fauna. The Marmi ceramic tabletop looked like something out of a kitchen design catalogue, but the scene around the dining room table as a whole was more of a *Saturday Evening Post* cover.

"Hi, Mom," Mara said, barely glancing in my direction. "Can you believe Cole has never made fudge before?"

Cole managed a quick "hello" but didn't look up from the pan on the stove. Part chef and part wizard, he was concentrating like a scientist whipping up a life-saving potion.

I went up to Mom and said, "I assume everything's okay?"

"Dinner will be a little late," she said. "We got distracted." She pointed to the refrigerator. "I made a spinach lasagna. It's in the refrigerator. It needs about an hour to cook. You could make a salad and some garlic bread to go with it. We should be done by the time the lasagna is ready."

Looking around at the happy fudge makers, it was clear that Jason, Mara and Mom had welcomed Cole into our family. Cole had cleaned up nicely, his hair pulled back in a ponytail, his face ruddy from the heat of the stove. He was apparently a couple inches taller than Jason though; his borrowed pants fell short of his ankles, but the look of pleasure on his face was super-sized. He seemed nothing like the frightened young boy I'd rescued earlier in the day. Everyone warned me not to get emotionally involved, but that was going to be hard.

I got the lasagna out of the refrigerator and took it downstairs with me. I needed to change my clothes, fix dinner and consider options for dealing with Cole. I knew that I was stretched about as far as I could go as a single mother with two teenagers and a demanding job, but I couldn't simply push him back into a system that had obviously failed him. Maybe there was some way I could be involved in identifying a family that was a good fit. I would have to see if I could find someone at DSHS that I could talk to on the QT.

When I stopped to set down the lasagna, No-name dropped the mangled remains of his African wild dog at my feet, apparently to let me know he needed another replacement. The orange and black clumps of fur still hung together, but not in the shape of any animal I'd ever seen. It hadn't even lasted a full week. Maybe I could get something that was really tough, like a dog toy made from a Michelin all-terrain truck tire. I wondered if there were any endangered species toys that came with warranties. I wouldn't require a life-time guarantee, but maybe a two-year limited warranty?

"No-name," I said in a tone that made him cower. Then I reminded myself that he was just a dog. "Leave it. It's okay; I'll get you another animal to hurry toward extinction."

The lasagna was in the oven, and I had finished making the salad and was setting the table when Jason came down. "Dinner's not quite ready yet, maybe in about 20 minutes, okay?"

"I want to talk to you." He sat down at the table, a troubled frown creasing his otherwise smooth forehead. In that instant, he looked remarkably like his father. The resemblance was unsettling. I had to remind myself that before Dan started secretly playing the stock market, he had been a good father and provider. It was only after he died unexpectedly from a heart attack that I learned he had used our savings for bad investments and left us penniless.

Now that I was back on my feet, it was probably time to let go of my anger.

"Sure." I put the silverware down and sat across from him. "What's up?" It was unusual for Jason to come to me for a chat. Usually, I had to engage in persistent hinting and probing to get him to talk about things that were bothering him. Even then, I wasn't sure he was telling me the whole story.

"It's about Cole."

"Oh, I'm sorry. I probably should have checked with you and Mara before bringing him here. He won't be staying down here with us; he'll be upstairs in your grandma's spare room. And it won't be for too long."

"No, it's not that. I like him. It will be fun to have him here. But …"

"But?" I had no idea where this conversation was going.

"He shouldn't be living on the streets." Jason's earnest concern made me proud that he was my son.

"I know. I'm going to see about helping him find a place to stay."

Jason took a deep breath and swallowed visibly before blurting out: "He's got scars."

"Scars?" This wasn't where I'd anticipated the conversation was heading.

"They beat him. He didn't want to tell me about it, but I kept asking. I saw them when he was trying on some of my clothes."

"That's terrible." I was stunned. I knew that kind of thing happened to kids, but the thought Cole had been a victim of violence while in foster care was not something that had crossed my mind.

"He's my age. I … I feel bad. My life is so good and his has been … well, pretty awful."

"Don't worry. I'm going to figure something out. Meanwhile, your assignment is to help him enjoy his stay with us. Okay?"

"But you can't send him back to where he was."

"Don't worry; I'll make sure that doesn't happen again." That was a promise I definitely intended to keep, no matter what I had to do to prevent it from happening.

"I don't suppose …," Jason said slowly.

"If you're going to ask if he can stay with us—"

"Why can't he?"

"Because he needs more care and attention than we can give him."

"He would be my friend."

"He can still be your friend after we find him a place to live."

"Yeah, I know."

"Meanwhile, do what you can for him while he's here, okay?

"Okay." With the resiliency of youth, he jumped up and asked, "When's dinner again?"

"Soon." It made me smile to see how caring he was and how self-reflective for someone his age. I sincerely hoped I could keep my promise to figure out some solution for Cole that satisfied everyone.

Soon after Jason disappeared back upstairs, Mom came down. "We need to talk." She sat down at the table and waited for me to take a seat across from her.

"Is it about Cole?" I asked.

"Yes, he's a sweet boy."

"So, no red flags?"

"Red flags? No. I just want to know what you plan to do about him. He says it isn't so bad being homeless, better than being in foster care. That doesn't sound right to me."

"It doesn't sound right to me either. We'll need to figure something out. But it's complicated. Let's talk after dinner, okay?"

"Just don't make any decisions until we've had a chance to discuss it." After assuring her we would talk about Cole's fate later, Mom went back upstairs, and I continued setting the table. I had just finished when Mara came in and asked if I needed help with dinner. Together we worked on the garlic bread.

"How was the fudge? Or are you saving it for after dinner?"

"We all took a taste," Mara admitted. "It was pretty good. You'll see."

"Looking forward to it."

Mara stopped chopping garlic and stared at me with a very solemn look on her perfect oval face. Studying her, I realized the thick eyebrows that she always complained about looked thinner. In the past, I'd refused to let her pluck them, but … they did look nice.

"Let me guess," I said. "You have something to say about Cole." Next, No-name would be taking me aside to give me his opinion.

"We can't let him return to the streets."

"Even though he claims it isn't that bad?"

"Mom. Be serious."

"Don't worry. That's not the plan."

"Then what is?"

"Well, I don't have one yet. But we'll come up with something. I promise." I always hated it when people said "I promise" or "trust me" when it wasn't clear that they could do what they were promising to do. But in this instance, I felt like I definitely had to come up with something, so I might as well "promise" that I would. Two things were clear—no one in the family wanted to see Cole go back into the system or on the streets. That meant I'd have to come up with something creative to fulfill my promise to myself and my family.

When everyone finally came down for dinner, I noticed a tiny smudge of fudge on Cole's cheek. When Mom wiped it off for him, it reminded me of Aunt Bea and Opie from Mayberry reruns. Only my mother was thin and classy, not particularly motherly looking, even though she still had on her yellow apron. The kids had removed theirs, but a faint aroma of chocolate followed them into our small kitchen.

Everyone dug in as if the fudge had only been an appetizer. Mom makes a great lasagna, but she usually limits herself to a tiny portion because she watches her calories. I watch mine too—as I devour them. Mom took more salad than the rest of us and eyed the garlic bread as it rapidly disappeared.

The kids seemed to be enjoying themselves. What Cole lacked in table manners he made up for with lively conversation. Mara, Jason and Cole talked about books while Mom and I listened. Jason and Cole shared a love of sea adventure stories, while Mara jumped in when they started talking about Jack London tales. Then she asked, "Did you have to leave your books behind at the encampment?" I was glad she hadn't seen where he'd been staying or she would have been embarrassed by her question.

Cole pursed his lips, like he was trying to decide what to say. "I read mostly at the library. It's nice there." Then he grinned. "And they have a great selection."

"Do you check out books?" Mara asked.

"I … I don't have a library card." He sounded both sad and uncomfortable.

Mara put a hand on the side of her face, as if she suddenly realized why her question was so terribly inappropriate. "I'm sorry. I wasn't thinking."

Cole quickly recovered. "Even though they won't let someone without a home address check out books, they don't mind if I read there." Then he grinned again. "And the lighting is better than under the trees at the camp."

"Well," I interrupted. "Jason has a few books I'm sure he'd be happy to loan you while you're here." This was feeling more and more like a Hallmark movie. Except for the kidnappers trying to find Cole, that is.

Yuri called just as we were finishing dinner. As soon as I answered, the kids wandered off and my mother used hand gestures to indicate I should come upstairs after I was off the phone.

"I've been thinking," Yuri said.

"What a nice change."

"Seriously. About Cole."

"You're going to adopt him."

"Nooo …"

"Well, if you're going to tell me we can't let him go back to the encampment, Mom, Mara, and Jason beat you to it."

"Really? Well, what I was thinking is that there must have been a reason he ran away."

"You're right about that. But that doesn't mean that all foster families are bad. He just landed in a bad place or two." I decided to fill him in on the scars Jason mentioned when we had more time to talk about Cole's future.

"The problem as I see it is that he's probably too old for most adoptions. If we send him back to some temporary situation, he'll probably just run away again."

"I don't mean to sound hard-hearted, but he can't stay here indefinitely. For one thing, it wouldn't be legal."

"I know. I mainly called just to see if everything was okay. Sounds like it is."

"You don't know anyone at DSHS, do you?"

"No, but I'll see if someone I know does."

"Sounds good. Meanwhile, tomorrow we need to figure out what the situation is with the alleged kidnappings. After that, we can work on finding a better home for Cole."

Before heading up to talk with Mom, I interrupted the movie the kids were watching to show Cole that I had his backpack and to say that I would take it upstairs to his room. The pack showed obvious signs of wear, smudged with dirt and grime, the once white unicorn defiantly rearing on its hind legs.

"That's great. Thank you," Cole said.

"What's with the unicorn?" Jason asked.

"You can't catch them," Cole said.

"They're a symbol of hope," Mara added. "And they supposedly have healing power."

"Well," I interrupted. "I'll take this good luck unicorn upstairs and let you finish your movie."

Mom had her spare room all set up for Cole. "I think I'll get him a haircut tomorrow," she said as I set the pack on the floor. "Then take him and Jason shopping, buy him a few things."

"Like what?" I asked.

"Some underwear and a pair of jeans that fit and a couple shirts. That's okay, isn't it?"

"Just don't shop at the mall. And have him wear a hat. Although they won't be looking for two boys with their … ah, a sharp-looking woman."

"You recovered nicely. If you'd said 'grandma,' you would have been written out of my will."

"I'm in your will? Your only daughter. That's nice."

"Just don't plan on me departing any time soon."

I had a sudden impulse to hug her, but that wasn't our style. When I noticed her eyeing the backpack, I warned: "Don't even think about washing his pack. I sure he wouldn't want you to. And you don't know what he might have in there."

"Have you looked?"

"No, and I don't intend to. He's entitled to a little privacy."

"Don't worry; I wouldn't touch his things. But I'm surprised at the unicorn. It reminds me of my hippie days."

I raised my eyebrows.

"That's a story for another time …"

I was about to press a little when my phone rang. This time it was Jenny. "Hi, I've been thinking," she said. I started laughing. "What's so funny?"

"You aren't the first person to be thinking about Cole's welfare tonight," I said. "I assume that's what you've been thinking about."

"Yeah. You caught me. It occurred to me he might want to stay at the farm for a couple days. After tomorrow, I'll have some free time. If you haven't found a place for him by then, he might enjoy spending some time here."

"First, I think that may be a good idea, but only if you let Jason come too, at least for a day." Mom was standing there at the entrance to the spare room, studiously following every word. "But I have to admit, I don't know how I'm going to as you say 'find a place for him.' It's really above my pay grade to use a cliché I've never liked."

"P.W. will figure something out."

"You think?"

"She's got connections."

"But she warned me not to get emotionally involved. Reminded me that I can't save everyone."

"Ha. Want a side wager on whether the message was for you or for herself?"

Mom caught my eye and asked me to put Jenny on speaker. When I did, she said, "Jenny, I want to pick up a few clothes for Cole. Then I could drop off Jason and Cole when you're ready to leave work tomorrow."

"Not at the office," I said quickly. The kidnappers could still be hanging around, hoping to find Cole again.

"How about at that Starbucks down the street from the mall?" Jenny suggested. They settled on a time.

Once we were off the phone, Mom asked me to join her for a glass of wine. We sat on a couple of stools at her counter, and Mom poured two glasses of a very nice merlot.

We sipped and chatted about this and that, relaxing, putting off discussion of the challenging issues that would still be there in the morning.

We had just finished our wine and were about to call it a night when I got another call from Jenny. She was laughing.

"I won the wager already. I just got off the phone with P.W. It seems she'd been 'thinking about Cole' and wondered if I'd be willing to have him stay at the farm for a while. She thinks it's best to hold off trying to find the right place for him until after you and Yuri figure out who's after him. But she's made some initial inquiries."

"Sounds like we all have our assignments," Mom said. "With a little luck, things may work out."

Lying in bed later, I kept going over the events of the very long day. Had it really been this morning when I came across Cole and the two men chasing him? So much had happened since then. If it felt to me like I'd lived through a week's time in one day, I could only imagine how Cole was feeling. From sleeping on the ground and running for his life to making fudge and having his own bed with bamboo bed sheets and a William Morris antique acanthus floral comforter. It must seem surreal to him.

As my mother had said, we just needed a little luck to figure things out. Unfortunately, none of us had actually touched a unicorn's horn, so we hadn't been blessed with good luck. There was never a unicorn around when you needed one.

CHAPTER 6
RUNAWAY

FRIDAY MORNING, I stopped for coffee at the kiosk near our office. When the barista handed me my coffee, she said, “Oh, I almost forgot—did the boy’s mother catch up with him?”

“Boy’s mother?”

“Yeah, a woman stopped by late yesterday afternoon looking for her son. She seemed nice and very concerned.”

“What did you tell her?”

“Her description of him sounded like the blond boy I saw you with, so I suggested she check with you.”

My heart did a little syncopated dance. A coincidence? Or did the two thugs call in help? “Let me get this straight. Some woman was looking for her son, and you told her you saw a boy fitting his description with Yuri and me?”

She must have sensed my alarm. “Yes. That was okay, wasn’t it? I assumed he was playing hooky from school or something.”

“Could you describe the woman?”

“Did I do something wrong?”

“The boy is trying to escape a bad situation, and since no one came to the office asking about him, there could be an issue with this woman looking for him. Could you give me a description of her, please?"

She closed her eyes and thought about it. When she opened them, she said: "Blue floral blouse and cropped jeans. Black sandals. Red toenail polish that matched her lipstick. Dyed red short hair with some brown showing at the part. No other makeup. Medium height and weight."

"Wow, you're good," I said.

"Thanks. And I'm sorry. She seemed so nice."

"You had no way to know. If you see her again, act natural. Just don't give her any other information, okay?" I handed her my card. "A let me know if you do see her again, even if she's just passing by. I'd appreciate it." I grabbed my coffee and hurried to the office.

Yuri was at his desk when I arrived. He started to say something, but I held up my hand and said, "We've got a problem." Jenny was there too. I waved her over and told both of them what the barista had said.

"You need to let your mother know right away and talk to P.W.," Jenny said. "I'll check the mall cameras and see if I can get a picture of the woman."

I quickly called Mom and told her to keep Cole at home and inside. "The men looking for him might know where he is. I'll call you back in a few minutes."

"Should I get out my Glock?" Mom asked. She has a pink Glock 43, lightweight and made for smaller hands, but with plenty of firepower. Before I took a job as a detective, she'd never owned a gun. But now she worries, and isn't about to let anyone hurt her family. Besides, whether she'll admit it or not, she likes the way it looks. I bet she's posed before a mirror with it to check out various stances.

I hesitated. "I hope you won't have to shoot anyone, but don't answer the door either, okay? And tell Jason and Mara without alarming them too much."

"Why don't you ask for something hard?"

"I'm sorry, Mom." The safety issues related to my job are real, and even though I try to minimize the risks for me and my family, from time-to-time situations arise that make me very uneasy. Especially concern for my kids' well-being. It's the main downside of my job.

"It's alright. We can handle it from this end."

Yuri was waving me inside P.W.'s office, so I said goodbye and joined him. "I've already given her the main facts," he said as we took chairs in front of her desk.

"First, if we get a picture off of one of the cameras, I'll see if we can track her," P.W. said. "Meanwhile, there are two options as I see it. We can put him in police custody or get him away to some place safe."

"He was planning on going to Jenny's," I said. "But if they know he was with me, they can obviously trace him there too."

"I don't like the idea of getting the police involved until we know more," Yuri said. "Besides, I don't think that would be good for Cole."

P.W. frowned, tapping her unlit imported Russian Kazbek Papirosi cigarette against the side of her vintage ashtray with an embossed double-headed Imperial eagle and the inscription "War 1914" inside. At one point we had hoped the cigarette brand or the provenance of the ashtray might help us discover something about P.W.'s secret past, but neither had panned out. Like all the other leads we'd come up with, they were dead-ends.

"What about that friend of yours on the island?" P.W. asked, looking directly at me. "Doesn't he owe you a favor."

The thought of Gary playing parent seemed out of character. Plus, he didn't really owe me a favor. He and his dog Bandit had rescued me when I was in a life-and-death situation on the island where he lives. I'd returned the favor by helping him out when he was on the run from some professional hitmen. So, we were even. Gary's actual "profession" is a bit vague, but based on the little I know about him, I think he might be referred to as a soldier of fortune. He and Bandit could definitely keep Cole safe though.

"I'll call him," I said. "If he's available, I'm sure he'll do it." Although even as I said the words, I had some doubts about the wisdom of the request. Then again, keeping Cole out of harm's way was more important than finding a nurturing family for him at this point.

I went into the conference room to make the call. Gary and I hadn't talked since I'd introduced him to Jenny and the sparks between them could have lit up a night sky. I wasn't sure if they still saw each other occasionally, and I wasn't sure I wanted to know. Although I confess to finding Gary almost irresistible, I'm not the "fling" type, and he definitely is. Not that I think casual relationships are necessarily undesirable; I'm just not built that way, especially since I have two kids. I want something a little more reliable, if not necessarily permanent. But there was one time when …

"Hey, how are you?" Gary said in his husky, sexy voice.

"I need help," I said, perhaps too abruptly.

"Well, you certainly got to the point fast enough. And I'm just fine too."

"Sorry, but it's somewhat urgent."

"Shoot."

"There are a couple of thugs trying to catch up with a 13-year-old boy who has been staying at my house. We thought he was safe there, but now we think they've connected him with me. We don't want to involve the police …" I hesitated.

"And you immediately thought of me as an ideal baby-sitter." I heard him chuckling.

"More of a bodyguard."

"That I can do. Okay. Let me check when I can catch a float plane to Seattle. I'll get back to you to let you know what time I'll arrive." He hung up without saying goodbye.

Yuri poked his head in. "He said 'yes'?"

I nodded. "It's a matter of what time we meet him." My phone started making noises like a grunting gorilla. Darn. Jason was fooling with my ringtone again. He thought it was funny, but at times it was downright embarrassing.

Yuri was smiling. "Better than the attacking hawk," he said as I picked up the call.

"That was quick," I said without looking at who was calling. When I realized it was Mom, not Gary, I felt a tingle of alarm by the way her voice quavered when she said: "Cameron."

Then she hit me with the bad news.

"Cole's run away." She sounded on the verge of tears. I immediately put the phone on speaker for Yuri to listen in. "When I explained to him that he needed to stay inside because there was a chance he'd been tracked, he got very upset. He said he didn't mean to put us in danger. And although I assured him that you had everything under control, I knew he wasn't convinced. Then … I only left him alone for a few minutes.

"When I couldn't find him, I asked Jason if he knew where Cole was. He didn't. Then I told Mara and Jason about what you'd said, and Jason immediately took off. Mara and I tried to stop him, but he got on his bike and was out of sight before we could catch up. We drove all around the neighborhood looking for him … and for Cole. We couldn't find either one. Oh, Cameron, I'm so upset and so very, very sorry."

"It's alright, Mom," I said, sounding a lot calmer than I felt. "Jason is just bicycling around the neighborhood looking for Cole. He'll be fine. And Cole—"

Yuri asked, "Did Jason say anything about knowing where Cole might go?"

"Get Mara," I said. "Maybe she has some ideas."

Yuri and I waited impatiently until Mara came on. "Mom, we looked everywhere." She sounded even more distraught than my mother, if that was possible. "He took his pack. And now Jason is gone too."

"It isn't your fault, Mara. It's not anyone's fault." Maybe mine for not anticipating this would happen. But there wasn't time for recriminations; we needed to find the two boys. "I want you to think carefully before answering. You've spent some time with him—is there anywhere you think Cole is likely to go? Is there any place he mentioned that he might consider safe?"

"The only thing I can think of is that camp. Until the problem with Bess, he said that he felt safe there."

Yuri said, "I doubt he would return to the one where he was living."

"I just thought of something," Mara said, her voice suddenly excited. "Earlier today, I overheard Jason and Cole talking about encampments in the area. I wasn't paying much attention, but I remember them talking about how the City is upset about the one at Carkeek Park. And," she added, "it's not too far away."

"You may be onto something," I said. "Yuri and I will check it out. Meanwhile, if you hear from Jason, please let me know immediately."

"Mom," I said. "Stay inside like we talked about before. The two men looking for Cole won't necessarily know he's no longer there."

"Got it. Go find them."

Yuri and I were halfway to my car when Gary called. I quickly explained what had happened.

"I'll let you know when I'm in your area," he said.

"You don't need to come until we find Cole."

"If you don't find him right off, I may be able to help. Like I said, I'll let you know when I get there."

He hung up before I could argue against him making what might turn out to be an unnecessary trip or to thank him for responding so quickly. I hated to admit that I found the idea of him helping us search for Cole reassuring. Yuri didn't feel quite the same though.

"I know you tried to tell him to wait until we got back in touch. But we don't need him."

"Unless we find Cole soon, he could be in danger." I didn't mention that we were looking for Jason too. No one in particular would be out to get him, but if he was headed to an encampment, he could get himself in trouble.

"I know. And I don't disagree. But Gary, well, he's a loose cannon."

"But he's used to dealing with … you know, challenging situations. Like hitmen and assorted bad guys."

"Okay, so he's Liam Neeson and I'm Steve Carrell. But we do just fine on our own."

"Yuri, my son could be in danger. If we find them before Gary gets here, that will be great. But if we don't …" Who wouldn't want both Liam and Steve on their team?

CHAPTER 7
A TOUGH LESSON

THERE WERE SEVERAL entrances into the park, including easy ways to intersect with some of the main trails. We assumed Cole probably either knew where the main encampment was or would be able to make a good guess based on his experience living in similar camps. Jason, on the other hand, wouldn't necessarily know where to look. Unless he ran into someone who could and would give him directions. Hoping he was still trying to get his bearings, we decided to start from the main entrance to the 220-acre park. As much as I was worried about Cole, Jason was my first priority.

Imagine my surprise when we saw Jason walking toward us on the road less than a quarter mile from the entrance. I was relieved and angry at the same time. Relieved to find him; angry that he had gone after Cole without telling anyone.

I pulled over and ordered him to hop in the backseat. He looked as surprised to see me as I had been to see him, but he instantly obeyed. As soon as he was inside, I headed for the parking lot so I could question him without blocking traffic.

Yuri turned to look at Jason. "You okay?" He sounded concerned. What had he noticed that I hadn't?

"Kinda," Jason replied, his voice a bit shaky.

That wasn't the answer I wanted to hear, but I refrained from bombarding him with the questions that were bubbling inside my brain until we reached the parking lot. As soon as I turned off the engine, I twisted around to look at him. He was hunched over, eyes downcast, like someone caught doing something wrong. "Want to tell us what happened?" I asked. I was relieved, upset, angry and troubled all at the same time. Then as I took in his appearance, I almost shouted: "What's that on your face? Did someone hit you? And why is your shirt dirty?"

Then it hit me that he had been on foot when we came upon him. "And where is your bicycle?"

"I'm sorry," he began, looking close to tears."

"Here," Yuri said to Jason. "You get in the front seat with your mother; I'll get in back."

When he got out of the car for the exchange, I got out too. Seeing how dejected he was, all my motherly instincts kicked in. I ran around to the other side of the car, pulled him into my arms and held him close. When he didn't pull away with an "Aw, Mom," I knew he'd been shaken by whatever he'd experienced. I patted him on the back. "Whatever happened, it's alright now. You're safe; that's the important thing."

Jason stopped trembling, stepped back, and gave me a thin smile. Then, we all got in the car—Yuri in back, Jason in front, and me in the driver's seat. Turning toward him, I asked: "Now, tell us what happened—start with whatever you think is most important."

"Well, they took my bike."

"Who did?"

"Some boys. I asked them where the homeless camp was and they … they started saying things. Then one of them dragged me off my bike, and they took turns pushing me back and forth until I fell down." Tears welled up in his eyes. "One of them kicked me. Then, they pulled me to my feet and punched me." He looked at Yuri. "I remembered what you said about not fighting back if you're outnumbered. You told me that it's best to act like you're done for and wait for an opportunity to get away, so that's what I did."

I didn't realize Yuri had given Jason advice on defending himself. I wondered about the circumstances.

"That was smart," Yuri said.

"But it didn't work out; I mean, I didn't get a chance to run away. Some runner came along, so they took my bike and my cell phone and left me there on the ground."

"Do you think you need to see a doctor?" I asked. "Your face doesn't look too bad, but you said they kicked you?"

"I think I'm okay. It hurts, but I can walk. Nothing's broken. We need to find Cole."

"I'm taking you home first."

"No, please. Let me go with you. Please. I should have stopped him."

Yuri and I exchanged looks. I knew it was up to me, so when Yuri didn't shake his head "no," I relented. In Jason's place, I'd want to go with us too. "Okay, but you need to stay right beside us; you run off and you're grounded until you graduate, understand?"

I'd never seen him so contrite, shoulders slumped, lips pursed, sad eyes. It made me feel guilty. After all, his instincts had been good. He'd been trying to look out for Cole. It was my "mom" gene that was making me sound like an uptight, controlling parent.

"First I need to call your grandma so she will know you're okay. You gave her quite a scare."

The phone barely rang before Mom picked up with an anxious, "Did you find them?" I put it on speaker and nodded for Jason to answer.

"I'm fine, Grandma. Sorry for worrying you."

"Are you coming home?"

I jumped in: "We're going to look around for Cole first. Just continue to stay inside and don't answer the door. Okay? And call me if there are any problems."

"Got it. Good luck." I pictured her in her floral apron holding her hot pink Glock. It was both reassuring and scary.

After studying the map on the park kiosk, we decided to take a trail that followed one of the creeks through a heavily treed area and led to another park entrance. Although there were no public facilities in that direction, and the trail was a favorite among runners, having easy access to fresh water might be considered a convenience by campers. Also, there was only one main trail heading in that direction instead of the maze of crisscrossing paths throughout the rest of the park. It seemed to us that might be preferable for squatters, so that's where we headed.

We had one big advantage—Cole didn't know we were following him, assuming we were in the right park. There was at least one other park nearby where the homeless had put up tents in the past. But we all agreed that if we were going to live in a city park in the area, this is the one we would choose because, even though there was heavy use by local residents, there were pockets of privacy among the trees.

It didn't take long before we saw a khaki-colored tent mostly hidden by trees and bushes. Jason and I stayed on the trail while Yuri went over to get a closer look. "No one there," he said when he returned. A little further on we came across a small cluster of tents that all looked similar in style and vintage. A few years back, a local outdoor retail chain had donated tents to the homeless, and my guess was that these were some of those tents. They were sturdy but smaller than most of the makeshift shelters we had seen at other sites. Those came in all shapes and sizes, cobbled together with tarps, sticks, lumber scraps, chicken wire—any material that could be scrounged in the area. Some looked almost permanent; others as if they would collapse in the slightest windstorm.

"There's someone," Yuri said, nodding his head to suggest which way to look without pointing.

Glancing in the direction he was motioning toward I saw a woman sitting in a deck chair in front of one of the tents. "She's alone," I said. "Maybe it would be best if I approach her by myself. You two stay here."

"Hi," I said as I got close. Except for the fact that her clothes were wrinkled, and her shoes had seen better days, much better days, she could have been someone from my neighborhood sitting on their back deck.

"You don't look like a cop," she replied.

"That's because I'm not." I pointed to Yuri and Jason. "We're looking for my son's friend who ran away earlier today. We think he's in trouble and want to help him."

"You want to turn him in, you mean." She didn't sound particularly sympathetic or cooperative.

I hesitated, then decided to be truthful. It was possible she knew something that might be useful, and at this point, the sooner we found him the better. "I don't know if you've heard about some encampment people disappearing ..." I paused to let her jump in, and when she didn't, I continued. "Well, my son's friend saw someone being kidnapped. He managed to escape. Now the kidnappers are after him. We need to find him first and get him to some place safe."

"What's your connection to him?"

She wasn't questioning the kidnapping piece, interesting. "I helped him get away from them initially. Then they found out he was staying with me and my family. He ran away to protect us. He shouldn't have. My son followed him here."

"What will happen to him?"

"I have a friend who lives off the grid. He's going to take him until we can figure out something more permanent." That was more information than I'd intended to reveal, but my gut said she knew something and was holding back. Perhaps to protect Cole.

"Off the grid?"

"He values his privacy and is, well, independent."

"Sounds like my kinda guy. Single?" Her tone had become more friendly, and her shoulders relaxed.

I grinned. "And sexy," I said.

"Well, feel free to tell him about me." She actually winked. Then, she gave me a long look before saying, "If it's that young blond boy with a gray backpack with the picture of a unicorn on it that you're looking for, I sent him down the creek a ways. There are a couple younger guys who hang out there."

"Thank you so much." We were not only in the right park but closing in on our runaway. "Thank you," I repeated.

"Just don't forget to tell your sexy friend he's welcome in my tent any time."

When I returned to Yuri and Jason, Jason said, "Mom, you're smiling."

I told them the good news, and we hurried down the trail. "Keep your eyes open," I said.

"Funny, Mom."

"You know what I mean."

"Think he'll run if he spots us?" Yuri asked.

"Let's be ready for that."

"I can catch him," Jason boasted.

"You agreed not to run off," I pointed out.

"If he runs, let me take the lead," Yuri said.

"Like you're in better shape than me," I countered.

"I'm not saying that."

The three of us were still arguing about who could outrun Cole when he stepped out on the trail ahead of us. "What are you doing here?" he yelled.

We froze. Jason recovered the quickest, "Cole!"

Cole backed up a few steps. "You shouldn't have followed me."

"Cole, listen," I said. "I've made arrangements for you to go with a friend to his place on an island where you'll be safe."

"They'll find me."

"Let me put it this way. If you go with my friend and they find you, they will be sorry."

"We'll explain everything on the way," Yuri said, glancing at his watch. "Come with us, and we'll take you to him." When Cole didn't say anything, he added, "We found you here; they can too."

I could tell Cole was struggling with the decision about whether to come with us. "I think the woman who directed you here knows about the disappearances. This is a bigger problem than you. We need to investigate. We can't poke the hornet's nest too much if we're spending our time worrying about you."

"Come on, Cole," Jason urged. "Gary's cool. And he has a dog named Bandit that is really smart. And, he lives in a cabin in the woods on this island that you can only get to by boat and …"

I cut him off. "We'll tell you all about him and what his situation is if you agree to come with us."

Cole didn't hesitate long before nodding agreement: "Okay." I assumed that meant he wasn't relishing starting over as a homeless person. Especially with a couple of thugs looking for him.

Yuri put his arm around Cole's shoulder as we walked up the trail together. "You made the right decision."

Back at the car, I called Gary. His floatplane was about to land. He would wait for us at the seaplane base. On the way there, I told Cole a little more about Gary and his cabin in the woods.

"He's a consultant," I said. That was a word I had decided on when explaining what Gary did for a living to Mara and Jason. "He's hired to find missing persons and provides security services."

"He's like a spy," Jason said.

"I wouldn't say that," I countered. Although Yuri and I have speculated that Gary might get involved in covert operations for government agencies from time to time.

"I wouldn't want him for an enemy," Yuri said. "He knows how to handle himself."

"He sounds kinda scary," Cole said.

"He's awesome," Jason said. "You'll like him." Then, "Think he'll have Bandit with him?"

"I'm not sure."

"Can he bring him on a plane?" Cole asked.

"Yes, Gary flies to and from the island frequently enough that he knows most of the pilots, and Bandit is a better passenger than some people, so they're willing to let him fly uncaged."

As we drew near the seaplane base, I hoped Bandit would be with Gary. Having Bandit there might make it easier for Cole to accept the situation.

Sure enough—the two of them were waiting for us when we arrived, Gary seated on the ground with Bandit next to him, a large and shaggy black dog with a strong muzzle and eyes that seemed to say "I see you" and "I know what you need." The instant Jason got out of the car, Bandit raced over to him, then quickly turned to Cole as if he knew that was the reason he'd made the trip.

"See," Jason said to Cole. "I told you, Bandit's amazing."

Cole was busy running his hands along Bandit's long back, and Bandit was acting like a puppy begging for attention. Meanwhile, Gary stood by watching. He caught my eye and smiled that warm, bad boy smile that made him so appealing. Yuri stepped in front of me and went over to shake Gary's hand. "We appreciate this." His "we" sounded rather proprietary. That irritated me a little, but it made Gary's smile show more teeth.

"Always glad to help out friends," he said, emphasizing the plural. That made *me* smile. Neither man was more than friend material for me, for very different reasons, but I was still pleased to see a little macho rivalry. After all, I wasn't committed to remaining single forever. Although after having a failed marriage that ended in an unexpected death and financial disaster, I wasn't eager to pursue another relationship. Being duped twice wasn't something I wanted to risk. But, I still had a few hormones that occasionally called attention to their presence.

Cole looked up when Gary moved beside Bandit, and Bandit quickly sat down, temporarily removing himself from the conversation. "I'm Gary." He held out his hand to Cole.

"I'm Cole." He shook Gary's hand. In that moment Cole looked very mature, a young boy, but one shaped by harsh reality. Whereas Jason occasionally had moments that hinted at the man he would become, the puppy in him was usually at the forefront.

"And you've already met Bandit." Gary turned to Yuri and then to me. "Are we good to go? Any instructions?"

"Keep him safe," I said.

"Bandit and I will be sure to do that." He looked at Cole. "Ready?" Bandit got up and nuzzled Cole's leg.

"Ready." The word sounded confident, but the voice betrayed some anxiety.

"Ever been on a seaplane before?"

"I've never been on any kind of airplane." Cole sounded excited and perhaps a bit frightened, or maybe just a bit overwhelmed. So much had happened to him in a short time.

"You're in for a treat," Gary said. "Bandit loves to fly. I'm sure you will too."

On the way home, Jason asked if we thought he would get his bike or his cell phone back. I told him that I'd report them stolen, but not to hold out hope.

"Life is full of tough lessons," Yuri said. "But you can always get another bike and another cell phone. You were lucky."

"And foolhardy," I added. "But lucky." And I was so thankful for that. With Jason back in the fold and Cole safe, we could continue to investigate. Unfortunately, the bad guys didn't know that Cole had moved on. I wondered if I needed to put a sign on my front door saying that he was no longer staying with us. I didn't relish getting a visit from the two men who were looking for him.

CHAPTER 8
SURVEILLANCE

WHEN WE REPORTED in to P.W. via phone, she said that I should not bother coming back to the office; that I needed to be with my family. I not only agreed but was relieved that I didn't have to ask permission to go home. P.W. was good that way. It was clear that she valued us as people and as employees, even though she never socialized with any of us, as far as I knew. Though I did suspect she had some kind of out-of-office relationship with Blake, maybe not dinner exchanges, more like an occasional coffee klatch.

We never included Blake in our speculations about P.W.'s past. In fact, none of us had asked him what he knew about it. He was one of us, yet he wasn't. We "pit dwellers" were a close-knit team. And so far, the Penny-wise pit-dwellers team hadn't even been able to find out P.W.'s current address let alone where she'd spent time prior to starting Penny-wise.

Nothing. No matter how much effort we put into it, we found nothing. Nothing at all. However, based on the data and support she'd provided on some of the cases we'd worked on, we were aware that she had some powerful contacts—government and perhaps extra-legal—that she could call on if necessary. Knowing that only whetted our appetites for information about her earlier years even more. Yuri in particular was determined to uncover her secret life. As for me, I kinda liked the fact that she had a mysterious past.

Blake at least had a visible past. We'd checked. Nothing unusual—we knew where he grew up and went to school, his work history—that sort of thing. Even though we hadn't identified a connection between him and P.W. before the creation of Penny-wise Investigations, that didn't mean Blake and P.W.'s paths hadn't crossed at some point in their lives. Not every detail of one's life is captured online. In any event, P.W. remained an enigma and her relationship with Blake another unknown.

I dropped Yuri off at the mall; then Jason and I headed home.

"Am I in trouble?" Jason asked shortly before we arrived.

"For leaving like that without telling anyone where you were going?"

"Yeah. And for losing my bike and my cell phone."

"If the same thing happened as before with Cole running off, what would you do?"

"You want me to be honest?"

"You'd follow him, right?"

"Yes, but I wouldn't stop to ask a group of boys anything."

I laughed. Jason and I were so alike. Then I said, "I would appreciate it if you thought about consequences before taking action, but I do understand that sometimes it's necessary to make snap decisions. Just remember, you're still young, and your family would like to see you live at least until you graduate from high school."

"You mean when you're no longer responsible for me?"

I laughed again. "I just don't want you to miss out on your senior year. Given societal trends, I could be 'responsible' for you until we reach a point where you have to take care of me."

"Well, I don't want to be kicked and beaten up, so I promise to think before doing something like that again."

"You do realize that you aren't getting off with just a few bruises, don't you?"

"What do you mean?"

"Your grandmother and Mara will not be as forgiving as I am. Brace yourself."

Within minutes of getting home, I was proven right about warning him to beware of his sister and grandmother. They'd apparently had sufficient time to be thankful he was safe, and relief had been replaced by anger at him for running off without telling them. "You can't imagine what it was like for us, Dumbro," Mara said. "We were frantic. We went up and down the streets looking for you." She turned to my mother. "Tell him, Grandmother." Then she took a second look at his face. "Did you get in a fight?"

"Someone hit me, but I'm okay."

My mother reached out and touched the red spot on his check before taking a deep breath and listing all the reasons he shouldn't have done what he did. They didn't even know yet that he'd lost his bicycle and cell phone because of his impetuous behavior. I decided not to bring that up. He was suffering enough.

In some ways it was nice to see someone else on the receiving end of my mother's ire. She dotes on Jason and Mara and always gives them the benefit of the doubt, but not this time. No one puts her grandson in danger and gets away with it, not even her own grandson.

Jason meekly accepted the duet tongue lashing while No-name retreated to the kitchen with his tail between his legs as if he too was being scolded. I followed and made myself a cup of coffee. I tossed No-name one of his favorite chew treats to improve his spirits. In spite of the fact that the chews were not intended as rewards, but to reduce tartar buildup and clean his teeth, he seemed to find them palatable. Although he usually lost interest fairly quickly and went searching for his latest soon-to-be-extinct endangered species toy.

We'd tried everything to wean him off his stuffed playthings. Bacon flavored "forever bones." "Long-lasting ostrich bone chews—from free range, ethically raised ostriches." "Made in the USA elk antlers." "Pig ears bully sticks." "Water buffalo cheek rolls." Every odd flavored bone or bone substitute that was supposed to last a long time and keep dogs from chewing things you didn't want them to chew. There was simply nothing No-name liked as much as his endangered species animals. He complained if he didn't have at least one available for destruction. It pained me to note that he was as determined and stubborn as the rest of the family.

We ordered pizza for dinner to celebrate Jason's safe return and Cole being under Gary's protection. Between mouthfuls, Jason asked, "Do you think Cole will like it on the island?"

"Who wouldn't?" Mara said. She tilted her head to one side. "I'd miss my friends though … and school … and shopping … and the city." She grinned and added, "And you, Mom." Looking at Jason, sauce dripping down his chin, she thrust a napkin at him. "But not you, weird, impulsive and lacking-in-manners brother."

Ignoring her comment, I said, "I think it will be like being at summer camp for him. Living in a cabin in the woods, but with amenities. He probably never went to a real camp before." His first time for making fudge, first time for bamboo sheets, first time on an airplane, and now hanging out on an island with his personal rifle-toting security guard and his trusty dog. That's a lot of firsts for a young boy, for anyone, for that matter.

"Think Gary will teach him to shoot?" Jason said.

"What makes you ask that?"

"Well, Gary's a tough guy. Maybe he'll teach him to fight too."

Mom interrupted. "Cole wasn't sent there to train to be a … a …" She couldn't seem to land on the right word.

"Soldier of fortune," Jason said, as if that was comparable to becoming President.

"Adventurer, free-spirit," Mara said

"Mercenary," Mom finally came up with.

"Gary does security work." That was what I'd decided to call what he did, what I thought he did, that is. It seemed like an acceptable professional label for children's ears.

"That means becoming good with weapons and being able to fight off attackers," Jason said. "Like FBI agents. Or undercover cops. Or covert ops. Or private detectives." He glanced at me and added, "I don't mean you, Mom."

My mother saved me from replying. "Security work is not glamorous," she said. "And unlike in the movies, real people get hurt. Furthermore, you can't dodge bullets like you see them do on TV. That just isn't realistic."

"And even tough guys don't always win fights," I added pointedly. "Especially if they're outnumbered." Hint, hint.

"Still, you have to admit, Gary's sexy," Mara said, wiggling her somewhat manicured, full eyebrows at me.

"Mara!" Mom said. "He's old enough to be your father."

"Ew," Jason said at the same time.

Mom quickly changed the subject. Thankfully, we stopped talking about masculinity and the appeal of the tough guy image. I didn't have to admit to them or to myself that I found Gary almost irresistible. But I felt that twinge of regret again.

I woke up, senses on high alert. Had I heard something outside? I glanced at my clock—1:00 a.m. My phone was lit up next to it. Even with the volume turned way down, I could still hear soft gorilla grunting sounds. Yuri. I tapped the phone image. "Hello?" I struggled to keep my voice calm. Early morning calls are seldom good news.

"Cameron. Get up. Now. Have the kids go upstairs with your mother. There are two men trying to break into your house."

"Huh?" I was confused, but I was already out of bed. I pushed my feet into a pair of clogs and grabbed my robe from the bench at the foot of my bed.

"Do what I say. I'm calling 911. But, I'm right outside, and I'm armed."

"I'll get Mom's Glock," I said.

"Good. Stay on the phone."

I woke Mara first. "Go upstairs," I ordered. "Now. I'll explain as soon as I get Jason. Wake up your grandmother and tell her we're coming."

Mara is usually a little slow to wake up, but not this time. "Should I get dressed?"

"No, just go."

I went to get Jason. When he didn't respond to my gentle "Jason, wake up," I put my phone in my robe pocket and shook his shoulder: "Wake up," I said a little louder. "We need to go upstairs right now."

Jason hesitated a moment, then seemed to come fully awake all at once and literally leapt out of bed. "What's happening?" he mumbled.

"I'll explain later."

Mom was waiting for us at the top of the stairs. She had her pink Glock in her hand. I was tempted to let her keep the gun, but I was going to be the first line of defense. She didn't resist when I reached out and took the Glock. "You need to get one of your own," was all she said.

"Stay up here. Yuri called 911." I took off down the stairs.

"Cameron." Yuri's voice came from my pocket. "They are coming in the front door. Do you have a gun?"

"Yes," I whispered into my phone.

"Stand to one side of the door. They've disabled the porch light. When they start to go in, I'll turn on my flashlight and tell them to stop or I'll shoot. Be prepared to back me up."

"Are the police on the way?" I asked, holding my hand over my mouth to muffle my voice.

"They should be. We're not waiting though. We need to stop these two men before they get inside."

"Right." I crept quietly and quickly down the last few steps and stood next to the door as Yuri suggested so I'd have a clean shot if they stepped inside. I assumed Yuri would take out the one furthest away from me if it came to a shootout. I'd never shot anyone before, but I wasn't going to hesitate under the circumstances.

No-name came out of nowhere and was standing next to me. What if he started barking? Why hadn't I thought about him when I was ushering my kids upstairs? I should have locked him in the kitchen. It was too late. I could hear a scraping sound as someone worked the lock on the door. We had a deadbolt too. Would they try to pick it or simply kick the door down?

No-name quit wagging his tail and stared at the door. Please don't bark. Please don't bark. I silently pleaded with him. He must have heard my thoughts because he was frozen in place, alert but quiet.

After a few minutes, I heard a muffled voice say, "Got it." The doorknob started to turn. I took a deep breath and held the Glock in position. I felt calm, but I could actually feel my heart beating. *Lub-dub. Lub-dub. Lub-dub.*

As the door opened, a bright light caught the two men in the act. "Put your hands in the air," Yuri yelled. His voice was loud enough to wake all the neighbors.

When I saw one of them nod toward the interior of my home, I said, "Don't even think about it. There are two guns trained on you. And we won't hesitate to shoot."

It was at that point that No-name apparently decided he'd had enough. He darted forward and bit the ankle of the man furthest away from me. I took advantage of the distraction to step forward and aim my gun at the stomach of the nearest man. "You heard the man, hands in the air." I saw a gun poking out of the guy's waistband, but he wasn't holding a weapon. He must have been the one picking the locks.

Yuri was holding a gun to the other man's head. Well, he was trying to. The man was hopping about, attempting to shake No-name off his leg. "You shoot the dog and you die," Yuri said as if he meant it. "Drop your weapon."

"Do it," the guy I was covering said.

The man dropped his gun. "Now get your damn dog off me," he pleaded.

"No-name, sit." I couldn't think of what else to say. We had no command for "let go of his ankle." He obediently sat, but held on to the man's ankle, jaws clamped into place.

At that moment we heard sirens. If we hadn't been there with our guns at ready, the two men would have taken off when the sirens screamed "the cops are coming."

"No-name, go see Jason," I said, hoping that would get him to release the hold he had on the man's ankle. It worked. No-name let go and headed up the stairs.

"He bit me. Your stupid dog bit me." The man sounded truly aggrieved, like I was the transgressor, not him.

"And what were you planning on doing with your gun?" I asked.

"This is a mistake," my guy said. "A misunderstanding."

"You wouldn't shoot us." The other guy looked like he was about to make a move even though Yuri was still holding a gun aimed at his head.

"Give me an excuse," I said. I must have sounded menacing because he stopped fidgeting. We stood there, a "don't move or I'll shoot" tableau, listening to the sirens. I knew it was going to take a few minutes for them to find us since our carriage house is shrouded by trees at the back of a large lot. Finally, the sirens stopped, and a few heartbeats later, an officer shouted, "Everyone drop your weapons."

"Not until you come and secure these two criminals," I yelled. "This is my house. And these two were trying to break in."

"And I'm the one who called you," Yuri said, looking over his shoulder.

"Get down on the ground," I said to the two intruders. When they didn't obey, I shouted, "NOW."

Both men knelt. I kicked away the gun the second man had dropped and lowered my Glock. Yuri took a step back and lowered his gun. The two officers quickly moved in.

"Thanks for coming so quickly," Yuri said.

"This man has a gun in his waistband in front," I said. "The other man's gun is over there." I pointed to where I'd kicked it away.

"You are?" the officer asked me.

"Cameron Chandler. This is my house. My mother and two children are upstairs."

"And I'm a private investigator," Yuri said. "Yuri Webster. I had the house under surveillance. When I saw them trying to break in, I called my partner to warn her."

The surveillance bit was a surprise to me—why hadn't he said anything?

"Any shots fired?"

"No," Yuri and I said in unison.

I suddenly felt a wave of relief and anger surge through my body. "You came to kidnap the boy, didn't you?" I asked the two men. They both looked away. "Well, you really blew it. He's not here."

"Fuck you," the second man said.

The officer said, "Kidnap?"

"It's a long story," Yuri said. "You can call our boss for verification."

"And Detective Connolly. He can vouch for us. He's …"

"I know Connolly," the first officer said as he tapped some numbers into his cell phone. I heard him call for backup. He turned away so I couldn't hear the second call he made.

The other officer handcuffed the two men and made them stay down on the ground while we waited for their backup to arrive.

"Is everything under control?"

I turned around. Mom was in the hallway wearing a long blue silk robe that shimmered in the flashlight the officer turned on her. She ducked her head away from the bright light.

"Ma'am, you should stay inside," the officer said.

"What happened to the porch light?" she asked.

"They unscrewed the bulb," Yuri explained. He turned toward the nearest officer. "Mind if I screw it back in?"

"Go ahead."

When the light came on, I finally got a good look at our two burglar/kidnappers. I felt certain they were the men who had been chasing Cole. For one thing, if they were thieves, what did they plan on putting their loot in? There wasn't a single "burglar bag" in sight.

"Who hired you?" Yuri asked. He was apparently hoping to get some answers before the two were hauled off.

"I want to talk to my lawyer," dirtbag number one said.

"Same here," dirtbag number two echoed.

The other officer came over and thrust his phone at me. "He wants to talk to you."

"Who?" I asked before taking the phone and saying, "This is Cameron Chandler."

"And this is Detective Connolly. I understand you had a little problem tonight."

"More like a big problem, but it's a long story."

"My office. First thing tomorrow morning. Both of you."

"I don't think you have the authority to ask us to come downtown first thing." I found his bossy demeanor extremely irritating, although I knew we would have to file a report of some sort.

"Let me rephrase that. Would you please come by my office some time tomorrow morning so I can figure out how to help you avoid getting killed?"

Until he mentioned the part about me getting killed, I was still mentally resisting his request. "We'll have to check with our client before we share certain facts with you."

There was silence at the other end of the line. "Okay, let's compromise. I'll come to your office tomorrow morning, and the three of us can have coffee and a friendly chat. How's that?"

"You'd do that?" I was touched.

"Based on my experience with the two of you, I imagine the 'long story' might be complicated. And knowing you …"

"You think you'll get more details out of me with honey than with vinegar."

"There's better coffee in the mall than here."

"And donuts."

"The cop-donut thing is more myth than reality."

"You don't like donuts?"

"I take my coffee black," he paused. "I wouldn't turn down a glazed donut either."

"It's settled then."

He hung up, and I handed the phone back to the officer who was grinning at me. I'm glad he hadn't heard both sides of the conversation.

Several more officers showed up, and the police turned their attention to the two would-be kidnappers. Then they took down our information, asked a few final questions, and departed. We went inside and re-locked the door. Obviously, I needed better security.

The kids came running down the stairs as soon as they saw my mother heading up. "What happened?" Mara said.

"We watched from the deck," Jason said.

"You went out on the deck?"

"We stayed down," Mara said. "We only went out after we heard the sirens."

I considered admonishing them for disobeying, but I caught the guilty look on my mother's face. She must have been with them on the deck.

Mom said, "We heard Yuri shout 'drop your gun.' After that, things got quiet, so we were fairly certain you had the situation under control."

"Okay, let's all go into the kitchen and have a cup of hot chocolate and talk about what happened. Okay?"

I knew Mom and the kids had a million questions, but there was only one at the forefront of my mind: why had Yuri been watching my house?

I quickly made a batch of cocoa with Ghirardelli Double Chocolate Hot Cocoa Mix, our favorite, while Yuri explained that he thought the two men had been looking for Cole. I agreed, emphasizing, however, that we didn't know for sure. As I poured everyone a cup of cocoa, Yuri described what had taken place from the time he called me to when we'd managed to subdue the two men. Everyone laughed about No-name biting one of them, and Jason gave him a chew treat as a reward. Once we'd answered all of the questions we could, we promised that after we talked to the police, we would fill them in on any details they shared with us.

Mom's eyes lingered on mine a second before saying, "Okay, why don't we all go back to bed and try to get a little more sleep?" The adrenaline bounce we'd shared seemed to suddenly deflate, and no one objected to returning to their rooms.

At the door, Yuri turned. "What did Connolly say?"

"Before I tell you, why don't you tell me about your surveillance on my house?"

"Well …" Yuri looked up and to the left briefly before replying. "P.W. and I agreed that they—whoever 'they' are—might think Cole was still here. We thought it was a good idea to keep an eye on your place."

"We?" Although the theory about eye direction when lying has allegedly been debunked, I still think there's some truth to it.

"She did think it was a good idea."

"But you suggested it."

"I may have."

"Don't you think you could have warned me?"

"I didn't want to alarm you."

"And you didn't think that a 1:00 a.m. call would 'alarm' me?"

"I was hoping I was wrong."

"Well, you owe me one for this."

"Don't you think it's the other way around? Maybe I saved your life."

"Let's not exaggerate." Then, I reached over and hugged him. "Thank you," I whispered. "For saving my whole family."

Yuri untangled himself and held me at arm's length: "Don't thank me yet. We still don't know who is behind this."

CHAPTER 9
LET'S STEP OUTSIDE

WE ALWAYS HAVE office coverage on the weekends because that's when we get a lot of mall traffic drop-ins. As a concession to me having young children, I was usually given weekends off—unless we were working on a case. This Saturday morning, I was there bright and early. Well, the day was bright; but according to how I felt and what I saw in the mirror when I tried to make my hair look half-way presentable, I was not a poster child for bright in the sense of being eager and ready for action. Yuri, on the other hand, appeared more than ready to face the day's challenges—hair slightly mussed, eyes large behind thick black-rimmed glasses, and wearing his kick-butt leather walking shoes with reinforced toes.

The morning would have gone a lot smoother if Detective Connolly and Gary hadn't shown up at the office at the same time. Blake often worked at least one day on the weekend so he could screen prospective clients, and when the two men arrived simultaneously, he called to let me know there were "two gentlemen" who wanted to see me: "Detective Connolly and a Mr. Gary Miles." Having him refer to Gary as "Mr." made me smile. However, my smile quickly faded at the prospect of the two men in our lobby at the same time.

"Just a sec," I said, motioning for Yuri to come over. "Connolly and Gary are both here. What should I do?"

"Have an affair with one and marry the other—your choice." I gave him the stink eye he deserved. "Okay, I'll take Connolly to the conference room, and you talk to Gary in the lobby. Law trumps other obligations. Tell Gary to come back in an hour."

"We'll be right out," I told Blake.

Yuri and I peeked into the lobby. At least in appearance, the contrast between the two men was startling. Gary's bushy, blond beard and his longish hair just brushing the collar of his plaid shirt made him look like someone from rural America who knew how to live off the land. Connolly, on the other hand, with his chiseled chin and short hair was the epitome of the "I could pose for the police calendar" image. To my surprise, the two men were engaged in what sounded like a cordial conversation, standing, not sitting, but both looking relaxed and comfortable. Blake, of course, appeared to be studying some papers on his desk, but I could tell by the way he held his head that he was taking in every word. I wondered if he would share what they talked about with me if I asked.

Yuri cleared his throat. They turned at the same time, then glanced at each other and then to me, waiting for me to make the call. Before I could say anything, Yuri jumped in.

"Detective Connolly. Why don't you come to the conference room with me. Cameron will join us in a few minutes."

Connolly gave me a questioning look before following Yuri into the pit.

"Let's step outside," I said to Gary. I didn't have any secrets, but I knew Blake had hearing like a greater wax moth—a bit of trivia about animals with extraordinary hearing that Yuri had once gone on and on about. Since I wasn't entirely sure why Gary was there, it seemed better to play it safe.

"Where's Cole?" I asked the instant the door shut behind us. My first thought had been that Cole had somehow managed to run away and Gary was here to find him.

"He's with my neighbors. They have a son about his age, and Bandit is with him."

I was relieved but puzzled. "So, why are you here?"

Gary smiled, a slow, sensuous smile—or so it seemed to me. "Cole and I had a long conversation about his situation, and he and I decided that you could use some backup talking to residents of homeless encampments because, well, you look a bit …"

"Official?" I filled in, not wanting to hear the label he might apply. Matronly? Conservative? Gullible? Vulnerable?

"I was going to say like someone who has never been homeless or ever would be."

I had to admit, he could probably blend in, although he looked much too fit to pass for homeless. "So, what do you suggest?"

"You talk to the handsome detective in there" — he smiled and nodded his head towards the door — "while I get a coffee. Then you, Yuri, and I put our heads together and come up with a strategy for approaching people in the encampments. Agreed?"

Handsome detective? "Detective Connolly is here because we caught two guys trying to break into my house last night. We think they were after Cole."

Gary suddenly looked concerned. "Did they get away?"

"No, they're in custody. We, ah, subdued them before the police arrived."

"Good to know." The skin around Gary's eyes crinkled. "I look forward to hearing about it when I return. Think your meeting with Connolly will take more than an hour?"

"It shouldn't."

"Time for a latte then. Maybe a croissant."

As I headed back inside, I was smiling. A mountain man who appreciates a croissant with his latte. When Blake looked up at me, I quickly put on a more serious face. "Got it sorted out," I said, as if he knew what had required sorting. Blake acted as though my comment made sense to him. Maybe it did—he had sharp eyes as well as exceptional hearing.

Yuri and Detective Connolly stopped talking when I entered the conference room. "Please, continue," I told them, taking a seat next to Yuri and across the narrow table from Connolly.

"Yuri has explained that he was watching your house and called you when the two men tried to break in. He's a bit vague about why he knew that someone might try to break into your house though. Why don't the two of you fill me in on some of the details leading up to last night. Then tell me what you did after he called."

I explained that we had a client who had seen something he wasn't supposed to and that we assumed the two men were looking for him at my house.

"You don't provide lodging for clients, do you?"

Yuri and I exchanged looks. "He's underage," I said. "And he only stayed one night."

"Let me see if I have this right: you have an underage client who saw something, something illegal?"

"We're investigating what he thinks he saw."

"And if you determine there's an illegal act involved …?"

"We will let the police know immediately."

Connolly glared at me. "You shouldn't be putting yourself in situations like this. That's what the police are for."

"We aren't sure what the actual facts are yet. Initially, we didn't think anyone could track our client to my home. After we found out that he was seen with me, we sent him someplace else. Apparently the two men who showed up at my place didn't know that."

"Obviously he was still worried." Connolly pointed to Yuri without looking at him.

"I was simply taking extra precautions," Yuri said. "It seemed like an easy thing to do."

"Easy perhaps, but not exactly foolproof if you anticipated they were there to … what? Kidnap or kill your client?"

"As soon as I spotted them, I called the police, then Cameron."

"And were you prepared to fend them off?" he asked me.

I looked to Yuri who flushed slightly before admitting: "I hadn't actually told Cameron that I was watching her house."

"He thought them showing up was a longshot," I said. I don't know why I defended him when I was angry that he hadn't told me he was going to be there.

"So, what did you do after he called?"

I explained about getting my kids upstairs and reluctantly confessed that I borrowed my mother's legally permitted Glock in case I needed to defend myself and my family.

"But neither of you deployed your weapons?"

Deployed our weapons? That sounded rather military, and dangerous. "No shots were fired. By anyone," I assured him.

"But your dog did bite one of the intruders." Was that the hint of a smile I detected behind the seriousness of the question?

"No-name has had his shots, and yes, he did bite one of the men on the ankle. He was defending me. He's never bitten anyone before."

"Don't worry, I have to include that on my report because the suspect has complained. Under the circumstances, you don't need to be concerned. Just make sure he doesn't make it a habit of biting strangers."

"Not unless they turn up in the middle of the night brandishing weapons. Better to deploy my dog than my mother's Glock, wouldn't you say?"

"I wish you didn't need a weapon for self-defense," Connolly said, sounding very serious.

"It comes with the job," Yuri said.

Connolly looked from Yuri to me and back to Yuri. "Okay, let's cut to the chase. Off the record, and without naming names, what's your client's problem?"

"I didn't think you could talk 'off the record,'" I said.

Before he could answer, Yuri asked: "Did either of the two guys who tried to break in say what they were up to?"

"Lawyered up on the way to the station."

"So, you don't know who they were working for? Because we're pretty sure they were hired by someone, not acting on their own."

"No idea. Unless they want a plea deal, we may never know … at least not if we're relying on them for all of the information." Hint. Connolly frowned at me, an angry cop face rather than a dashing Romeo.

Yuri and I had discussed whether we could trust Connolly to let us handle Cole's situation if we shared the circumstances with him—at least until we or the department identified the source of the problem. Unfortunately, we had decided we couldn't. Not because we didn't trust him as a person, but because he was committed to upholding the law, not bending it when it suited him. Still, he'd said "off the record."

"Off the record?" I asked. Connolly nodded, and Yuri gave me permission with his eyes. "They're after a 13-year-old homeless boy who may have witnessed a woman's kidnapping. We're trying to track the woman we think they abducted. We have the boy stashed somewhere safe. That about sums it up."

"Oh, that's all, huh? A homeless boy, a possible abduction, and two hired thugs."

"Your sarcasm isn't lost on us," Yuri said. "You know how these things evolve from one tiny incident and then morph into something bigger."

"Witnessing a possible kidnapping doesn't seem like a minor incident."

"Well, we don't know for sure that's what it was. It could have been related to a drug deal gone bad or a disagreement about something, anything. We don't know at this point."

"But it was serious enough that they are trying to lay their hands on the boy to prevent him from telling anyone about what he saw and possibly identifying them to the police."

"That's what we assume," Yuri said. "But that doesn't necessarily mean they want to physically harm him. Depending on what happened to the woman, it's possible they think it's sufficient to threaten him to make sure he keeps quiet."

"You think they only want to talk? They tried to break into Cameron's house in the middle of the night for a conversation?"

"Okay, so we think it's more serious than a conversation. That's why Cameron's friend who you met in the reception area is here. He knows his way around places we may not be able to maneuver in on our own."

"You know that what you're planning on doing could be dangerous."

"That's why we have backup," I said. "Gary's a security, ah, specialist."

Connolly sat there in silence for what seemed like hours but was only a matter of a minute or so. Time stretches out when you're trying to think of ways to minimize admitting your own fears and avoid lying or having to tell the whole truth.

Finally, he said: "I can't stop you from doing what you do, but please call me if there is something I can help with. And ..." He looked directly at me. "... please consider your own safety and that of your family. Just because we've captured those two men doesn't mean that whoever hired them isn't going to send someone else after the boy …" He left the sentence hanging, but it was clear he was suggesting they could return to my place as the last place the boy was known to have been. Then he stood up, "I'll let you know what, if anything, I learn from the two guys we have in custody."

"Thanks," Yuri and I said, just ever so slightly out of synch so that it came out as "ththananksks."

Yuri stayed behind while I walked detective Connolly to the entrance under Blake's watchful presence. "Could you step outside a moment?" he asked. Once outside, he turned to me and added, "You know I worry about you, don't you, Cameron?"

"You don't need to," I added, feeling both pleased and annoyed. Was he saying that simply because I was a woman?

"I know it's unwise to …" He stopped in mid-sentence. "After this is over, I'd like to have a talk with you." Before I could respond, he took off.

Talk with me about what? The words hung in the air like skywriting, hard to decipher and fading so quickly it was difficult to recreate the moment.

Before I could go back inside, Gary appeared. Had he been lurking nearby waiting for Connolly to leave?

"He has a thing for you," he said. "You could do worse."

"Like you?" I asked before I could stop myself.

Gary laughed. "I'd be a lot worse."

I knew a red flush had stamped my face with embarrassment, so I turned and went inside with Gary in tow. Jenny wasn't in the office today, so I didn't have to suffer further embarrassment by seeing if the two of them were still an item. Yuri took one look at my face and raised an eyebrow in question. I simply shook my head, and he fortunately didn't press. He may be a tease, but he's also a supportive friend.

"Okay," Gary said, taking a seat. "Here's what I learned from Cole."

CHAPTER 10
A NEW CLIENT

"COLE COULDN'T BE too specific about why he thinks the two men were after Bess, because the encampments are a target for all sorts of criminals. Drugs, prostitution, angry gangs who hate the homeless or just want someone to beat up. He's heard that young kids are taken from parents and sold to the highest bidder. Then there's mental illness and disease. You name it, it's a tough life.

Still, he talked about acts of kindness and camaraderie, the reason he'd rather be there than trapped in foster care. He's been lucky enough to be befriended by a number of residents, Bess included. She's given him food on numerous occasions and advice on where to stay to be safe. He said that the place where they were staying was supposed to be one of the safest in the greater Seattle area. Far enough from downtown so as not to attract too many gangs looking for trouble, with easy access to bus and light rail transportation."

"So, what's his best guess about why they came after Bess?" Yuri asked.

"He thinks she might have been dealing drugs, not just using. If so, she could have gotten in trouble if she started selling in someone else's territory. Or maybe she ran up a tab she couldn't pay back. She could even have been cheating someone in the sales chain or selling bad stuff. You never know. Nice people who get addicted do crazy things."

"Wouldn't someone at the camp know if she was selling drugs?"

"They might know, but they might not want to say," Gary shook his head. "You don't mess with some of those people involved. To them, life is cheap."

"You don't think she's dead, do you?" I asked. That was the fear I was trying to suppress.

"Hard to say. When someone is hauled off like that, and then whoever took her comes after the kid who saw it happen—"

"But all we found in her tent was one bottle of pills," Yuri said. "P.W. had someone check them out. They were prescription opioids. But there was no label on the bottle, no indication where she got them."

"Maybe they took her stash when they grabbed her. They could have missed a bottle she set aside for personal use."

Blake interrupted us. "We have a client who wants to talk to someone about a missing person. Cameron, why don't you take it?" I wondered why Blake had picked me instead of Yuri. Maybe it was simply my turn. Blake had an unspoken process, and no one complained because it seemed to work.

"We'll give P.W. an update and wait here until you're through," Yuri said. "By then we'll have a plan."

I went out to reception to meet our prospective client. She was middle-aged with mousy brown hair, stylishly cut, and she wearing a pin-striped navy pants suit with a light blue blouse. Nothing fancy, but very professional. I introduced myself and suggested we should meet in the conference room. By the time we got there, Yuri and Gary had moved into the smaller room, leaving the larger, yet still smallish space, for me and our new client.

"Please have a seat." She sat, and I took a chair across the table from her.

"My name is Elinor," she said. "Elinor Easton. I believe you've been asking around about my sister, Bess."

Wow, I thought, small world. "Has your sister been living in a homeless camp?"

"Yes, that's her. I, um, I..." A tear trickled down her cheek. "Bess has had a drug problem for years. I can't tell you how many rehab programs she's been through, but she always ends up back on the street." She sniffed loudly. I reached for the box of tissues we always keep handy and put it in front of her. "Thank you," she said. "This is so difficult for me."

"I'm sorry." I waited for her to continue.

"I'm here because I want to hire you to find her."

"You know we are already looking for her. For another case."

"But I want to hire you to focus on finding her, not look for her as a part of something else." She dabbed her eyes. "I'm worried. She often moves around, but she wouldn't leave her stuff behind."

"You've been to the camp?"

"Yes. I live in Portland, but I came here about a week ago on business and decided to check up on her. She wasn't particularly, ah, interested in talking to me. When

I went again yesterday to tell her I was leaving, one of the residents told me she was missing, and that you had been asking questions about whether anyone had seen her lately. I couldn't just go home without knowing what's happened to her."

"If her things are still there then the other residents must think she's coming back."

"The ones I talked with weren't too hopeful. But she's out there somewhere. I can feel it. You see, we're twins."

"Oh." I didn't know what to say. I know there are stories about how emotionally connected twins can be, but I wasn't certain how reliable that was under the circumstances, especially when one of the two is a homeless drug user. "She's already a priority with us," I said. "And we plan on interviewing people at other camps to find out what they know about her and others who have gone missing."

"But as a client, you'll keep me up-to-date, right? I'm staying at a downtown hotel. Luckily, I'm able to work remotely for a while, and even if I have to leave before you find her, I'm only a few hours away."

I was torn. It seemed somewhat unethical to charge her for something we were already doing, but on the other hand, we were currently looking for Bess for free. This would be a paying client, and having her as a client would lend legitimacy to our investigation without naming Cole. That meant we could work with the police instead of "off the record."

The big question was whether I should tell her that we thought her sister had been abducted. I wasn't entirely sure how I would do that without revealing that we had an eyewitness. Waiting until we had a few more facts wouldn't change the situation, and telling Elinor that we believed her sister had been forcibly removed from her tent would only cause her more pain. At the same time, I worried that my desire to protect Cole might at some point conflict with my responsibility to Elinor as a client.

"You do understand that we were asking around about your sister because of another case that we're working on, and that we could end up with a conflict of interest. Although I don't see how."

"Are you trying to arrest her for drug use?"

"No, we have no direct knowledge that she is engaged in anything illegal. We won't know more until we locate her."

"Does your other client want to see her arrested for any reason?"

"No. He just needs some information from her."

"Then I want you to proceed. You already have a head start, and I trust you to tell me if a conflict of interest arises."

"Yes, we will definitely do that. Being able to tell camp residents that we are acting on behalf of Bess's sister will be helpful. It makes the search more personal." She didn't need to know that was the ploy we were already using.

"Good, it's settled then. I'll expect progress reports."

"Absolutely. We like to keep clients informed. Before you go though, I have a few questions. We're talking to people in the camps, but is there any other place you think she might have gone? Anyone she might have been in contact with? Friends? Relatives? Or somewhere she may associate with pleasant memories?"

"All of her friends have long ago given up on her. The same is true of our relatives. She left home as soon as she graduated from high school, and I don't think she's ever looked back."

"But you've kept in touch."

"She has a tendency to show up when she needs something. Usually at an inopportune moment." She took a deep breath. "Sorry, that's unfair. She has an addiction, and she is my sister. I desperately want you to find her. Maybe this time rehab will work."

I felt like she didn't really believe that this time was any different than all of the other times. I could also understand the guilt that goes with not doing something you feel you should be doing. Whether hiring us was a sincere desire to locate her sister or the result of guilt-laden feelings of responsibility, it probably didn't matter. It was taking action that counted.

"Is there anything at all you can think of that might help us find her?"

"No, I've thought and thought about this, but no."

"Well, if you do think of anything, let me know." I handed her a card. "Meanwhile, I'll have Blake get your contact information and walk you through our standard agreement, okay?"

"Yes, thank you."

After I took her to see Blake, I returned to the tiny conference room and joined Yuri and Gary. "We're done," Yuri announced. "Want to hear the plan?"

I held up my hand. "Before you tell me what you think we should do, there's something you need to know about our new client."

CHAPTER 11
SORRY, NO BOOZE

IRONICALLY, GARY and Yuri had decided that Yuri and I were going to continue using Bess as our excuse for talking to people in the encampments. They thought that seemed like the most straightforward approach and were pleased to find that we actually had a client we could truthfully name in doing so. Meanwhile, Gary was going to see if he could find out who was selling drugs in the camps and loosen tongues by offering some free weed. I didn't question why he was in possession of enough weed to share around. I assumed it was more likely that he had grown what he was using as bait rather than buying it, either legally or illegally.

Yuri and I chose a rambling, large encampment near where Bess and Cole had been staying originally as a place to start. It was on a wooded hillside that sloped upward from the freeway. Just the other side of the hill were middle-income houses with tidy yards, many filled with playground equipment for young children, others with dogs corralled behind low fences.

The trail that led to the encampment area ran behind a row of houses next to a freeway off-ramp. It looked like the kind of city trail that kids on bikes would use, except for the excessive amount of litter. It was almost as if someone had hauled a garbage-filled dumpster along the path leaking bits and pieces of this and that everywhere. My first thought was that the debris probably attracted all sorts of animal scavengers—crows, raccoons, possums, rats and who knew what kind of bugs. Not somewhere I'd want to linger—or have my kids riding bicycles.

This particular homeless camp had a history of being "swept" due to on-going complaints by locals who considered it a health hazard and because much of it was visible by those driving by on the freeway. Given all the trees around, it surprised me that the homeless residents didn't make more of an effort to keep their makeshift dwellings out of sight and avoid calling attention to the path they used to get back and forth. Was it their way of thumbing their collective nose at authority? A plea for help? Or just not worth the effort given the temporary nature of the encampment?

Although, because of the constant sweeps, it was a strange sort of "temporary." Within days of the police dismantling their dwellings and disposing of any belongings left behind, the homeless returned. There were very few locations with so much undeveloped land this close to the city and local stores, including a large Goodwill. In addition, the stretch of vacant land was difficult to access because of the terrain, thus discouraging random passersby. Overall, a desirable and convenient place to camp.

We parked our car halfway up the hill in front of a row of small, older homes overlooking the freeway and wended our way over to the trail. Several crows working on whatever had been left in a discarded McDonald's bag angrily hopped aside to let us pass. We followed the trail to a dirt access road that had been cut into the hillside above the freeway. As it curved around clumps of trees, the road was occasionally hidden from passing cars. It reminded me of an abandoned logging road you might come across in the foothills. I assumed the city used it, probably for maintenance access to the freeway as well as for the periodic removal of unwanted campers and debris. But it also made it easy for them to return.

There were tents and crude structures on both sides of the road, some grouped together, others set apart from the rest. There seemed to be a lot more litter everywhere as compared to Cole's encampment, but maybe it was just more visible because there was less underbrush.

As we drew near the first cluster of dwellings in a level clearing alongside the road, there were some unpleasant smells I avoided trying to identify. When lots of people camp in one place over a long period of time, it's difficult to deal with food and human waste. Some locals favored putting up porta potties and providing running water for the homeless encampments, as much for the convenience of the homeless as for sanitation generally, but that was costly, so the idea never seemed to get much traction with the legislature or city councils.

Although we passed a number of tents and make-shift dwellings, we didn't see any people around at first. Then we came upon a woman in an ancient lawn chair next to a lean-to composed of various tarps draped over a tree limb on one end and propped on the other sides by pieces of lumber of different heights and shapes. It looked like a good wind could easily knock it all down. The woman in the chair also looked like a good wind could knock her down. She was tiny, insubstantial, with Applehead doll face wrinkles that could have been the result of age or a combination of age and living outdoors year-round. Her hair was covered by a red scarf that matched her shirt.

Yuri and I were both wearing backpacks full of snack food, bottles of water and a few odds and ends, including duct tape, some plastic containers, Band-Aids, twine balls, and a few paperback mysteries. We also had cash in small denominations spread out in pockets and in the packs so we didn't have to pull out a wad of bills and peel off a few as incentive for information if it seemed appropriate.

The woman looked us over as we approached. Yuri took the lead. "Hello, my name is Yuri, and this is Cameron. We're looking for a woman named Bess. Mind if we ask you a question?"

"You just did … ask a question. Got more?"

Yuri squatted down in front of her, but I remained standing a few feet behind and to the side. "Yeah, I have several. First, what's your name?"

She gave him a big smile, showing the gap where her two front teeth should have been. The rest were yellowed with age. "Nora," she said.

"Well, Nora, Cameron and I are investigators, and we've been hired by Bess's sister to find her. She was living at a camp not far from here in the Rainier Valley, but she's disappeared. Her sister is worried. I have a picture of her—would you mind taking a look?"

Nora nodded and Yuri showed her the picture. Bess was smiling into the camera. There was a birthday cake on the table in front of her, the candles all lit, waiting to be blown out. Elinor had told us she'd taken it on their 18th birthday. It was one of the last times they'd been together as a family.

"No, I don't know her."

"Well, she's older now. Maybe you've heard of someone named Bess living in the area?"

"Nope."

I took a step forward. "I know that people come and go, but has anyone you know suddenly vanished lately?"

She looked up at me but didn't respond right away. I waited, not wanting to interrupt her thoughts, hoping that her hesitation was because she had information and was trying to assess either whether or how much to tell us. Finally, she said, "Maybe. People come and go all the time."

"We're interested in anyone who didn't go away on their own. People who might have been forcibly removed. Ever hear of that happening?"

"There're some rumors."

"What kind of rumors?"

"People disappearing in the middle of the night."

"Has anyone seen someone being taken away like that?"

"Not sure."

"Are you afraid for your own safety?"

"God's will."

"Or the demon's work," I said.

"Amen."

"Well, we'd better move along," Yuri stood up. "Would you like a candy bar? Maybe a bottle of water?" Yuri motioned for me to turn around so he could get into my pack.

"No booze?"

Yuri laughed. "Sorry. Just snacks and drinks."

"I could use a little whiskey, but I wouldn't mind a bag of chips, if you have any. And a water."

Yuri got out the chips and water and thanked her for talking to us. He then handed her his card and said if she spotted Bess or heard anything about her, she could either call him or tell Bess to get in touch with her sister.

I saw her tuck his card in a pocket next to a cell phone. It seemed strange to me that so many homeless people had cell phones. I knew there were some social programs that occasionally handed them out to the homeless so they could keep in contact with doctors' offices and call 911 in an emergency. There were also inexpensive options through various government programs, but I found it hard to believe that these programs accounted for the statistic that 94 percent of the homeless own a cell phone. I also had a hard time figuring out how they managed to keep them charged, especially if they weren't near a shelter, library, or a store or coffee shop that didn't mind them mingling with better-dressed clientele.

We passed quite a few more tents and improvised shelters but didn't see another person for about an eighth of a mile. Finally, we spotted three people, a woman and two men, seated around a small fire. I could smell the coffee before I saw the pot on a grill positioned at the edge of the flames.

Yuri gave them our spiel, and they suggested we sit down and asked if we wanted coffee. I shook my head "no," but Yuri said he'd love some. One of the men came up with a tin mug and filled it from the pot. "It smells good," Yuri said, then sipped it.

"Hey, I have some cookies to go with that," I said, feeling guilty for not accepting their hospitality. I took off my pack and came up with a package of Oreos and handed them to the woman on my left.

"My favorite," she said. She ripped off the end of the package, took three cookies and passed them along.

"There seem to be a lot of people along this road," Yuri said. "Maybe you've seen Bess passing by. Her sister is looking for her." He handed them Bess's picture. "She's older now," he added.

The second man to check out the picture said, "You say her sister is looking for her?"

"Yes, her name is Elinor. She's Bess's twin."

"Wish I had someone looking for me," the woman said.

When no one added anything, Yuri asked about people disappearing.

"People don't stay," the older of the two men said.

"Well, some do. Like you," the woman said. "And me."

"There are a few regulars," the man admitted.

"Anyone you think we should talk to who might know something about Bess?"

"The Doc," the woman said.

"Is that a nickname?" I asked.

"No, he's the doctor that comes by from time to time. A good guy. Checks in on us. Gives us medicine."

"What's his name?"

"He's Doc."

"Here," the woman said, thrusting her phone at me. "This is his number."

I took out my phone and copied his number. "Thank you."

"He goes to all the camps—if anyone has seen her, it would be him."

When we got up to leave, I got out another package of Oreos. "Since they're your favorite."

She took them and tucked them in her jacket. "Thanks."

One of the men said, "I could use some more cookies."

"How about chocolate chip?" I handed him a package. Then I handed another to the remaining man.

As we left, they all wished us luck in finding Bess.

"I didn't expect them to be so forthcoming," I said to Yuri as we got out of voice range.

"I'm not so sure they were. Didn't you feel the tension when I asked about people going missing?"

"Kinda. But I assumed it had something to do with the lack of stability in their lifestyle. You think there's more to it?"

"Yeah, I think there's a story there. And by giving us Doc's phone number, they were trying to help. They might not want to get involved, but he has nothing to lose by talking to us."

"Whereas if they tell us something and it gets back to the wrong person …"

"Exactly."

"Maybe it's a good lead."

"Let's hope so."

We came across and talked to a half dozen or so others before we reached a turnaround for the road with a narrow path continuing through the trees. We'd given away snacks, a couple of five-dollar bills and a Starbucks gift card I'd been meaning to use. I wasn't sure Starbucks would thank me, but the young man specifically asked for any gift cards.

I thought it was strange, but I was glad they would be used for something. Maybe there was a gift card exchange, like I've heard some people do with coupons. Another eyed our packs until I felt uncomfortable and started holding onto the shoulder straps on mine. One man seemed to want to touch me—my hair, arms, torso. It didn't feel sexual, just weird. We didn't linger with him.

On our way back, there was no one in sight. "I think we've worn out our welcome," I said.

Then we came across an old man who was dancing and singing something off-key. When he saw us, he yelled something unintelligible.

"Maybe we should give him some food," Yuri said.

"I don't think he's rational."

"He can still eat."

Yuri removed a bottle of water and a couple of candy bars from his pack and approached the man. When he continued to gyrate to his own music, Yuri put the stuff on the ground, and we continued on our way.

"A friend of mine works downtown," Yuri said. "There's a woman who hangs around on a streetcorner near his office and occasionally takes off all her clothes and screams at passersby. Eventually she puts her clothes back on. Sometimes the police come by, but all they can do is make her put on clothes. Apparently, the funding for mental health care workers for the homeless has been cut."

"What kind of a society are we that we don't have health care for everybody who needs it?"

"After we finish with this assignment, I think I may do some volunteer work."

"Feeling guilty?"

"Lucky. Privileged. And a little guilty."

"I think I should have Mara and Jason do some too. It's too easy to forget that the homeless are people. Not all rational or healthy people, but flesh and blood people who don't deserve to suffer.

We were almost back to my car. "Where to next?" Yuri said. "I understand there is quite a grapevine between camps. The next one will probably be expecting us."

"I hope Gary is having better luck."

"We could also try a couple of shelters," Yuri said. "Or food banks."

"And the Doc."

"Yes, the nameless doctor. I wonder if he wears a white lab coat when he visits the encampments."

"You sound skeptical."

"He's either a saint or has some ulterior motive," Yuri said.

"Let's see if we can find him. I've never met a saint."

CHAPTER 12
THE SAINT

NOT ALL DOCTORS are available on weekends; in fact, in my experience, few if any are. Nevertheless, we called the number we had for "Doc" before heading to our next encampment. Worst case scenario, if all we got was a message, we might still learn his name or the name of the clinic or practice where he worked. But we were in luck. The person who answered the phone said, "Zander, Lee and Walsh, how may I help you?" My first thought was that I got a law office by mistake.

"Ah, I'm trying to locate a doctor who donates time to helping the homeless. Do I have the right number?"

"That would be Dr. Walsh," the receptionist said without missing a beat.

Yuri was busy pulling up their website while I explained that I was a private investigator and had been hired to find someone who had been living in one of the encampments. "I was told that if anyone would know where this person might be, it would be Dr. Walsh. Is there any chance I could have a few minutes of his time to ask him about this?"

"Dr. Walsh is committed to helping the homeless, so I'm quite certain he would be willing to talk to you," the receptionist said. “Let me check.” She didn’t say whether he was in the office or not, but it sounded as though she anticipated he would respond quickly to my inquiry.

While I was waiting, Yuri showed me the website for Zander, Lee and Walsh. Their office was near Harborview where Dr. Walsh was listed as a part-time emergency physician. There was no mention of his work with the homeless on the website. However, it did give links to several articles he’d written on depression and addiction.

A few minutes later the receptionist came back on the line. “He has some free time in about an hour. Could you drop by then?”

“At the office?”

“Yes. He’s in today.”

“Thank you. We’ll be there.”

“Well,” I said after clicking off. “That was easy.”

“Walsh must be a workaholic—a full-time practice, part-time emergency care doctor, provides health services to the homeless and still has enough energy left over to write articles for medical journals. A Type A personality or overachiever for sure.”

“Or maybe he does qualify for sainthood.”

“I’m reserving my opinion.”

An hour later, after fighting—and cursing—downtown traffic and finally finding a cramped parking spot on the seventh floor of a poorly lit garage with disturbing black smears on the cement wall next to the space, we arrived just in time to meet with Dr. Walsh. He was a small man, short and slender, with dark brown hair and caramel brown eyes. He took us to a break room and offered us coffee, which we declined, while he ate a sandwich and poured himself coffee from a pot that smelled like it had been left on a heater element too long. "I hope you don't mind if I eat," he said. "I don't get many breaks."

"We appreciate you taking the time to meet with us," Yuri said. He took out the picture of Bess and put it on the table in front of Dr. Walsh. "We understand you regularly visit residents in a number of homeless encampments. Any chance you recognize this woman? This was her eighteenth birthday; she's older now."

"Her sister hired us to find her," I added.

He barely glanced at the photo before replying. "Yes. That's Bess. She's one of my regulars." He took a bite of sandwich.

"One of your regulars?" I asked.

"She's a drug addict. Primarily opioids. I've been trying to ween her off. Mostly I treat her anemia and other health issues. She's in pretty bad shape."

"Have you seen her recently?"

"Let me think." He chewed with his eyes closed for a moment. "It's been about a week," he said finally. "I can be more specific if you need to know exactly. I keep records of my visits."

"Do you visit her at the camp in the Rainier Valley?"

"Yes, the one on the hillside on the main route to the freeway."

"Her tent is still there, but she isn't," Yuri said. "You wouldn't happen to have any idea where else she might be?"

"If she's not at the Rainier Valley camp, then no. I can give you a call if I run across her. I try to go to the different camps on the same day each week, so they know generally when to expect me, but it doesn't always work out. Sometimes my regular patients forget what day it is or happen to be somewhere else when I arrive. And I'm sometimes called at the last minute for mental health consults at Harborview."

I interrupted by placing pictures of the two men who had snatched Bess on the table. Yuri had snapped the pictures just before the police took them away. "How about these two men—have you seen them at any of the encampments?"

Dr. Walsh studied the pictures before shaking his head. "No, I don't think so."

Yuri broached a new subject: "I noticed you write about depression and addiction, and you have a degree in psychology as well as an M.D. Do you treat people with mental health problems in the encampments?"

"Yes and no. Recently, I've been doing research on anxiety and depression. It's been on the increase since the pandemic—across all social and economic levels. Addictions too. So, I try to address whatever health issues patients have. It isn't always possible to be of much help given how little time I have to spend with them. Obviously, those with serious problems who have health insurance I can refer to specialists. But for the most part, the homeless have neither homes nor insurance. I do what I can, but it's never enough."

"I would imagine the homeless population provides a lot of anxious and depressed subjects for your research," Yuri said.

Dr. Walsh put down his sandwich. "I don't think of my patients as 'subjects.' They are human beings suffering from a variety of health issues, many of the issues interrelated."

"Sorry, it was a bad choice of words. I'm curious, though, what drew you to working with the homeless?"

"Nothing too surprising, really. My father ran off when I was young, and my mother was an itinerant farm worker during the summer and did waitressing during the winter months to keep food on the table and clothes on our backs. We moved around a lot, and I became quite familiar with the problems of poverty and homelessness. We lived out of our car occasionally when she couldn't find work. I was lucky though. I managed to beat the odds and get a full scholarship to college. Now I'm a doctor, and I feel it's time I help those less fortunate than me."

"That's admirable," Yuri said. I thought I detected the slightest touch of sarcasm in his tone, but Dr. Walsh either didn't pick up on it or chose to ignore it.

"I don't think of it that way. The Hippocratic Oath sets an ethical standard, but it doesn't address the reason that most people become medical professionals. One becomes a doctor to help people live better, healthier lives. Along the way, you find pockets of great need and try to address them."

He sounded like someone destined for sainthood to me. I put my card down next to his sandwich plate. "If you see Bess or hear anything that might help us track her down, we'd appreciate getting a call." I smiled, and he smiled back. He had a piece of lettuce caught in his upper teeth. At least it was something healthy.

Yuri and I stood. "Thank you for your time," Yuri said. "And I just want to say how much I appreciate what you do for the homeless."

I mumbled agreement, and we left him there finishing off his food.

"Well?" Yuri asked. "What did you think?"

"I think we need more doctors like him."

"He isn't a little too good to be true?"

"If he was a little taller, I'd ask him for a date."

"Isn't that a sexist response?"

"So, I'm not a saint like him."

"I guess I've never understood why someone would become a doctor. It's one thing to help people by finding them housing or giving them food, but dealing with their physical and mental health is … ah, messy. There are too many things that can go wrong. Too much to know. Too much responsibility. Too much, I don't know, just too much."

"I agree. It's the same sort of impulse I had for wanting to be a teacher—to help people better themselves. Only with doctors it can be a life-and-death commitment."

"Say, speaking of teaching, whatever happened to that professor you were dating?"

"Not enough sizzle."

"Hmmmm." I could almost hear Yuri's mind searching for the right comeback.

"Don't go there—I'm already sorry I said it."

"You remind me of … Goldilocks: too hot, too cold … too short … still looking for the 'just right.'"

His characterization of my love life or lack therein was closer to home than I wanted to admit. Fortunately, there were more pressing things for us to discuss, so Yuri didn't pursue his Goldilocks analogy further. My recollection of the story is that in the end, she escapes and runs away. A happy ending for Goldilocks if a disappointing one for the bears — perhaps a bit too close to home for the story of my relationships with men, although not necessarily always a happy ending.

That evening, Mom fixed dinner for Mara and Jason so I could meet with Gary and Yuri to talk about what we'd learned and make plans for the next day. We met at a crowded Thai restaurant and were lucky to get a table without reservations on a busy Saturday evening. The restaurant had tall, dark wood booths that created a sense of privacy even when the restaurant was packed with customers. We ordered a lot of food and started drinking the tea before it had properly brewed because we couldn't catch the waiter's eye to order something else to drink.

"This all makes me feel a bit guilty," I said, motioning at nearby tables crowded with platters piled high with food, their aromatic clouds drifting our way, increasing my hunger pangs. "So much abundance."

"And a lot of it will be taken home in little white containers, stored at the back of someone's refrigerator, eventually becoming crusted with mold," Yuri said. "At least that's what too often happens to me."

"It's a matter of who you compare yourself to," Gary said. "I'm sure there are people who create a lot more waste than you do. That being said, it does sound to me like you need to clean out your refrigerator more often."

Yuri conceded the point with a lopsided grin.

"Visiting the homeless encampments does make me feel like I should be doing more for people in need," I said.

"We probably all should," Gary said. "And there's lots to pick and choose from. Last year I spent a month helping build a school in a small village in Kenya. It made me feel good to be contributing something other than money.

Although that group of kids there need so much more than a school. It's hard to know where to start and when your conscience will let you say, 'that's it for now.'"

Gary mentioning his Kenyan project surprised me a bit. At first, I had a hard time envisioning him slinging wood as a volunteer, but on second thought, it did fit with the positive vibe under the tough guy exterior. He is definitely a complicated man.

"Imagine if you were Bill Gates. All those resources, but you can only target so many causes," I said. "What would you make a priority? Elimination of certain diseases? Education? Food distribution? Clean water? Climate change projects?"

Gary shook his head. "It's more than I can wrap my mind around. I usually get involved by accidentally coming across some project in progress, something tangible."

"That's why Jimmy Carter wanted to eliminate the Guinea worm," Yuri said. "It was a huge goal, but one he could actually achieve."

"And did he?" I asked. I didn't remember reading anything about the worm project, but of course that was the kind of weird fact Yuri would know.

"Last I heard there were only six cases in Africa. That's down from 3.5 million when he started the eradication program in 1986. I'd say he succeeded."

"Well, we have to think smaller," Gary said with a short laugh. "Much smaller. Like helping one young boy."

"And finding out what happened to Bess for her twin," I added. "If we can do that, we will probably help Cole out of his dilemma at the same time."

Gary frowned. "If I had to guess, I'd say she's gone for good."

"Why?"

"Well, after I spread a little free weed around, a number of people got a bit chatty. The homeless have never been a stable community, but they confirmed the rumors that there have been some surprising disappearances lately. Not just your normal ebb and flow of people."

"Gang related?"

"Lots of drugs, but not much muscle around according to the few I talked to."

"Serial killer targeting the homeless?"

"Could be something odd like that. But I need to get more info. From what the people I talked to shared, I couldn't deduce a pattern. Most serial killers have a type and a consistent MO."

It struck me as interesting that Gary was familiar with serial killer MOs, but that might be the kind of expertise you'd need to do security or bodyguard work. The bottom line was that we didn't have a good lead, or any lead, on what had happened to Bess, and, in turn, we were no closer to ensuring Cole's long-term safety. "Do you think if we spend more time talking to camp residents that we will learn anything helpful?" Maybe there was a more productive line of inquiry we were overlooking.

"You never know when you'll get a break," Gary said. "I say we keep nosing around."

"I agree," Yuri said. "Count me in for another day of guilt for having a good life and not doing enough for the needy while handing out processed food snacks."

CHAPTER 13
A BODY

SUNDAY WASN'T DESTINED to be a day of rest. Yuri was scheduled to come by around 10:00. I'd set my alarm for 9:00 but woke up before it went off when I heard my kids in the kitchen fixing their own breakfast. I was too tired to feel guilty enough to drag myself out of bed to join them.

When the ringtone gorilla grunted, I ignored the call, barely managing to get in a few extra minutes of snoozing before No-name decided it was time for me to get up. He slipped into my bedroom, jumped on the bed and licked my face. "Call your dog," I yelled to Jason.

Moments later, Jason appeared in the doorway: "Mom, it's time to get up."

I looked at my clock—8:30 a.m. In my opinion, that wasn't exactly late on a Sunday morning, even if it was a working day. It was slobber from No-name's tongue on my face and pillow that convinced me I couldn't continue lying there. "Okay," I said out loud, mumbling "I give up."

I took a quick shower before heading to the kitchen for coffee and toast. The call I'd missed was from Detective Connolly. Apparently, he didn't get weekends off either.

His message said that the two men who chased Cole and attempted to break into my house were trying to negotiate a plea deal. They claimed they didn't know who had hired them. All of the arrangements were made from a burner phone that the tech team had not so far not been able to trace. The payment for services was in cash, delivered in a small box with a numeric key code. Someone left the box on the receptionist's desk in a downtown church when the receptionist stepped away for a few minutes. There were always lots of people milling about because the church offered free coffee, bottled water, and cookies to anyone who came by, and there were no cameras in the immediate vicinity.

"We're going on the theory that the person who left the payment has been in the church before," Connolly said. "Apparently a lot of large churches have similar setups with reception areas where people come and go freely. They only lock up rooms or place cameras where there is something to steal. In this instance, someone went to a lot of trouble to remain anonymous." He ended with, "Call me when you get a chance."

I waited until my coffee was ready before calling him back. Initially he seemed hesitant to share more details with me, then, for whatever reason, he must have decided "why not?" "As part of their plea deal, they admitted to forcing Bess to go with them."

"You mean they admitted to 'kidnapping' her."

"No, their lawyer helped them shape the wording. They 'forced her to go with them.'"

"That's kidnapping in my book."

"I'm confident a judge or jury would see it your way, but sometimes you have to make concessions to get the information you need. Anyway, they allegedly left her in a playground next to an elementary school in a Seattle neighborhood near Lake Washington. They claim they have no idea what happened to her after that. I tend to believe they are telling the truth, about that at least. They would have dangled more bait if they'd thought it could get them a better deal."

"Unless they did more than drop her off."

"We're looking into that. But they strike me as 'for hire' types, not masterminds or psychopaths."

"What I don't understand is how someone they don't know figured out how to hire them online. If I wanted to find someone for something like that, I wouldn't have a clue how to go about it."

"My guess is that it's someone connected to some kind of illegal activities. These two may be known in those circles as guys eager to make a buck and who aren't too particular about what they have to do for it. What puzzles me the most is the secrecy surrounding their hiring and payment."

"Maybe they aren't known for being trustworthy. Willing but weak links."

"So, it all comes back to why someone was interested in Bess."

"You've obviously searched the area where they dropped her off." I said it as a statement to encourage him to tell me more.

"Yes, we checked it out and didn't find anything helpful. With kids playing there, the ground was too scuffed up to identify shoe prints. Nor did we find anything else of interest. We also questioned the neighbors, but it was the middle of the night when they left her there. The alleged drop-off spot wasn't next to any houses. Not surprisingly, no one saw anything."

"Would you mind if Yuri and I took a look?"

"Be my guest." He gave me the address and said to be sure to let him know if we did find something. I could tell by his tone that he didn't think there was any way we would succeed when his officers didn't. And I mostly agreed. But it still seemed worth a try.

As soon as I hung up, I called Gary and told him the news. He said that he wasn't too far away from the place they had supposedly left her, so he would swing by and take a look for himself. When I told him Yuri and I were planning on stopping by too, before heading to some of the other encampments, he said he'd keep an eye out for us.

"Even if we don't turn up any evidence," he said, "… it might suggest a line of inquiry. You don't know until you've been there."

Before I had a chance to make any toast the doorbell rang, and Jason yelled that he would get it. I started gulping down what remained of my coffee. Since I had agreed to let Yuri drive, I probably should have taken a Prozac instead of filling myself with caffeine. Yuri is a notoriously distracted and inconsistent driver. When he's behind the wheel, I'm always working the passenger side brake and bracing myself for an accident. I'd agreed to let him drive because it was Sunday, and I was hoping traffic would be light. Besides, my street doesn't get a lot of traffic because it isn't a main route to anywhere other than the houses in the neighborhood. That was a good thing, because Yuri didn't bother checking for other cars before pulling out and doing a U-turn. I inhaled deeply and made sure my seatbelt was snug.

When I told Yuri about Connolly's call, he agreed we should stop by the site. We were just pulling up to the school when I got a call from Gary. He asked where we were, and when I told him our location, he said, "Don't stop there. Drive on down the hill. There's a path that begins at the southeast corner of the block and goes up the hill toward the playground. You might not see it right off because of the brush, but it's there. Park your car and follow the path to the remains of an old foundation with a partial wall at one end. It's about halfway up. I'll meet you there." He clicked off before I could ask any questions.

It took Yuri several tries—at my insistence—to park his car close enough to the sidewalk to be safe from cars turning onto the street. After that, it didn't take long to find the narrow footpath and climb upward through the tangle of brush and evergreens. It's always surprising to find an area so near to downtown Seattle that remains untouched by development and riddled with rough paths. But, if you walk around the neighborhoods, you find them here and there, especially on steep hillsides.

Just about half-way up the hill we came to some stone steps leading to what had once been the foundation for a house. There was a fireplace at one end where part of a wall still pressed against the embankment. Gary was there waiting for us.

Without any greeting, he got right to the point: "I found her body," he said. "It looks like someone beat her badly, then dragged her off into the woods and covered her with some tree limbs and brush."

"Oh," was all I could manage to say. I'd been holding to the hope that we would find her alive. Her death would upset both Cole and her sister. For me, the thought that she had been beaten and left in the open near a school where kids could easily happen upon her body was particularly disturbing.

"Where?" Yuri asked.

"We need to call Connolly," I said. He wasn't going to be pleased; not only because Bess was dead, but because Gary had discovered what his officers had missed.

"If you're okay with it, I want us to have a quick look around first," Gary said. "I've examined the body—you don't need to do that. And don't worry, I didn't touch anything. But we can cover the surrounding area faster with the three of us. We may not find anything, but it's worth a shot."

"Do we tell Connolly we searched the area?" I asked. "What if we contaminate evidence?"

Gary smiled. "You've been reading too many crime novels. Besides, he knows we came here to search the area. He doesn't have to know how much searching we did before rather than after I stumbled across the body.

"If we find something, like a cigarette or a shoe print or whatever, don't mess with it. Take a picture. You can even call Connolly's attention to it if you want. As for me, all I'm going to admit to is finding the body and suggesting you call Connolly rather than 911."

"Obviously, our footprints will be everywhere since we were canvassing the area when I found the body."

"He won't like it," Yuri said. "But let's do it anyway, okay?"

We spread out and started searching. I couldn't help glancing at the partially leaf-covered body as I passed nearby. A faint fishy odor hung in the air mixed with the smell of rotten fruit. Connolly couldn't blame Gary for brushing a few leaves aside to determine whether there really was a body under the unnatural hump. But that was definitely as close as I wanted to get; I didn't need to see her for myself, especially after Gary described her as having been beaten.

I didn't have a clue what I should be looking for as I scanned the brush near Bess's body, so I followed the hillside path down the hill, this time looking for anything that stood out. The path obviously wasn't well traveled, and as near as I could tell, the brush alongside the path hadn't been disturbed recently. Clingy weeds and prickly blackberry vines extended onto the path from both sides. The sidewalk leading up the hill was definitely more convenient, but anyone could have taken the trail as a shortcut to the school. If it had been a high school rather than an elementary, kids might have been sneaking off into the woods to smoke or drink or have sex. Elementary kids seemed more likely to hang around the playground equipment I'd glimpsed before we headed down the hill. Still, how would I know if something had been left behind by Bess's killer rather than some child or other passerby?

Using a stick I found alongside the trail, I started occasionally pushing vines or bushes aside, careful to avoid nettles and blackberry thorns. It wasn't until I was back to where I'd started from that my efforts exposed a latex glove caught in some berry bushes. As I leaned close, I could make out some dark stains across the back of the glove.

I took a picture and texted Yuri and Gary, waiting impatiently for them to join me. When they did, we speculated on the significance of my discovery and whether to report it to the police.

"The killer could have dropped it and not noticed it was missing right away." Yuri snapped a couple of pictures from different angles.

"If this glove belongs to the killer, that suggests the murder was planned, not a crime of passion." Gary pointed at the dark stains. "The police will be able to identify whether that's Bess's blood. They might even be able to get prints from the inside of the glove. Unless the killer was smart and wore regular gloves underneath the latex gloves."

"Should we mention the glove to the police or assume they will search the area thoroughly now that they know there is a body here?"

"Let's give them a chance to find it," Gary said. "That way they won't worry that we've disturbed anything." He turned to Yuri. "You okay with that?"

"Yeah, as long as Cameron is."

I nodded, then called Connolly and told him we were at the playfield and that Gary had found a body. He said to wait for him and quickly signed off.

We didn't talk again until we were standing near the spot where the two men claimed to have left Bess. "Leaving a glove could be a breakthrough for the police," Gary said. "I doubt they will find any prints on the stick she was beaten with."

"She was beaten with a stick?" Yuri asked.

"There was a hefty piece of wood in the brush by her body that appeared to have traces of blood on it. With only a superficial examination of the body, I can't tell whether the beating was post-mortem or not. I can only guess that's what killed her." He paused. "Not a quick way to die. It has the feel of a personal kill to me. Either that, or a very twisted sociopath who wanted her dead."

"I wonder if there have been other beatings like this in the area," I said. "Maybe it is gang related or some hate group targeting the homeless."

We were still speculating when the police arrived with Connolly in the lead. Gary walked them down the path to show them the body while Yuri and I waited. "Elinor will be devastated," I said.

"Oh, I think she probably suspects the worst. An addict living in a homeless camp is on the edge already. I'm sure her sister knew that."

"I assume Bess was Elizabeth. Elinor and Elizabeth. It must have been hard to see your twin sink so low."

"I wonder why she was looking for her now. Didn't you say that she told you Bess only got in touch when she needed something? And that friends and family had pretty much given up hope of getting her to stay clean?"

"That's what she said, yes. My guess is that she probably checked up on her periodically to make sure she was still alive and to see if there was any receptivity to being helped. That's what I would have done after so many failed attempts in the past."

Gary and Connolly came back together. "Is there anything you want to tell me before you leave?" Connolly asked.

"Nothing," Yuri said on behalf of both of us.

"Except that we need to tell Elinor, our client, about Bess's death," I added.

"Technically, I should be the one to break the news, but it might be better if you did, as long as I can be there."

"Would you mind coming to our office?"

"That works. Call her right away and let me know when she's coming in or if we need to go to the hotel where she's staying. We need to tell her before her sister's death makes the news. And I need to question her as soon as possible."

Gary was parked near the sidewalk, so we walked with him to his car. "It's smart of Connolly to let you break the news to the sister. That will give him an excellent opportunity to observe her response. Let me know if he holds off telling her he's with the police—I'm curious."

"He's a good detective," Yuri said.

"He strikes me as competent," Gary said. That seemed like high praise coming from him.

"And he has a thing for Cameron." Yuri wiggled his dark, bushy eyebrows and twirled a pretend mustache.

"Why would he want to observe her response?" I interrupted before the two of them could start discussing my relationship or lack thereof with Connolly. "He can't possibly suspect she's involved in her twin's death."

"You have to consider everyone who knew her as a possible suspect," Gary said. "You know that."

"Are you still going to ask around about Bess?" Yuri asked Gary.

"I don't like to walk away from something like this. Besides, there's Cole to think about. I'll give it a little more time."

"We'll let you know how it goes with Elinor."

"Thanks. I'll check in with you later."

As we headed down the sidewalk to our car, Yuri called Elinor to see when she could come by the office for an "update," or, if she preferred, we could drop by her hotel. I could tell he was struggling not to sound like there was "no hurry" while at the same time avoiding making it seem like we needed to talk to her "right away." He didn't want to make her suspicious about the reason for the call and then feel forced into giving her the bad news over the phone.

Elinor chose our office for the "update." They agreed on 2:00. Then, Yuri called Connolly to let him know.

"Lunch?" Yuri asked as he reached the car.

I wasn't sure I could eat with the scent of Bess's decaying body lingering in my mind, but I did feel hungry. We stopped at a fast-food place Yuri likes near the office, and I ordered clam chowder while he got a burger and fries. I was feeling kinda low and didn't do my usual fry snatch.

"You okay?"

"Not terribly hungry," I said.

"I can take the lead with Elinor if you prefer."

"No, she's technically my client. I'll do it."

"Afterwards we can check out another camp. Show pictures of Bess and the two men around. You never know what you might learn. No one will know that she's dead yet."

"We'll be working for ourselves again. The police will probably want us to stay out of their way. But you're right. We need to find out who's behind this for Cole's sake."

"On the other hand, if we keep Cole out of the picture for long enough, maybe they'll give up on him."

"You don't really believe that."

"Well, the two men who screwed up Bess's kidnapping have been neutralized. Now that Bess's body has been discovered, whoever is behind this may be feeling a little more cautious. It's even possible the person who hired the men might not know that Cole saw their henchmen in the first place. Those two may have been hoping to take care of Cole as a loose end on their own, especially if they weren't in communication with whoever hired them."

"'Taking care of him' with threats? Eliminating him? What do you think?"

"Hard to know. If the police can't trace either the initial phone call or the payment made to those two—"

"It comes down to whether the person responsible for her murder can be identified some other way."

"And whether the two men told anyone about Cole. Someone who might feel a need to follow up on their behalf."

"You agree that Cole could still be in danger."

"Well, let's put it this way: I'm not sure he's completely safe yet."

Two o'clock came around far too soon. The only other person in the office was Norm. It looked like he was working on a couple of reports and being available for any drop-ins. Sunday tended to be slower than Saturday. Blake usually took Sunday off. We had a sign on the door for anyone who wanted to talk to someone to ring the doorbell. That way, whoever was on duty could stay in the pit and work on other things rather than sitting at the reception desk.

Connolly showed up just minutes before Elinor. When she arrived, he introduced himself as simply Cormac

Connolly, without any explanation of what he was doing there with us. Score one for Gary, I thought. He'd guessed that Connolly would want to observe Elinor's reaction rather than have her on guard by knowing he was police. Elinor barely gave him a glance before following me to the conference room. Maybe she assumed he was a Pennywise investigator.

Although I was worried about the upcoming conversation, I was distracted by having heard Connolly's given name for the first time. I wondered if friends called him Mac — "Cormac Connolly" was quite a mouthful.

It felt crowded in the conference room, perhaps more because of the purpose of the meeting than the fact that there were four of us. The room could easily accommodate more. Since I had agreed to tell Elinor about her sister, I sat directly across from her, prepared to hand her the box of Kleenex if she needed it. I had barely opened my mouth to speak when Elinor said, "She's dead, isn't she?"

"Yes, I'm sorry."

She started to sob, turned to Connolly who was sitting next to her and leaned into him. He looked uncomfortable for a moment before putting one arm around her and patting her reassuringly. He raised his other hand in a questioning way as he stared at me over the top of her head. I had no advice.

"We're sorry for your loss," Yuri said, the cliché hovering overhead like a cloud hiding the sun. "I'll get you some water." He got up and went into the other room, leaving Cormac and me with the grief-stricken twin.

Yuri returned with a glass of water at about the same time Elinor was pulling herself away from Connolly.

I pushed the Kleenex across the table, and Yuri placed the water in front of her. "We're so very sorry for your loss," I said, repeating the platitude. I couldn't think of anything else to say. She wiped her eyes with a Kleenex and straightened up in her chair.

"Where did you find her?" she asked.

"A colleague found her near a school playground."

"That's odd. How did she die?" Elinor had gone from hysterical to unnaturally calm. We all respond differently to death and stress, so you never know what to expect when you give someone bad news.

"We won't know for sure until the medical examiner gives us cause of death," Yuri said.

"I see."

At that point, Connolly finally spoke. "I'm with the police, Ms. Easton." She quickly looked over at him with a hint of … what? Surprise? Disappointment? Dislike? "I'm afraid I need to ask you a few questions. Is that alright?"

Elinor regained her composure and said, "Of course. Anything I can do to help you investigate my sister's death. Although I imagine it was an overdose. That's what I've always feared." She dabbed at her eyes with the Kleenex that she had twisted into a soggy mass.

Connolly went through a litany of questions that sounded almost memorized. When did you last see your sister? Did she seem anxious or behave differently than usual? Did she mention anyone she was upset with or someone she'd had a recent disagreement with? Was there anything at all that struck you as unusual when you met with her? Do you know if she had any enemies? Did she owe money to anyone?

Elinor answered his questions directly and calmly. Finally, she paused, looked him in the eye and said, "Why are you asking me these questions? Was there something strange about my sister's death? Something you haven't told me?"

"There was evidence of a struggle …"

"Was she raped?" Elinor sounded horrified. "Tell me she wasn't raped."

"There was no external indication of that," Connolly said cautiously. "I'll be able to tell you more in a day or two."

"Can I see her?"

"I'll let you know when that's possible." He handed her a card. "Call me tomorrow and I'll be able to give you more information. Also, I need to know how to contact you if we have more questions."

She nodded and wrote her contact information on a pad of paper I offered for the purpose. After Connolly read it, he thanked her and stood. "I'm very sorry for your loss," he said. That was three "sorrys." I imagined she would hear quite a few more in the days ahead.

When Connolly started to leave, Yuri joined him. "I'll see you out." The two men disappeared.

"I wish this had turned out differently," I said to Elinor.

"You did what I asked, you found her." She looked directly at me. "Did you see her body?"

"I only glanced at it. I'm afraid I can't tell you any more than Detective Connolly did."

"Will it be in the paper or on the news?"

"I didn't see any reporters at the scene. I know they listen to police scanners though. Maybe they call contacts after the fact."

She sat there, hands folded on the table, eyes downcast. I hesitated to interrupt her thoughts and didn't know what to say anyway. Finally, she spoke. "I can't think right now, I'm afraid. I know there are things I'll need to do, but right now, all I want is to go back to the hotel."

"I understand."

"I need to settle my bill …"

"Don't worry about that; there's no hurry. Blake will invoice you."

At the front door she turned and gave me an A-frame hug, awkward because of the difference in height. She was at least five inches shorter than me. "Thank you. At least I know where she is." Then, she walked away.

I was back in the pit when Yuri returned. "She gone?" he asked.

"Yes. I assume you had a chat with Cormac."

"That will take some getting used to. I had him pegged as a Cillian or a Liam."

"Seriously?"

"More romantic than Cormac."

We fell silent.

Norm pushed away from his desk and came over. "That meeting didn't look pleasant. Why was Connolly here? Everything okay?"

We explained about what had happened—finding the body, having to inform our client, not having any answers as to why someone had killed her.

"I feel drained," I said.

"Cases like this squeeze the glamor from the job," Norm said. "Not that finding lost pets or domestic surveillance is glamorous." Norm was the master at being nondescript, so he did a lot of our surveillance work. It was strange; even though I'd worked with him for several years, I always had a hard time remembering what he looked like.

"Nor doing background reports or writing up reports," Yuri added.

"Discount detection doesn't even sound glamorous," I said.

"So," Norm said, "we aren't in it for the glamor …"

"Or the money," Yuri added. "Maybe the occasional adrenaline rush?"

"What about the satisfaction of helping ordinary people solve ordinary problems?" I offered.

Yuri and Norm looked at each other and laughed. "Oh, that too," Norm said. He shook his head. "Ever the optimist." He gave me a quick hug and returned to his desk.

"Let's go get a coffee and take a break before we move on, okay?" Yuri said.

"This is a real downside to our profession, isn't it? Breaking bad news to people. Whether it's about an errant spouse, a pet that will never return, or an employee who's been committing fraud."

"Hey, you said it before—we do good, too. Sometimes the spouse isn't cheating, we find the lost pet, or we prove someone innocent … or guilty. At least there's variety and interesting challenges. Now, let's go get some good coffee and figure out how we're going to keep Cole safe."

We waved at Norm and headed out. "I can't imagine what it must be like for a police detective. How do you set the grim reality aside and live a normal life at the end of a day like this?"

"Maybe he's married to a Barbie, lives in a pink house and has a houseful of kids to lighten his days. I'm going to put that on my 'to do' list—investigate Cormac's marital status."

"Your time would be better spent working on your own marital status."

"I've been thinking about that. Maybe one of those online apps where you swipe your preferences and see if they swipe you in return."

"I can see it now: 'adventurous male obsessed with trivia seeks bosomy woman who shares passion for hamburgers, fries, and demolition derby.'"

"I only went once, out of curiosity. Or maybe twice. I'm more of a 'walk on the beach' and a 'glass of wine before a candlelit fire' kind of guy."

"That might get you to a first date … until they learn the truth."

"Maybe I should add 'cougars acceptable if wealthy.'"

"Sure … let's get that coffee and hit the road."

CHAPTER 14
BLUE MONDAY

I WOKE UP in a bad mood. To make it worse, when I rolled over, I found No-name laying there, snoring, his pink tongue poking out between his canines.

"No-name," I screamed. "Get off the bed."

He jerked and twitched a moment, then relaxed and continued to make snuffling noises, like he was having a dream about something pleasant. He woke up instantly when I pushed him toward the edge of the bed. Before jumping off, he turned hurt eyes in my direction.

Suddenly Jason was standing at the foot of my bed. "What's wrong?" he asked. "Why are you yelling at No-name?"

"Because he was on my bed."

"You must have left your door open."

"Like it's my fault?" I knew I was being irrational, but I didn't like having No-name in my bed.

"He's a dog. He doesn't know any better," Jason, my wise son said as he turned toward the door. "I'll go see if he's okay."

"You do that," I mumbled to his retreating back. I dragged myself up and decided to skip a shower and go straight to the coffee phase of my morning. Maybe I'd feel like facing the world after a cup of coffee.

The cupboard where my Keurig cups should have been was empty. I reached in and felt around as if a magician's trick had hidden my coffee under a veil of invisibility and I could break the spell with touch. That's right; I suddenly remembered—I needed to go shopping. Well, that could wait. First, I needed to drive to the mall and buy a Grande Americano before settling in for the day at the office.

I managed a heart-felt apology to my son and to No-name before leaving, experiencing a wave of guilt when No-name wouldn't come out from behind Jason. Hopefully, his little doggie brain would soon forgive and forget. In the future, I would remember to securely close my door when I went to bed.

Mara barely looked up from her computer when I poked my head in to say "have a good day." She must have been listening to music while she worked because her head was bobbing, her shoulders swaying rhythmically back and forth.

The drive to the mall didn't help my mood. It seemed like every stoplight turned red before I could hit the gas and sneak through. Once there, I almost gave up on getting an Americano when I saw how long the line was at the kiosk. Then, I remembered the office coffee's unremarkable blend and decided to wait. I needed something better this morning.

I swear that every person ahead of me had some complicated order or couldn't make up their mind or were just being slow to irritate me. Then Yuri came from behind and scared me half to death when he said, "Will you get one for me?"

"That's like crowding," I said when I recovered. The next person in line was scowling but apparently too polite to complain out loud.

"If I texted you and asked you to get coffee for me, no one would know the difference." Yuri looked pointedly at the man behind me. Then he said directly to him, "Sorry, but it's not a great Monday morning. I really need a cup of good coffee."

"Don't we all," the guy said. After a brief pause, he added, "That's okay. Go ahead. Just don't ask for anything fancy. I need to get to work."

"Black," Yuri said to me. "I have sugar and milk in the office.

I looked at his empty hands. "No donuts?"

"I got up late. Sorry."

"At least you didn't wake up next to a dog." I could sense Yuri trying to come up with a snarky comeback. Before he could get his mind in synch with his mouth, I said, "Do not comment. I'm not in the mood."

The guy behind me piped up again: "It sounds like both of you need to lighten up."

We glared at him in unison. Then Yuri said, "Advice like that makes me want a Baby Yoda Frappuccino with a shot of soy and topped with …" He either ran out of irritation or descriptors before shaking his head and apologizing. "Sorry, I don't mean to take my problems out on you." He looked at me. "Black is fine."

We waited in silence until I got our coffee and two blueberry muffins. Jenny was in the pit when we arrived. Sitting across from her was Gary. I felt tiny pangs of jealousy in spite of telling myself that I had expected him to be staying with her. I envied their casual "take it as it comes" attitude toward their relationship.

Gary saw us entering, grabbed his mug of coffee and motioned for us to meet him in the conference room. We had put off debriefing our day's activities the night before because I had to get home for Sunday evening dinner with my family, and Gary had said something about wanting to make a few more stops anyway. One of the stops was probably Jenny's farm. "You two look grim," he commented as we took our seats.

"Yesterday was not the greatest," Yuri said.

"But it's TODAY," Gary said.

"You trying out to become a motivational speaker?" Yuri mumbled.

"I hear it pays well, but I'd have to shave my beard." He was refusing to let Yuri's funk dampen his mood.

When Yuri didn't come back with another volley of downers, I said, "Sorry, Gary. I can't speak for Yuri, but I just can't shake the feeling that we're letting Cole down. I mean, we're no closer to knowing who's behind this than we were when we started. And, Bess is … dead." I had a hard time saying the word "dead" because an image of her battered body was imprinted on my brain even though I'd barely glanced in her direction. Gary's reference to a stick with blood stains on it was suggestive enough for some part of my subconscious to fill in the gory details. "Unless you've discovered something encouraging."

"I take it that means you didn't make any headway yesterday afternoon."

"Zip. Nada. Nothing." Yuri tapped his pen on the table as if emphasizing our failure.

"Well, I didn't gather any startling information either, but I confirmed some things we already suspected. For one, I think someone is abducting young kids from homeless camps, the younger the better. Probably selling them to prospective parents or pedophiles."

"Well, that certainly makes me feel better," I couldn't help saying.

"And it doesn't explain why Bess was killed," Yuri said.

"The two issues may not be connected, but when you come across something like this, you can't simply turn away. These kids and their parents need their stories told. You never know what might pop up if you poke around enough. However, my guess is that Bess's issue was drugs. Like her sister said, she was a user and maybe also a dealer. According to someone I talked to at the morgue, the most common cause of death for the homeless in this area is bad shit or overdosing."

"You talked to someone at the morgue?"

"Yeah, as an undercover agent, I needed to know whether Bess had opioids in her system when she died." He smiled. "People who work with dead bodies don't get out much—not like it's portrayed on TV. They like the occasional visitor bearing coffee and snacks. It was a bit early for a definitive answer, but they'll know more after they do the autopsy tomorrow. I'm welcome to drop by."

"I hope Connolly doesn't find out you were impersonating a DEA agent."

"I wasn't too specific—if they jumped to conclusions about my identity, I can't help that. Besides, it isn't uncommon for a DEA investigation to overlap with a case being pursued by the police. In some states that's a problem, but not here. They're encouraged to work together and share information. So, I doubt anyone gave much thought to me dropping by to ask a few questions. No worries, okay?"

Gary was probably right, and we had no control over his part of the inquiry anyway, so despite my doubts, I let it go. Since Yuri was keeping quiet, I guessed he had come to the same conclusion.

"Let's say that Bess got in over her head and owed someone money," I said. "Why murder her? As a warning? I've never thought that made sense. Unless the dealers she was buying from thought she knew too much about their drug business at the encampment, and they were worried she might be about to cooperate with the DEA in return for … something …" As soon as the words were out of my mouth, Yuri shook his head in disagreement.

"Nah, they would have used their own thugs to nab her."

Arguing against my own speculation, I said: "And even if that was the case, why beat her like that? And why go through the rigamarole of hiring outsiders to pick her up and drop her off?"

"I agree, it feels like we're missing something," Gary said. "Although I can think of a couple of options we haven't considered. For instance, maybe those two guys weren't instructed to beat her but did it for some reason known only to them. She died, and they stashed her body and ran. Killers aren't necessarily rational people."

"Or maybe, someone just happened to come along, found her tied up there, and beat the crap out of her for fun," Yuri said.

"A wandering sociopath. A couple of drunks. A gang of kids. It's all possible."

"If it's something random like that, we will have a hard time finding the killer or killers."

"The homicide clearance rate in Washington is at about 51 percent, give or take," Gary said.

"What's with all the statistics?" Yuri asked.

"I like to know what I'm working with. That doesn't mean it isn't worth trying to improve those stats."

"About Cole," I said, interrupting the exchange between the two men. "Gary, have you already told him about Bess?"

"No, not yet."

"Do you plan on telling him what happened to her when you go back to the island? Or do you think we should tell him right away?"

"I'd like to tell him in person. I don't imagine a few days will make any difference. You two okay with that?"

Yuri and I were nodding agreement when my phone rang. "It's Connolly," I said. The two men indicated I should take it. "We're in the conference room—Gary, Yuri and me. I'm putting you on speaker." I set my phone down in the middle of the table and clicked speaker.

"Good morning, everyone." He sounded chipper.

Yuri laughed "Are we Connolly's Angels?"

"Hmm. I can't quite see your three faces on a TV ad."

"More like 'Get Smart,'" I muttered.

"Moving on … I'm calling because I got an identification on the woman who questioned the barista about your young client. Adele sent me a photo off a mall camera, but the woman wasn't in any of our databases. However, when I showed the picture to our two guys who abducted

Bess, it seems there was one detail they left out of our deal agreement. The woman just happens to be the sister of one of the two men. They said they were hoping to keep her out of it because she has a couple of small kids, had no idea why they wanted the information, and only did it as a favor to them. I think they may be telling the truth. We'll talk to her, of course, but she's likely a dead end.

"Also, when I informed them that Bess was dead, I believe they were sincerely shocked. They immediately started denying any involvement, repeating what they'd already told me. Asked if they needed to have their lawyer present before saying more. That kind of thing."

"Would they have admitted to dropping her off there if they were the killers?" Yuri asked.

"Killers aren't necessarily smart," Connolly said. "But I doubt it in this instance. They seem truly clueless to me. I think the killer or killers are still out there."

"We keep wondering why they were approached to snatch Bess. Do you think they've been involved in any other illegal activities at the camps?" Yuri asked.

"They're both construction workers. Hard to know what they do for supplemental income. The deal we made with them ended our background research."

"We'll keep looking at our end, but I'm not hopeful," Yuri said.

"So, we're nowhere," I said, feeling a wave of Blue Monday wash over me again.

"Anything on the autopsy?" Gary asked.

"It should happen this afternoon. Even if they find drugs in her system, it's the brutality of the attack that leaves me with questions."

"Have there been similar attacks?" Yuri asked.

"Some fairly brutal attacks, yes. Similar, not really. No pattern that I can discern. There has, however, been a slight uptick in the number of homeless disappearing."

"You think there's someone trafficking in children?" Gary asked. "Or body parts? Or both?"

"Those are possibilities. That seems to be what some of the homeless think. The shelter volunteers have heard the same rumors. It would explain the disappearances, although we're not talking big numbers here. Both are little more than a trickle. But then, it's human lives at stake, so we don't take it lightly."

"And that doesn't necessarily explain what happened to Bess," I said. "All it does is suggest that there are some pretty sick people preying on the homeless in our city."

"That's what we should do," Yuri said to me. "Visit food distribution centers or shelters. See if anyone knows Bess."

"Are they no longer called soup kitchens?" I asked.

"They serve a lot more than soup these days."

"You two should offer to help out in a kitchen at a free meal location," Gary said. "They're always looking for volunteers. That will give you a chance to do some eavesdropping and talk to people. Maybe I'll stay at a shelter tonight, nose around a little."

"Good idea," Connolly said. "Safer than roaming around encampments.

I knew the "safer" comment was aimed at me, and I resented it. I still thought it was a good suggestion, though, and I couldn't help but feel a bit relieved.

As Connolly was about to hang up, he said, "By the way, City Council is having an open meeting to discuss the increasing problem with the homeless tomorrow at 2 o'clock. You might want to attend."

"Maybe even testify," Gary added.

Connolly signed off, and Gary said he was leaving. "I'll check in later." Out of the corner of my eye I saw him swing by Jenny's desk and noted the big smile on her face as he leaned down and said something to her.

"You could do an online dating app too," Yuri said. He must have noticed me checking out the interaction between Gary and Jenny. "Unless you think Cormac …"

"How many times do I have to tell you that I'm not trying to meet anyone. I have enough on my plate as it is."

He held both hands in the air in surrender. "Grab your coffee and let's go. I'll drive."

CHAPTER 15
VOLUNTEERING

"NO THANKS. I'll drive," I said with more intensity than I intended. With Yuri driving, the day could go from lousy to total disaster in no time. For once Yuri didn't question my decision about who was going to drive. The scowl on my face must have looked like a Halloween fright mask for him to have given up so easily. He didn't mention Cormac again either. That was a bonus.

By the time we reached the park-and-ride where we dropped my car off and caught the light rail to downtown, I was feeling in better spirits. My coffee had kicked in. I'd set aside my resentment over Gary's interest in Jenny, and I was relieved that we were headed for a food distribution center rather than another encampment.

Unfortunately, it didn't take long for my spirits to plunge into a downward spiral—ironically, it was going "up" that made them go "down." The walk from the light rail to the center was up one of Seattle's steep hills. The kind where I always worried about getting stopped at a light while in my car, and through some klutzy maneuver end up sliding backwards when the light changed. Yuri grumbled about the climb, but I was too breathless to do much complaining.

We didn't have to check the address or read the sign over the door to know when we'd reached our destination. The people clustered around the building or sitting on the sidewalk out front weren't dressed for downtown office work or shopping. There were mostly men, but some women, and a few mothers with small children. The majority were engaged in conversations in small groups, although there was one man napping up against the building, another playing a battered guitar, and a woman moving from one foot to the other singing to herself—totally out of synch to what the guitarist was playing.

"I think some businesses who need day workers come by here in the morning," Yuri said. "Maybe if they don't get work, they hang around until they get something to eat."

When we tried the front door, it was locked, and someone yelled that they weren't open yet. We walked around to the side of the building and found a door marked "deliveries." It too was locked, but when we knocked, someone answered after a few minutes, looked us up and down and asked, "What can I do for you?"

"You need any help today?"

"You cook?"

"No, sorry. But anything else that needs doing."

"We can always use extra hands. Especially today. We have a couple people who didn't show. But let me warn you, the work won't be glamorous."

"Glamor is overrated," Yuri said. Remembering our earlier conversation, I couldn't help but smile.

"Well, come on back, then. I think I can fix you up with menial but necessary work. How does that sound?"

"Like most jobs," Yuri said.

Five minutes later I found myself chopping vegetables for soup. Yuri was assigned to washing dishes and setting out clean plates, bowls, and utensils for the noon meal. Everything was being done in a hurry to get ready for the noon rush. We didn't have any time to talk to any of the other staff or volunteers, and I was beginning to wonder if we would get anything useful out of our effort. At least we were doing something distracting and worthwhile.

When they started serving lunch, Yuri got the job of keeping bread and crackers available and taking the cookies out of the oven, putting them at the end of the counter. Meanwhile, I was told to mingle and make sure people had what they needed and collect used dishes and return them to the kitchen. "They're supposed to bus their dishes, but most don't."

"I suppose they don't leave tips either," I said.

The kitchen manager acknowledged my joke with an eye roll. "Watch your pocket more likely."

The first chance I got, I stopped to talk to a small group of friendly looking, older men. "A friend's sister asked me to find out if anyone here remembers seeing a woman named Bess lately. She used to come for a meal now and then. She seems to have vanished. Any of you know her?" It was a longshot, but that's often how the detective business goes. You poke here and probe there and hope you get a scrap of information you can follow up on.

"Sometimes people disappear. Here one day, gone the next," a man with weathered skin said. He reminded me of photographs of Clarence Darrow with his deeply lined face and the unruly lock of hair hanging down one side of his forehead.

"Where do you think they go?" I asked.

The men glanced at each other as if to decide who if anyone was going to respond.

"They move on," another guy shrugged.

I waited, hoping someone would add something, but no one did. Instead, they looked down at their food, dismissing me. I was about to give up when Clarence Darrow glanced at me and asked, "Bess, you say. She gone?"

I hesitated. I wanted to learn more about her before telling them the bad news. "Her sister knows she has a drug problem. That's one of the reasons she's worried."

"She was okay last time I saw her."

"How long ago?"

"About a week, I'd say."

I decided to push a little harder. "Someone told her sister they'd seen her leave the camp with two guys, maybe not willingly. Think it could be drug related?"

"You with DEA?"

"No, seriously, I'm just hoping to find Bess and make sure she's okay."

"Did she leave anything behind?" a man wearing a faded baseball cap with a Seahawks emblem on it asked.

"Her tent and all her belongings are still where she's been staying."

"She wouldn't do that," the man said, and the others nodded agreement.

I took a deep breath. "Ever heard of people being kidnapped at encampments before?"

"Rumor is you need to hold onto your kidneys and other bits and pieces." This time the comment came from a man slouched over in his chair, like he was too weak to sit up straight or had back problems. "Wouldn't think our 'parts' were in great shape, but that's the rumor." Several men laughed.

"Hope she turns up. She's a nice 'un. Shared whatever she had." They all nodded in agreement again. They not only knew her but obviously liked her. I hoped Elinor would find that comforting.

It felt wrong to question them and not tell them what had happened to Bess, but they would find out soon enough that she was dead. I couldn't face being the bearer of bad news again so soon.

Yuri and I stayed to clean up, and because they were still short-handed, we decided to hang around for the evening meal. That turned out to be a wise, yet tiring move. It finally gave us a chance to talk to the other volunteers. Six of us gathered around a table and shared a plate of cookies with freshly made coffee. Both were surprisingly good.

"Starbucks donates coffee," one of the volunteers explained. "Not enough to serve it all the time, but fairly frequently."

"Not sure our customers notice the difference, but it gives Starbucks bragging rights."

We introduced ourselves by first names: Ken, Julie, Bogart, Fran, Yuri and me. Ken was older than the others, probably in his mid-sixties. Julie and Fran were possibly late-forties, and Bogart was at best thirty. All except Bogart said they were regular volunteers.

"I live nearby and work from home," Bogart said, "but I can only take off a day here and there."

Ken was retired and happy for something meaningful to do. Julie was employed part-time at one of the local restaurants, and Fran was "between jobs." When Yuri admitted we were PIs looking for a missing homeless woman, they were all immediately interested—in our profession and in who we were looking for.

"Is it exciting?" Bogart asked.

Yuri laughed. "This is as exciting as it gets."

"We talk to a lot of people," I said. "Ask a lot of questions." I took out the picture of Bess. "This is the woman we're looking for. Her name is Bess. Anyone recognize her?"

"I'm usually cooking," Ken said as he passed the picture on to the others. Fran and Julie both recognized Bess but said they hadn't talked with her other than to say "Hi" and "How are you doing?" Bogart shook his head "no." No one recognized the two men.

Then we asked them about the rumors of missing people, and they had all heard a little something, but no one had any specifics. "I thought it was mostly made up," Julie said. "Gives people something to talk about. Then I heard about a baby that disappeared." She turned to the others. "Remember Glenda's baby, Gwen? She was kinda sickly and always crying." They all nodded. "I gave her a couple of toys I had in storage. Then one day a cop comes in and is looking for the baby. They'd found Glenda on the street, dead. OD'd, or so they said. I thought she was clean since she had Gwen."

"Do you know if they ever found Gwen?"

"Not that I know of."

Our chat was cut short by a request from the kitchen to get started on dinner. From that point on we were busy with our chores. During the evening meal we were kept hopping and had no time to chat with anyone. When we got everything squared away, the volunteers and other staff quickly departed. We'd considered asking one or two to have drinks with us to pump them for more information, but we didn't think there was much more to learn from them, and besides, we were dead on our feet. It had been an exhausting day.

We were tempted to Uber to my car, but decided since it was downhill to the light rail that paying for an Uber was extravagant. "It's amazing how everyone has heard the rumors about kids and people going missing and just seem to accept it as a way of life," Yuri said as we trudged downhill. Downhill might be easier on the lungs, but it was definitely harder on the knees.

"I bet it would be different if people from Mercer Island started disappearing."

"Life has never been fair," Yuri said.

"I know. And you can't save everyone."

We both fell silent. I was thinking of Cole and wondering whether we could keep him safe and help him launch a new life or whether he would end up shuffled from one place to another until he finally ended up back on the streets. And I assumed Yuri was having similar thoughts. Shared silent moping.

What started for me as a blue Monday ended on a blue note, flat, half-way between sad and deflated.

CHAPTER 16
TESTIMONY

TUESDAY MORNING Yuri, Gary and I met for coffee and pastries at a Starbucks near the mall to reconnoiter and regroup.

"You look rested," I said to Gary. "How was the shelter?"

"It all depends on what you compare it to," he said with a quick grin.

"I bet you've been in some uncomfortable spots," Yuri said. He always tries to get Gary to talk more about what he does for a living, but Gary deflected as usual.

"What about your day at the food kitchen? Enjoy yourselves?"

"I'm thinking my kids should help out on some holiday," I said. "They don't necessarily appreciate living in a bubble of comfort."

"Interacting with people who are either temporarily or permanently homeless can help humanize the issues, but it can also reinforce stereotypes. The homeless do include a lot of misfits, addicts, and even some con artists."

Yuri agreed. "But developing empathy for those less fortunate, even those who may never be capable of leading a 'normal' life—however you define 'normal'—is part of what it means to be human. That said, the homeless in Seattle could definitely use better PR people."

"By the way," I said, "we did get a message from Detective Connolly about cause of death. As we suspected, Bess was using, but the beating is what killed her," I took a breath. "She apparently didn't die quickly." I wished he hadn't told me that. He also mentioned they found some latex gloves at the site, but they didn't get anything useful from them. My big discovery was a bust.

"There are both violent criminals and mentally deranged people out there," Gary said.

"But why would someone pay those two guys to leave her there if they intended to kill her all along? What could she possibly have done to deserve that kind of retribution?"

"Maybe someone did want a kidney or a couple of corneas but got spooked when Cole saw the two men. They could have been playing it safe." Yuri sounded like he didn't believe what he was suggesting.

"But if the two men are telling the truth, this is the first time they've done something like that," I said.

"It's possible everything they've told the police is a lie. Maybe they're part of a gang picking up people to sell for body parts."

"Then why make up such an elaborate lie about the payment method?" I asked.

"Maybe that was decided in advance, in case they were caught."

"I don't buy it," I said. "But based on the scuttlebutt we heard yesterday, at least some of the homeless are spooked by the possibility that there are people preying on the homeless for body parts. They don't think the police or anyone else cares enough to stop it."

"And the few who knew Bess thought she was a kind and generous person. Which is consistent with Cole's experience with her," Yuri said. "Did you talk to anyone who knew Bess?" he asked Gary.

"An older man who said he talked to Cameron earlier at lunch. When I realized he didn't know she'd been killed, I told him that Bess was dead. He was pretty upset. I figured he'd find out sooner or later. He was relieved to know her body was intact."

"He asked?"

"Yes."

"Did he have any theories about what might have happened?"

"He thinks it was a hate crime. Said that a lot of locals are angry about the homeless taking over parks. They consider them a blight on the community."

"That could explain the savageness of the attack, but not the elaborate kidnapping."

"The problem is that there are probably several things going on in the encampments," Yuri said. "Hate crimes, drug use, illegal body part harvesting, child kidnapping. Who knows what Bess either saw or was involved with? I'm not sure we will solve this no matter how hard we try."

"But if we don't find answers, what does that mean for Cole?"

"I've been considering that and have an idea," Gary said. "But you may not like it."

"Go ahead," I said.

"It's feeling more and more like we aren't going to find out who hired the men who were after Cole. So, I suggest we leave him with my neighbors on the island. They like him, and he's a great companion for their son. And, he seems to like it there. They can homeschool him with a couple of the other kids on the island. No one is likely to look for him there. After a few years, whoever is after him will probably give up trying."

"That's not legal," Yuri pointed out.

"No, but the legal way isn't safe for Cole."

"Think about it, Yuri," I said. "If he stays on the street, there won't be any record of him either. At some point, he'll have to get things sorted out so he can make a living. For now, at least, he would get some schooling and good food … and be with people who care for him."

"My neighbors might be willing to act as foster parents or maybe even adopt him, but I don't think that's a good idea just yet."

"It's only been a few days—how can you be so sure this will work?" Yuri asked.

Gary laughed. "I'm a quick study." Then he got serious. "I've known my neighbors for a long time. They really wanted children and when they finally had a son, they were thrilled, but they wanted more kids, and it didn't happen. Then, Cole comes along. Serendipity, I suppose."

"What do you think P.W. will say?" I asked Yuri.

"She's a stickler for doing things right, but we've seen her bend the rules too. I think she'd consider Cole's well-being over what's technically legal."

"Technically legal? I'm not sure there's such a thing." Nor was I sure I disagreed with his assessment.

Gary jumped in. "I'm afraid I walk that line more often than I'd like. Why don't you avoid drawing a line in the sand for a while. Tell her it's a temporary solution until you can be absolutely sure Cole is safe."

"But we're not sure that is going to happen."

"Another technicality," Gary said.

Yuri and I looked at each other. "I'm okay with this if you are."

"P.W. will know what we're up to."

"But if she doesn't authorize it, she has some level of deniability."

"The same is true for both of you, too," Gary said. "This conversation isn't being recorded, and we won't put anything in writing or mention the arrangement online."

"What about leaks from the island?"

"I don't anticipate that will happen, but if it does, it won't prove we intended the arrangement to be anything but temporary."

"Should we pinkie swear?" Yuri said.

"We could take a blood oath," Gary said. I half expected him to take out a mean-looking pocketknife for the purpose.

"I'm okay with a pinkie swear," I said quickly. "Mentally, so no one sees it. NOW." I paused. "Got it?"

The two men smiled at me, and Yuri wagged his little finger. "Deal," he said.

"Deal," Gary echoed. Cole's "temporary" fate was decided.

Gary was going to poke around one more day before heading back to the island. I figured that meant one more night with Jenny, but I forced myself not to think too much about that. Yuri and I went to the office to catch up on a few odds and ends and update P.W. before catching the light rail to the City Council meeting on homelessness that Connoly had suggested we attend.

"Should we sign up to speak?" I asked Yuri as we entered the Council Chambers in City Hall.

"I thought we were here to listen."

"What if we decide we have something to say?"

"I suppose we can sign up and then relinquish our time if we don't want to talk."

"I feel like I want Council members to know they have serious issues they should be addressing to help the homeless. They aren't in positions of leadership simply to satisfy community sensibilities."

"You want an encampment next door to where you live?"

"No, but I'm willing to pay to set up some proper living areas with toilet facilities and garbage pick-up."

"Glamping?"

"At least decent camping amenities."

"Where? In our parks?"

"Why are you arguing with me?"

"I'm not. I'm sharpening your arguments."

"I'm not the one being paid to come up with answers."

"If we're going to set up mini reservations for the homeless, someone has to live near them. That's part of the problem from the neighborhood perspective."

"I agree. But, almost anything is better than what we're doing now."

"Okay, let's sign up to speak before it's too late."

Only twenty minutes was allotted for Council members to get comments from local residents, specifically about a proposal before the Council on how to deal with drug use among the homeless. We picked up copies of the proposal and skimmed it before the meeting got underway. The assumption was that if they got rid of drugs in the encampments, they would be eliminating one of the major challenges in dealing with homelessness in the city. To me, however, it seemed like the proposal was little more than a Band-Aid for a major wound.

As it turned out, it was a good thing we had signed up to speak, because as the meeting progressed, both of us became increasingly upset with the limitations of the discussion. When it was my turn to speak, I used my two minutes to point out that although overdoses supposedly counted for the majority of deaths in the homeless population, when you talked to homeless people, they were even more concerned about illegal organ trafficking, hate crimes, and children being taken from their mothers and sold by human traffickers. One of the council members stopped me before I could turn over the microphone to Yuri.

"Why have you been talking to homeless people?" she asked.

"I'm a private investigator," I said. "We were hired to find a client's sister who was living in a homeless encampment. My partner and I have been talking to encampment residents to try to find out what happened to her. Unfortunately, it turned out that she had been brutally murdered. The police have no solid leads as to who did it or why."

"Thank you. Next."

When there was no comment or follow-up from the council member, I felt like I'd been stomach punched. Why had she bothered to ask that question in the first place? I didn't know anything about her other than what I read on her nameplate: Amanda Smythe. Her name was a mouthful, but it had a nice lilt to it.

Yuri took the mic and spent his two minutes suggesting that city regulations should be adapted to accommodate better living facilities for the homeless rather than chasing them from one location to another. He pointed out that it's hard to get a job when you have no address and no place to clean up to go to an interview. The council members looked bored, but I saw several reporters typing furiously on their laptops. I wondered if they had taken down what I had said too.

While we were listening to the rest of the testimony, a young man came over and handed me a note from Councilwoman Amanda Smythe. She wanted to know if we could talk for a few minutes at the end of the meeting. I wrote a "yes" at the bottom of the note and gave it back to the young man, after first showing it to Yuri.

The rest of the meeting seemed to last forever. I kept wondering what the councilwoman wanted to talk to me about. When the meeting was finally adjourned, people milled about, but the majority of council members made quick exits. Councilwoman Smythe waited for us while we wended our way through the exiting crowd to the front of the room.

"I just have a couple of questions," she said. She glanced at Yuri with eyebrows raised.

"We're partners," he said by way of explanation. "Both PIs," he added to clarify. That seemed to satisfy her.

"What I want to know is whether you have any proof about illegal organ trafficking or children being kidnapped and sold."

"Other than what some of the homeless people we talked to told us, no."

"I would think the coroner's office would know if there were bodies missing organs," Yuri said. "Unless there is a mass grave somewhere."

"We do know that the woman we were looking for was badly beaten, but we don't know the killer's motivation."

She looked from me to Yuri and back to me again, as if considering carefully her next question. Then she took out a card and asked, "I assume you have a card?"

I took hers and gave her mine.

"Penny-wise Investigations?"

"Vigilance you can afford," Yuri said with a smile.

"I need to know more about this. I may get back to you."

"Do you have a personal interest?" I asked. Her attitude suggested to me that she might.

She hesitated a moment, then said, "I have a cousin who was living on the streets and disappeared. The family …" She took a deep breath. "No one really looked for him. We've all assumed he moved to another city."

"How long ago?"

"It's been over a year."

"We've been told that most homeless people move around a fair amount. Especially since no one wants them in their neighborhood," Yuri said. "A year is a long time though."

"Let me get back to you, okay?"

We mumbled a couple of "fines" as she turned and hurried off.

"He could be anywhere," I said to Yuri.

"Even in a mass grave with a missing kidney."

"If she asks us if we'll look for him, should we tell her it's hopeless?"

"She probably knows it is, but I don't think that's the message she wants to hear."

"The moral dilemmas are piling up, aren't they?"

"If by 'moral dilemma' you mean it may be unethical to take on a case knowing it's hopeless but do so simply because the client doesn't want to face the truth."

"Oh, oh, I sense a trivia rant coming on."

"I got a bit bored during the hearing and my mind started wandering."

"And whence did it go, my liege?"

"I was thinking about unicorns—because of Cole's backpack. You see images of them on kids' lunch boxes and T-shirts and in children's books—always as symbols of good luck and purity. Surrounded by rainbows and small Disney animals."

"So?"

The elevator seemed to be staying for a long time on the first floor. I impatiently jabbed the button even though I knew it wouldn't do any good.

"So … why don't we see more about the black unicorn?" Yuri asked. "Are we trying to ignore the darker side of unicorn symbolism? Focusing on the positive while running from the negative? For the sake of children? Or ourselves?"

"What do you mean?"

"Well, the black unicorn is linked to the devil in folklore. Known as witches' mounts."

"And …?" I don't usually encourage his trivia rants, but, although I vaguely remembered seeing pictures of black unicorns, I didn't know anything about them. And the elevator was still not headed to our floor.

"Some people think unicorns use their horns to drink human blood."

"Yuk. You mean they use them like a straw?"

"Poke and sip."

"Gross."

"Both white and black unicorns are known to be aggressive fighters and not always liked by other creatures as Hallmark cards and cartoons would have you believe."

"Anything else?"

"Since you asked … If you happen to come across a white unicorn and it bows its head to you, that's a good sign. But if it indicates it doesn't want you to touch its horn, you need to back off immediately, or there will be consequences. Bad consequences."

"So, you're telling me that there's a dark side to unicorns, whether white or black."

"Maybe the moral is not everything is as it seems."

"Or, that even the nicest seeming person has a dark side; some people are just better at keeping it hidden."

"That too. But since black unicorns are considered harbingers of death, I say we avoid them."

"You always have such good advice."

The elevator doors opened. We stepped inside and pushed the down button. But the elevator went up instead. Our karma wasn't good even without having annoyed a unicorn.

CHAPTER 17
ANOTHER CLIENT

THE ELEVATOR went up two floors before stopping. The doors opened, but no one was there. Yuri punched the first-floor button with more vigor than necessary, but the doors opened again on the floor we had started from. A man in his 40s was standing there, staring at us. "I've been looking for you," he said. "I thought I'd missed you."

The elevator doors started to close. Yuri stuck his hand out at the same time as the man did, and the doors bounced back.

"Both of you are private investigators, right?"

"Yes," Yuri and I said at the same time.

"Do you have a few minutes?"

The doors started closing again as we quickly stepped out. I thought I remembered the man from the council meeting, but I wasn't sure. His stylish haircut and dark navy suit suggested a downtown office job, but his light blue shirt was unbuttoned at the top, his stark white undershirt peeking out. I guessed he'd done that and removed his tie to look more casual.

We moved a few feet down the hall away from the elevator before the man said anything more: "Your testimony suggested you're familiar with the homeless community in the city."

"We've been investigating a homeless woman's disappearance," I said.

He nodded as if assessing whether that was sufficient expertise before continuing. "I assume you can be discreet. I mean, if I hire you, will you keep it confidential?"

"It depends," Yuri said. "We won't cover for a criminal act. But otherwise, we try to honor the privacy of our clients." Yuri handed the man a card. "If you want to come to the office and discuss our services, we could give you a better idea about what to expect."

The man studied the card as if hoping to find answers in the fine print. "Do I need to make an appointment?" he asked.

"We'll be there first thing tomorrow morning, but otherwise it's best to make an appointment to ensure we are around. We do a fair amount of field work." I had to suppress a smile, because the way he said it made it sound like we were in high demand.

"Could we talk at 9:00 tomorrow?"

"That sounds good."

He immediately turned back toward the elevator and walked briskly off. We were a little slow out of the starting gate, and the elevator doors closed behind him before we got there. I pushed the down button, perhaps a little too firmly. "Maybe we should take the stairs. Have you seen a sign showing where they are?"

"No, let's wait." We both stared at the elevator car indicator. It stopped at the main floor and started up. "Should we have asked for his name?"

"I thought about it. He'll either show or he won't. My gut says he'll be there; he's obviously very stressed about something related to the homeless community."

Yuri was already in the pit when I arrived Tuesday morning. Norm was at this desk, and Will and Grant were in the small conference room. I said hello to Norm and asked how his kids were doing. He's divorced and doesn't see his two boys as much as he would like, but he makes an effort to remain part of their lives. We often share little stories about the achievements and foibles of our kids. This morning he took out a picture of one of his boys playing soccer. "He's pretty good," he said proudly. After a brief chat with Norm, I went over to where Yuri was making coffee.

"The line was too long," he said. "Bad coffee is better than no coffee, right?"

"I hate to spend more on coffee than on my kids' school clothes. So bad is good."

"It adds up." He handed me my mug. "Did you notice all the Starbucks' cups at the encampments?"

"If you can't make your own, you need to get it somewhere."

"Maybe they do make their own and pick up cups, creamer and sugar at Starbucks."

Blake interrupted us. "Cameron, Yuri, you have a potential client waiting. Says he has an appointment."

I glanced at my phone. If it was the man from the elevator, he was early. "I'll go get him, you pour coffee for us and make sure there's enough left over for our 'client.' Although he's probably used to better."

This time the man was wearing his full official outfit: dark suit, light blue shirt, and striped tie. I invited him in, asked if he wanted coffee, and guided him to the conference room where Yuri was waiting for us. "Coffee?" Yuri asked. Our potential client had turned me down and apparently hadn't changed his mind. He still didn't want our coffee, but his eyes lingered on Yuri's mug with the fornicating penguins around its base. P.W. had warned him not to use his mug in front of clients, but he'd either forgotten or didn't care this morning.

"I'm not here because you offer a discount," the man said by way of introduction. "I need someone who knows their way around a homeless camp and can keep their investigation confidential."

"Why don't you tell us what you would like someone to do for you, and we can discuss what's possible." I thought Yuri's tone was a bit abrupt. I could tell he wasn't wild about the man, but you didn't have to like someone to work for them. Especially when they looked like they could more than afford our services.

"It's an uncomfortable, personal matter." He shifted in his chair and touched the knot of his tie. He was definitely uncomfortable. "You see, last year I had an affair. My wife doesn't know. I ended it when I realized how foolish I was acting. But, it was too late. The woman I was seeing was pregnant and refused to get an abortion.

"I warned her that I wouldn't support her and the child, but she was determined. At the time, she was a waitress. That's how I'd met her.

"When she refused to listen to reason, I broke off all ties with her and didn't return to the restaurant. Recently, I started wondering about the child and went by the restaurant to see if she still worked there. That's when I found out she had lost her job and had been living in her car with the baby. I felt terrible."

"Didn't she have any family or friends to turn to?" I asked.

"Her parents live in Georgia, very strict Christians from what she'd told me. No siblings. And she'd just moved out here when we met. So, no close friends in the area."

"Did you catch up with her?"

"Yes, stoned out of her mind and with no idea what had happened to the baby."

"That's why you're here," Yuri said.

"Yes, I want to know what happened to my child."

His use of the phrase "my child" seemed somewhat ironic under the circumstances.

"What do you propose to do if we find the child? By the way, is it a girl or a boy?"

"A boy." He sounded almost proud. "And I'm not sure. I just want to make certain he's safe."

"Did she tell you his name?"

"Eddie. She said it was Eddie, not Edward. What kind of name is Eddie?" He seemed almost as disturbed by the name as by the fact that his former girlfriend had no idea where the baby was.

"Do you know the date of birth?"

"I'm not sure. He should be about two, maybe three months."

"That's pretty young to be living in a car," I said. I personally couldn't imagine how she'd been coping. It sounded like maybe she hadn't.

"Do you and your wife have children?" Yuri asked.

"No, we've been trying but haven't succeeded so far."

"Would you consider taking Eddie into your home?" Yuri said.

"I don't know. I just don't know."

"Well, if we are going to look into this for you, we'll need your name as well as your, ah, former girlfriend's name and current location."

"I'm Broderick Kendall. Her name is Siana Campbell. She moves around some, but I can write down information about the car and where I found her recently."

"And if there is anything else you can tell us about what she said about the boy. You never know what might be helpful."

"She wasn't terribly coherent when we talked. I could hardly believe she was the same person."

"She wasn't on drugs when you were with her?"

"I wasn't actually with her. But, no, she wasn't. We always had a few drinks, nothing to excess."

"Well, why don't you write down what you know." Yuri pushed a pad of paper and a pen bearing a local bank logo over to Broderick. Ignoring the promotional pen, the man removed his own expensive looking one from his shirt pocket and wrote while we watched. When he finished, Yuri said, "Blake will go over the standard terms of our contract with you, and if you find it agreeable, then we'll see what we can do."

"You won't refer to me by name while you are asking around, will you?"

"No, we'll work up a cover story and keep you out of it."

Yuri accompanied him to see Blake, while I reviewed what he had written down. A father belatedly concerned about the fate of his son. In some ways, taking the case posed another moral dilemma for me. The mother in me wanted to lecture him on the responsibilities of parenthood. I also wanted to tell him that, in my opinion, we had little hope of finding his son. Self-interest won out over truth, however. His case would give us a reason to nose around some more. I'd been feeling guilty about simply walking away from rumors of some of the serious problems the homeless were facing. Maybe we could learn something that would justify police intervention. And although I had little hope of finding Broderick's son, I didn't feel guilty about having him pay a little to further our investigation. After all, if he had taken responsibility for his behavior sooner, his girlfriend and son might not have ended up living in a car.

CHAPTER 18
ADDICTION

JUST AS WE WERE getting ready to go in search of Siana, Gary called to tell us that he was heading back to the island. He had a job assignment and wanted to check on Cole and Bandit before taking off. He estimated he would be gone for a couple of days to a week. "I think I'll wait until I'm back to mention Bess's death to Cole," he said. "I'd like to be around awhile after I break the news. He might be upset, as well as concerned for his own safety."

"You still feel like he's okay staying with the neighbor?"

"Absolutely. I've explained that they shouldn't tell any outsiders that Cole isn't their son. And Bandit will stay with him."

"Well, we have some news." I told him about our latest client and how we acquired him.

"Keep testifying on homelessness and this could become a booming business for you," he said.

"You serious or giving me a bad time?"

"A little of both. "Statistically, about 600,000 people are declared missing in the United States each year. Most are found or return on their own fairly quickly. There are also 4,000 to 5,000 unidentified bodies found each year.

With the large homeless population in Washington State running at around 25,000, there's bound to be quite a few who fall into both camps—the missing and the dead."

"I'm impressed with the fact that you know all this."

"I do a few missing person's cases from time to time."

Now that was interesting, but I had the feeling the missing persons he looked for weren't like our usual runaways and errant parents.

"If I had to guess," he continued, "that baby already has another family, and they probably paid dearly for him."

"You don't think we can find him? I mean, I have some serious doubts myself."

"I think you need more resources than you have to crack that kind of criminal enterprise. But you're resourceful, so you never know. Just be careful. There seems to be more than one group taking advantage of having so many homeless around."

I hated to admit even to myself how sorry I was to see Gary leave. It was reassuring to have him as backup, even though there were others on our team that we could call on. Dealing with possible kidnappers and organ traffickers felt a little out of our league.

Yuri and I started our new assignment by trying to find Siana Campbell's gray 2019 Ford Flex station wagon. Adele had found the license number for us, so when we came across a battered 2019 Ford Flex covered in leaves and grime, all we had to do was check the plates to verify it was hers. It was parked just a few blocks away from the strip mall where Broderick said he'd caught up with her before.

"Well, that was easy enough," Yuri said.

"Maybe she's low on gas."

We didn't see anyone inside as we slowly drove past. There were only a few cars parked nearby, but it was a fairly busy street. "Seems a bit public for a baby snatch," Yuri said.

"It probably happened at night. There may not be many people around after dark. If she was kinda out of it, she might not have put up much resistance."

We parked across the street to wait for her to return.

"Wish we'd brought coffee and snacks," I said.

An hour later, there was still no sign of her.

"I need to stretch my legs," Yuri said. "I think I'll stroll over and have a look in her car."

"I'll go with you. If we see her coming, let's wait until we're close to say anything."

Yuri laughed. "You're thinking of those FBI shows where they yell '*STOP, FBI*' from 100 feet away, aren't you?"

"I know they're trying to set up a chase scene, but it always irritates me."

"Well, there's no reason for her to do a runner …"

"Unless she thinks we're DEA or the police."

"You're right. We'll be cool."

We strolled across the street and slowly started to make our way past the car. "Oh no," I said when I saw her slumped down on the back seat.

"Maybe she's just sleeping."

"In that position?"

Yuri tried the handle and the door opened. Then he leaned in and shook her shoulder. "Siana, you okay?" When she didn't respond, he reached down and checked her neck for a pulse. "She's alive," he said. "Pull the car over here. I think we need to take her to the hospital."

As I hurried to get our car, I wondered if we should be calling 911. We weren't that far away from a hospital, though; we could have her there in no time.

"No sign of her son," I commented as we hurriedly transferred her to our car. She didn't weigh much and was totally limp. It was more like moving a prop than a live woman.

"Under the circumstances, it may be a good thing that we didn't find Eddie with her."

The next half hour was a blur of activity. With Yuri in the back seat with Siana, I drove as fast as I dared to a nearby hospital emergency room, pulled in behind an ambulance and ran inside to get help. When an EMT team came with a cart, we told them we thought her condition was possibly drug-induced and that she had been unresponsive since we found her. They quickly took her away, and we were given some forms to fill out about her status and health history. We had to explain that except for her name, we didn't really know anything. And "no," we didn't know whether she had insurance. I was tempted to say that I highly doubted she did since she'd been living out of her car, but I wasn't sure it was in her best interest to reveal her inability to pay for services, so I kept my mouth shut.

After that, we moved our car to a parking lot and then hung around the waiting room, hoping someone would get back to us with good news. If she didn't recover, there was even less chance we would find Eddie.

Yuri said he was going to the snack bar for coffee and something to eat while we waited, and I told him to get something healthy. When he came back with his hands full, I asked, "You think one banana balances out two bags of flavored chips, a package of pepperoni sticks and a couple candy bars?"

"The candy is dark chocolate—that's good for you."

To be honest, I was surprised at the banana and had been secretly hoping for junk food. In my experience, most junk food takes time to crunch and chew and is better for passing time than more healthy fare. Of course, if my kids made that argument I would scoff.

While we worked our way through our assortment of goodies and drank coffee that was "blacker than a thousand midnights," Yuri and I took turns asking at the desk to see if they knew anything yet, trying and failing not to be impatient. I also called the office to let them know where we were. Finally, a doctor came into the waiting room to talk to her "next of kin." I explained that we had been hired to find her and that we were the ones who brought her in.

"Can you tell us her status so we can report to our client?" I asked him.

"Well, we gave her some Naloxone and managed to bring her around, but she will need to have someone look after her for a while. Is she going home with you?"

"No, we need to ask her a few questions as to the whereabouts of her baby, but we won't be taking her with us."

"Her baby is missing?"

"We were actually hired to find her baby and wanted to start by talking to her," Yuri said. "We'll contact our client, but he's out of town. Are there any local facilities that can keep her while she's convalescing?"

"She's been living in her car," I added.

"I can keep her here for a couple of hours, but then we'll have to discharge her."

"Let us talk to her. Maybe she can suggest someone we can contact on her behalf."

"Okay. Go on in."

There were two patients in her room. Siana seemed to be dozing when we went in. The old woman on the bed next to her said, "Dearie, you have visitors." Siana blinked a few times before her eyes focused.

"Hi, Siana," I said. I was about to ask how she felt, but one look at her tangle of long dirty hair and face as pale as the inside of a coconut, I stopped myself. I started to say "you're lucky to be alive" and stopped myself again. I wasn't sure she would agree.

Yuri got right to the point. "Eddie wasn't with you in your car. Do you know where he is?"

"Eddie," she said, as if not certain who that was.

"Your son, Eddie," I said. "We've been hired to find hm."

"You're looking for Eddie?"

"Yes, do you have any idea where he is?"

"I woke up and he was gone."

"You didn't see who took him?"

She shook her head. "He was gone," she repeated. "I told Broderick, and he got very angry." Her eyes darted around the room. "How did I get here?"

"We brought you," Yuri said. "You're going to be okay, but we need to find Eddie."

"He disappeared," she said.

"Had anyone been asking you questions about him before he disappeared?"

She frowned, appeared to give the question some thought, then said "no."

"Did someone give you some drugs or alcohol just before he went missing?"

"I don't do drugs," she said, apparently either lying or in denial about having just been treated for an overdose.

"Were you parked on the street or near an encampment when he went missing?"

Her frown deepened. "I don't remember." Her eyes filled with tears. "Poor Eddie. No one wants him."

"Don't you want him?" I asked.

"He doesn't like it in the car. He cries all the time."

I could barely imagine what it had been like for the two of them living like that. How had she been changing him? And she looked so undernourished, I wondered if she'd been able to breast-feed him. If not, what had she been giving him to keep him alive? I said, "Was there anyone who showed an unusual interest in him recently?"

Again, she seemed to think for a moment before saying "no." But it was possible she was having trouble processing even simple questions.

"Can you describe him?"

"He's a baby."

"Any distinguishing marks?" Yuri asked.

She shook her head. I wanted to ask if she would recognize him if she saw him, but I was afraid of her answer if she was honest. So instead, I asked, "Is there someone we can call to come for you?"

She shook her head.

I left Yuri behind and stepped out into the hall to call Broderick. He didn't answer, so I left a message. Then I called the office and asked if Adele could find a state-funded rehab in the area where we could send Siana.

When I went back in the room, Siana seemed more focused, but when I told her we were trying to find a place for her to go to recover, she balked.

"No way. I want to go back to my car."

"We can't do that," Yuri said. "It isn't safe for you."

"You can't tell me what I can and can't do." Where she had been foggy before when asked about her son, she was now very clear about not wanting help getting her life back on track.

"Well, we won't help you destroy yourself," I said. "Don't you want to know what happened to Eddie?"

"I want to go back to my car," she repeated.

Yuri turned to me and signaled that we should go. "Good luck," he said to Siana.

Once out in the hall, I said, "We can't just leave her like this. That's heartless."

"She's an adult, and we don't have the authority to commit her. There are lots of homeless people in similar situations."

"And if we give her license number to the police?"

"Unless they arrest her on drug charges, they will give her a warning and she will move her car, and the cycle will repeat itself."

"How will she even get back to her car from here?"

"Maybe the hospital will refuse to release her if there is no one here to take her home. That would be the best outcome."

"I can't believe there's nothing we can do."

"Well, we can keep trying to get in touch with our client. Maybe he will relent and try to help her. And, we can look for Eddie."

"I know you can't save someone from themselves; they have to want to be saved. But I feel like we are abandoning her."

"It's called tough love."

"I understand the concept, but …" The thought that this was the kind of decision Elinor had been forced to make with her sister again and again over the years made me feel sorry for her and every other relative who had to deal with a loved one's addiction. "As for Eddie, I'm not so sure that he isn't better off wherever he is. If we're right about these traffickers, at least he's supposedly with people who wanted him enough to pay for him."

"I agree to some extent. People will do desperate things to get a child, except we don't know if the people who have Eddie are 'good people' or child abusers. I think we have a moral obligation as well as a contractual one to try to find him."

CHAPTER 19
SEARCHING FOR EDDIE

I LEFT ANOTHER message for Broderick, hoping he had enough compassion for the mother of his son that he would be willing to help her get back on her feet. I told him what the doctor said about her needing someone to look out for her after her discharge, and if he didn't want to do that, maybe he could call someone about getting her to a rehab center. Otherwise, she was going to try to go back to her car on her own. I explained that she'd had keys and a wallet in the pocket of the jacket she was wearing when we found her and that we'd looked in her wallet for insurance information. All it contained was her drivers' license, an expired VISA card, and a couple one-dollar bills. That wasn't going to get her far. Meanwhile, we would continue searching for Eddie.

"Do you think he will try to help her?" I asked after leaving the message.

"Worse odds than winning at Keno," Yuri said.

"I assume you mean you don't think he'll come through."

"I'd place a hefty bet on it. Interested?"

"I hate to bet against something I would like to see happen."

"I can see why you wouldn't do well in a football pool."

We decided to swing by my place to pick up No-name before heading to the encampment. People have a tendency to talk more willingly when you have a dog with you. It instantly gives you something in common. For people who like dogs, that is. And a lot of homeless people seem to have dogs. That surprised me at first, but it made sense. Dogs are both companions and protection.

On the way, we stopped at the strip mall near where Siana was parked. We asked around, but no one we talked to remembered seeing her car. A middle-aged clerk in the mini-mart knew who she was though. His eyes narrowed as he described her in very unflattering terms as a druggie who he had to keep his eye on or she would fill her pockets with everything from snacks to cue-tips. One time he even caught her trying to lift a roll of paper towels by stuffing them in her pants. Furthermore, when we asked if he had ever seen her with a baby, he assured us that he would have reported it to whoever was in charge of child welfare in the state if he'd seen her with a kid because he didn't think she was capable of taking care of one.

It was late afternoon before we got to the homeless encampment. We knew that a hit-and-miss wander around approach looking for someone who knew or had seen Siana enough times to remember her was a longshot. Still, it seemed possible that she was parking nearby because it was a convenient place to buy drugs. If so, we might come across someone who either knew her or could direct us to someone who did. We doubted anyone would give us a dealer's name, but they might talk to us if we kept the focus on Eddie being missing. Still a longshot by any measure.

It was also possible that no one even knew she had a child. From the mini-mart clerk's response, my guess was that she left Eddie in the car when she went shopping—whether for legal or illegal goods. In fact, I was starting to wonder why she wanted to keep the child in the first place, and why she didn't turn him over to foster care once she was living in her car. Mother love versus drug addiction—that left both mother and son teetering on the edge.

Even if no one remembered seeing Siana—with or without Eddie, they might be able to confirm whether the child abduction rumors in general were true or just speculation. We didn't anticipate anyone would have any concrete evidence, but they could have seen something or know of specific instances that we could follow up on. Maybe that would give us something to pass along to the police and also provide a lead on finding Eddie. Although if, as Gary had suggested, we were dealing with professionals, fear could keep people from speaking up. There was also another possibility, that taking Eddie was a one-off done by someone who simply took advantage of the situation, finding him unattended in an unlocked car. If that was the case, tracking them would be extremely difficult, if not impossible.

No-name was excited to be on an outing and squeezed out the door before it was fully open. His leash got caught on something, and he was jerked to a stop. He stood there glaring at me as if it was my fault. I untangled him while Yuri filled his backpack with the remaining snacks we had in the car from the last time we'd tried to encourage conversations with reluctant camp residents by handing out goodies. Armed with food and accompanied by an eager dog, we began looking around for tents.

Late afternoon turned out to be a good time to find people "at home." There were several groups visible from the street. They were gathered around small fires. It looked like they were cooking — maybe sharing an early dinner or gathering to socialize around the comfort of a campfire. One group was composed mostly of women. We immediately headed for them. I didn't have to check with Yuri to know that we were in agreement: women might be more likely to have noticed a baby. Sexist, perhaps, but based on my experience, it was also reality.

No-name seemed to know exactly why he had been included. He bounded over to a youngish woman wearing overalls and a red handkerchief headband. "Whoa," she said as he put his head on her thigh. "And who are you?" No-name wagged his tail and gave her his "everyone loves me" look. She rubbed his head. As I came alongside her, she asked: "What's his name?"

"I'm embarrassed to admit that my two children couldn't agree on a name, so we started calling him 'No-name,' and it's stuck."

The older woman next to her said, to no one in particular: "Sounds like her kids are a handful."

"They can be," I said. I squatted down next to No-name in front of the fire.

The smell of coffee perking in one of those old aluminum pots was tantalizing, the light brown bubbles popping up in the glass dome. I noticed there was a large iron pot of what looked like stew hanging by a rusted handle from a bar positioned across one side of the fire. It was supported on each end by a couple of wood boxes. I must have been obvious in sniffing the air because the woman fondling No-name offered me a cup.

Yuri had been silent to that point. "I have some cookies that would be good with a cuppa." He pulled a package of cookies and a cup out of his pack. "Cameron and I can share some coffee," he said, handing me the cookies to pass along. "I'm Yuri by the way."

"Connie," the woman in the overalls said.

"What else you got in there?" an older guy in patched jeans on the other side of Yuri said. "Any beer?" He looked hopeful.

"No beer; just snacks. How about some peanuts?"

"Sure. Too bad there's no beer—peanuts go good with beer," he said. I was almost sorry we hadn't thrown in a six-pack.

Someone asked Yuri if he had any chips. Yuri took several small bags of different kinds of chips out of his backpack and passed them around. I let go of No-name's leash and he started making the rounds, begging for attention. "In case you didn't hear, the handsome beast hoping to be petted is Cameron's dog, No-name."

"His name is 'No-name'?" a woman with a deeply wrinkled face under a battered Mariners baseball cap said. "What kind of a name is that?"

"No name," the woman next to her said, giggling and poking the woman in the ribs with her elbow.

One woman pushed No-name away, but she was the only one who seemed to object to his attention. He recovered from her rejection quickly and continued on his networking journey.

It felt a lot more comfortable drinking coffee and chatting to residents than I'd anticipated. The question of why we were there was definitely the proverbial elephant in the room, or in this case, at the campfire. Finally, someone brought it up.

"What 'ha want?" The man seemed to be missing most of his front teeth, and he made a slight whistling sound as he spoke.

"We're looking for someone," I said.

The woman who had pushed No-name away said: "You can't buy information here with a few bags of chips."

Ignoring her hostile response, I explained, "We're here on behalf of a homeless woman named Siana who had her baby stolen. She's been staying in her car about a half block away. You may have seen her and her son, Eddie."

A woman in a blue-checked shirt who seemed to be in charge of stirring the stew, looked hard at both of us and said, "You don't look like someone she could afford." I didn't know whether to feel flattered or just be honest.

"The father of the baby hired us when he learned Eddie had gone missing. We located Siana's car. She was inside but unconscious from an overdose. We took her to the hospital. She'll be okay, but she doesn't have a clue where Eddie is."

"Kids sometimes disappear around here," the woman in the checked shirt offered. "It's not a safe place." The words sounded like a warning … or a threat.

"I assume these disappearances get reported," Yuri said.

"Like to the police?" the man in the Mariners cap said. "That's a laugh."

"So, no one keeps track of disappearances?" I asked. "Any guesses as to how many kids have gone missing in the past year?"

They started whispering back and forth, whether to come up with a number or decide whether they wanted to continue the conversation, I wasn't sure.

"They take 'em at night," the woman in the checked shirt said.

"What happens to the parents?"

"Sometimes they disappear too."

"But not always?"

"No, if they're drunk or high, they wake up to find their kid gone. There's nothing they can do then."

"One here and there," the woman who had pushed No-name away said. "No one counts, but they add up over time."

"And no officials have tried to stop it?" I knew the answer but had to ask.

Several made scoffing noises, and no one bothered to reply. I wanted to defend the police; I knew they got lots of pressure from neighborhoods to clean up or get rid of homeless sites but no resources to protect them. Besides, my guess was that there were a fair number of officers who saw the homeless as more nuisance than human beings. The animosity between the homeless and the police was regrettable, if in some ways understandable.

"Look," I said. "We can't make any promises, but we are looking into the disappearances, starting with trying to find Eddie. If we get any leads, we have some contacts who will follow up." I paused, then added, "I wish we could do more."

"We just want to be left alone," Connie said. "Is that too much to ask?"

"Unfortunately," Yuri said, "some criminals consider encampment residents vulnerable targets. They think you can't or won't fight back. You need to keep an eye on each other. And if you see something bad going down, call 911. Or call me." He took out a clutch of cards and passed them around.

"What are you going to do? You Superman?" They all laughed.

"I wish I were. I prefer him to Batman or the Hulk. Green isn't a good color for me."

A couple of people chuckled.

"Why not Batman? You against gays?"

"I don't like bats. You have any around here?"

"Just mosquitoes and squirrels. Squirrel meat's okay." No-name perked up at the word "squirrel" and looked around. When he didn't see one, he settled back down between Connie and me.

"I had a dog, Bouncer," an older man who hadn't spoken before said. He was probably in his late 60s, his skin weathered from being outdoors so much of the time. "He was a good squirrel hunter, but he didn't like to skin 'em." He smiled, showing a row of even, gray teeth.

"And, as I recall, he didn't mind eating them raw," the woman stirring the pot said. There were a few guffaws and snickers.

"What happened to Bouncer?" I asked.

"Lost him during a sweep."

"I'm sorry." I didn't know what else to say.

"Wanna leave your pooch with me?" he asked.

"My kids would never forgive me."

"Shelters won't give any of us dogs," someone said.

"Well, that's one thing I can do," Yuri said. "I know someone who might be able to get you a dog. Tell me how to find you if I do."

Yuri and the man stepped away from the circle and exchanged information. As I considered the individuals huddled around the fire, waiting to share their communal dinner, I thought I understood why they resisted going into shelters. Their camp was primitive, and probably not safe, but in some ways they were a family. Not by blood, but by shared circumstance. People trying to survive, a little lower on Maslow's Hierarchy than the people I associated with normally, but with similar interpersonal needs. At the same time, I didn't want to accept that drugs were an inevitable and unstoppable part of the lifestyle for so many of the homeless, and I could empathize with neighbors who worried about the camps being a crime and health hazard. It's like Oscar Wilde wrote, "The truth is rarely pure and never simple."

CHAPTER 20
BOTTOM'S UP

THERE WERE TWO dogs in the second group we approached. We didn't see them until No-name put on the brakes and either growled or simpered—maybe it started out as a growl and sank to a simper when he saw that one was a German Shepherd and the other a Pit Bull. Neither was on a leash. Both leapt to attention when they saw us coming in their direction. No-name decided he didn't want to be left behind, but he glued himself to my leg, making it difficult to walk.

"How about we skip this group?" I said. Like No-name, I was apprehensive about the odds if attacked. But what reason would they have for attacking us? Or did they need a reason other than that we obviously weren't members of the homeless community?

"Let me go first," Yuri replied.

No-name and I hung back while Yuri went over to the handful of men sitting on wood stump rounds of various heights facing a fire that was struggling to catch hold. The man working to get it going stood up when he saw us and asked: "Can I help you?" He had an accent that I couldn't quite place. And his tone suggested we weren't going to be offered coffee this time. We would be lucky if they didn't sic their dogs on us.

"I'm Yuri and that's Cameron." He pointed back in my direction. "We're looking for a missing baby taken from someone who's been living nearby in her car, a 2019 Ford Flex station wagon. Anyone hear anything about someone suddenly showing up with a baby? The baby's name is Eddie, and he's only three months old. He needs his mother."

The men looked around at each other and shrugged. "I'm Hari," the man lighting the fire said. "Why don't you and your friend join us."

Yuri glanced at the two dogs who were standing stone still, like snipers calculating when to take their shot. "What about your dogs? Ours is more of a lap dog; not used to being around large dogs."

There were a few snickers at the phrase "lap dog."

"Duke. Bull. Sit."

Duke and Bull? That didn't sound too friendly, but I was impressed when both dogs immediately obeyed and sat. Although they were still on alert.

I took a seat on a log next to Yuri. No-name was sticking so close I almost expected him to live up to Yuri's description and climb on my lap. I didn't embarrass him—or me—by telling him to "sit," because he never listened to commands. Still, he wasn't taking any chances; he laid across my feet and kept his mouth shut. Smart, but cowardly dog.

The men were passing around a bottle of something in a brown bag. When it got to Yuri, he handed it to me. "112 days sober," he said. "I feel good."

Thanks a lot, I thought. What was I going to do? All eyes were on me, including Yuri's. "She's more of a chardonnay woman," Yuri said with a chuckle. When everyone laughed, I quickly passed the bag on.

"I appreciate the offer," I mumbled, feeling awkward. Still, better to be the brunt of a joke than to take a swig of who knew what kind of liquor from a community bottle.

"I know the car," someone said. I followed the voice to a young man with a shock of bleached blond hair and slightly bulging eyes. "Her baby cries a lot."

"You know them, then?"

"Not really. She bummed some pills off me once or twice. I would've hung out with her, but I didn't like the kid."

"Did you know that he went missing?"

"I heard something about that."

When he didn't continue, Yuri prompted him: "What did you hear?"

"That wherever the kid went he was better off."

"But you have no idea who took him?"

The blond man shook his head.

Hari asked, "You sure she didn't sell her kid?"

"She told us he was snatched," I said.

"Well, if she sold him for drug money, that's what she would say, righto?"

Righto? Wasn't that Australian slang? "I don't think she did that."

"Maybe she doesn't remember doing that," Hari suggested.

"Let's say for now that Eddie was taken rather than part of a drug buy, any idea who might have done that?"

There was a lot of head shaking but no one said anything.

Yuri tried another tack: "Any of you heard rumors about a child trafficking gang operating in homeless camps?"

"You cops?" someone asked.

"No, we're just trying to help out the ex-wife of a client. We're private investigators."

"Her too?" The her was me. Not an advocate for women's equality, I guessed.

"Yes, me too," I said as confidently as I could manage. Maybe we needed to call No-name something tough like Brute or Marmaduke or Rambo to give him—and me—some street cred if we approached other all-male groups with dogs who might consider No-name an hors d'oeuvres. At least then, being referred to as a "chardonnay woman" wouldn't make me feel like I should be auditioning for a role in Desperate Housewives.

"Rumors, yeah. But none of our business."

"I understand," Yuri said. "You have to pick your battles."

"Some people don't like it when you get in their way. You might want to think about that." It sounded like a friendly warning, but it could have been more sinister.

Yuri poked me in the ribs and No-name's head snapped up. "Thanks," Yuri said as we stood up at the same time, like we were joined at the hip. He didn't give out any cards. We just slowly walked away with No-name slinking along between us.

At the main trail we simultaneously turned back toward the entrance rather than continuing further into the camp. "Maybe we should call it a day," I said.

"That's what I'm thinking."

"Otherwise, you'll get a reputation as a camp teetotaler."

"Want to stop for a quick glass of white wine on the way back?" Yuri smiled. "Don't say I never do anything for you."

"I did appreciate that. In a twisted sort of way."

"For a minute I thought you were going to take a swig."

"So did I."

"Probably wasn't a good idea. I doubt it was quality whiskey."

"But I felt so …"

"White middle class? The quintessential Yuppie?"

"Yeah, privileged. Like someone who only drinks chilled white wine."

"When you're hunkered around one of those campfires, the idea that 'you can't save everyone' feels kinda thin, doesn't it? Hard to know whether it's a way to rationalize doing nothing."

"On the other hand, adults have the right to make decisions for themselves, unless there are mental health issues involved. Even then, there are laws to prevent someone from being institutionalized against their will."

"Multi-layered, tough issues."

"Why don't we ask the saintly doctor about missing children?" I said. "That might save us some time."

"Good idea. Why don't I give him a call while you drive me back to my car." He glanced at his watch. "It might be too late, but we can leave a message."

As I took out my keys to unlock the car, a voice called "Wait!"

No name raced around to the other side of the car as I turned to see Duke bounding toward us a few feet ahead of the young blond man from the all-male campfire group.

Yuri opened the passenger door for a frantic No-name before turning toward my side of the car to see what the man wanted. I almost jumped inside too, but I couldn't let Yuri face Duke and blondie on his own … could I? Although since Yuri remained on the passenger side of the car, it appeared that I was the first line of defense against the fast-approaching man and his mouth-drooling, incisor-barred dog.

"Sit," the man ordered as he got closer. It took me a second to realize he was talking to his dog and not me. Thankfully, Duke sat before I could. At that point, Yuri joined us, reluctantly, I thought, while No-name watched from the safety of the car.

The blond man came up alongside his dog and took a few seconds to catch his breath before blurting out why he'd chased after us. "I just wanted to tell you that you shouldn't let Siana go spooking around looking for her kid. She could end up missing too, if you get my drift."

My knees were still shaking, but his comment sounded more like concern than a threat.

"Look, Siana is out of control. Hari was right—she could have handed Eddie over to someone for drugs or cash, but I don't think she did. There are children who go missing. People of all ages too from time to time. Even though we try to watch each other's backs." He paused. "I just wanted to make sure you understood that you should take Hari's warning seriously."

"You like her, huh?" I asked. I couldn't think of any other reason why he would bother telling us this.

His neck turned red. “She’s nice when she’s not high.” He looked down. “I’ve been clean for six months. The Doc gave me some pills that helped.”

“Did you try to get him to help Siana?”

“She wouldn’t go along with it. She’s really messed up.”

“Anyone you think we should talk to?”

“I think you should just walk away.”

“Do the others know you came to warn us?”

“No, and please don’t tell anyone.” He turned and hurriedly headed back the way he had come, Duke trotting along at his side. The German Shepherd didn’t look nearly as threatening moving away from us instead of lunging in our direction.

“That was strange,” Yuri said.

“It confirms that we should talk to the Doc, righto?”

“Righto.”

Once on the road, Yuri placed the call. To our surprise, a receptionist answered. When he gave her our names and said we had a couple of quick questions for the doctor about kids in homeless camps, she said she would put us through and to hold on.

“He apparently works late,” Yuri said. “Here, I’ll put him on speaker.”

Classical music interrupted by occasional static crackling noises unpleasantly much louder than the music filled the car. Still, it was better than listening to an advertisement or being told every minute that our call was valued, just not enough to hire sufficient staff to handle in-coming calls in a timely manner.

The music ended and a pleasant male voice said, “This is Dr. Walsh, how can I help you?”

"Thanks for taking my call," Yuri said. "You're on speaker with Cameron."

"Hi, Cameron."

Without giving me a chance to reply, Yuri continued. "When we talked to you before, we were looking for a missing woman; this time it's a missing baby."

"Oh no. When did this happen?" He sounded sincerely upset.

"We're not sure of the timing, but the reason we're calling is not only to ask if you know anything about the child we're searching for, but whether you've heard rumors of other children of homeless parents who've gone missing."

"I'm afraid the homeless are not a stable community especially those with children. They generally try harder to move on, to find more permanent housing. Overall, there aren't a lot of kids in the camps. When I run across any, I try to make sure they are vaccinated against common diseases. And I give their parents lists of shelters that will accept children."

"So, have you heard anything specific about an organized group trafficking in young children?"

"No, that's not something I've encountered. I hope the rumor isn't true."

"That's what we're trying to find out."

"Sorry I can't be more helpful."

"One more question about this specific case," Yuri said. "Any chance you came across a young woman named Siana? She was living in her car with the baby we're searching for, a little boy named Eddie. He's about three months old."

"You say she was living in her car with a three-month-old baby? That sounds tough. Sorry. It doesn't ring any bells either."

"Well, thanks for your time. If you do hear anything about Eddie, or other kids going missing, give me a call, okay?"

"Right away. And good luck."

Yuri cut the connection.

"Another dead-end," I said, feeling deflated.

"Don't you think it's strange he didn't admit to hearing rumors about kids getting abducted? I mean, he's spent a lot more time in encampments than we have."

"I don't remember anyone just volunteering the rumors. We've brought up the idea by asking about it."

"Still, I got the impression our blond friend may have mentioned Siana to him. Didn't he say something about how the doctor gave him some pills that helped him get off drugs and that he tried to get Siana to see the doctor about her drug problem?"

"When it became clear that Siana wasn't interested in giving up drugs, maybe he decided not to talk to the doctor about her. It's also possible the doctor doesn't pay any attention to the rumor mill. His mission is to deal with health issues."

"You think he's a doctor first and human being second?"

"Could be he lacks good bedside manners. Doesn't need it for his specialty. Fix them fast and move on to the next."

"He's saving the world, one person at a time, but doesn't really care about who they are as people?"

"Well, I doubt he's sharing a bottle of whiskey around a campfire."

We both laughed before falling silent. Finally, Yuri said, "I hate not making any progress. I think I'll run in and see if P.W. is still around. Maybe she'll have some suggestions. You go home to your kids. Be a good mother so they don't end up living on the streets."

CHAPTER 21
CLIENT NUMBER THREE

AFTER DINNER with the kids, Jenny called to tell me she had heard from Gary and that he was returning on Friday. I felt a flash of irritation—why hadn't he called me directly? Why channel a message through Jenny? Although I knew the answer and rationally knew it made sense, I was still ticked. It's like not being asked to a party you didn't want to go to in the first place. You always want the option of turning down the invitation.

Then I got another call, a surprising call. From Dr Elliot Walsh. At first, I thought he had remembered something he wanted to tell us, but, no, he wanted to get together for dinner … with me. Dinner? With Dr. Walsh? Was he asking me out on a date? He couldn't be—I was a good three inches taller than him. I might even weigh more. Even as I thought it, I knew it was a politically incorrect and old-fashioned response, like something from an old Hallmark rom-com.

"I would like to talk to you more about the homeless situation in our city," he said. "And it would give me a chance to relax over dinner instead of eating on the run. Friday evening? Does that work for you?"

"I'll have to check with my mother," I said. Suddenly realizing how that sounded, I stammered: "She lives with us. I need to see if she can fix dinner for the kids."

"You have children?"

"Yes, two, Mara and Jason."

"Well, let me know if you can make it. I know of a wonderful Ethiopian restaurant that serves amazing beef tibs. Their specialty is a spicey chicken stew, or if you prefer, their beyaynetu, a vegetarian sampler, is quite good. Oh, I could go on and on. I spent a year working in a clinic in Ethiopia, and I really miss the food."

"You're making me hungry. I've never had Ethiopian food before, so that sounds interesting. I'll get back to you tomorrow, okay?"

If it was a date and he didn't mind being shorter than me, why should I care? Except he wasn't my type. It was okay to have "types," wasn't it? I didn't find him physically appealing. But maybe it wasn't a date, just two people talking over a shared meal. Was that a thing? He'd mentioned that it would give him a chance to relax, as if I had a more leisurely life. Or maybe that was his way of making it easy for me to say "yes." I sat there for a moment thinking about it before finding myself calling Yuri.

"Is everything okay?" Yuri said instead of "hello."

"Everything's fine, but I just got an interesting call."

"From …?"

"Elliot Walsh."

"Oh, what did he tell you?"

"He didn't 'tell' me anything. He wants to have dinner Friday evening."

"With us?"

"No, just with me."

Yuri laughed, a deep-throated, husky sound. "You're kidding, right?"

"I wish I were."

"If you didn't sizzle with the good-looking professor, I doubt you will sizzle with Elliot." After a brief snort-laugh at his own mocking comment, he asked, "What did you say?"

"That I had to check with my mother." I might as well let him get a really good belly laugh out of the situation.

"You didn't." Snort-laugh, snort-laugh.

"I did."

"Did he rescind his offer?"

"No, and upon reflection, I think he has a hidden agenda. But I can't imagine what it could be. What do you think?"

"Well, it isn't as if you aren't good date material; I mean, you're the right age and attractive enough—"

"That's flattering."

"And, in my experience, doctors tend to be arrogant. Maybe he thinks he's a catch."

"Seriously? That's what you think?"

"Maybe he finds you irresistible."

"I would have picked up a vibe."

"You can be a bit dense."

"Thank you for that."

"There is another possibility. Maybe he simply wants to talk about what we've learned about the homeless community. After all, he spends a lot of his time with encampment residents. Or maybe he's lonely for adult, homeowner companionship. Or, maybe he's tired of eating alone. Where is he taking you?"

"An Ethiopian restaurant. He spent a year in Ethiopia."

"Don't they eat with their hands?"

"I think they do, but they use their bread as a scoop."

"Well, just remember to wash your hands first."

"I suppose I need to go, don't I? He did mention that he would like to talk about the homeless situation."

"There you go—not a date then. Or, maybe an excuse for a date. Hard to know."

"Want to come with us?"

"No, thanks. I'm sure he would have mentioned it if he wanted me to tag along. If he does have an ulterior motive, you'll have a better chance of discovering it on your own. Of course, if it's you—body and soul—that he's after, well, I wouldn't want to interfere."

"You're not much help."

"Just make sure you're home before your carriage turns back into a pumpkin."

"Thanks for the sage advice, Dr. Ruth. See you tomorrow." I hung up, even more suspicious about the saintly doctor and even less interested in going to dinner with him on Friday evening. But Yuri was right, I needed to do it. If he did have an ulterior motive, it might be linked to the missing baby. Although, why he would hold back information about that or anything else related to the homeless was beyond me.

Two minutes later I called Yuri back.

"I think you speed dialed the wrong attractive male. I'm the tall one," he said.

"Not funny. I forgot to ask what P.W. had to say about our investigation."

"Not a lot. She agrees it's probably a dead-end. She had Adele call hospitals in the area as well as Child Protective

Services to see if any unidentified babies had been left with them on the off-chance Siana had 'misplaced' him. Nothing turned up. Blake is going to invoice Broderick for time spent with a discount for lack of success."

"So, that's it."

"That's it. Case closed. So, I went ahead and finished off the snacks we've been passing around. Some of the candy was pretty good, but we should have spent more on the cookies."

"It doesn't feel fair."

"You mean because I got all of the leftover snacks?"

"Be serious. You know what I meant."

"I do. But we have to look on the positive side."

"Which is?"

"Cole has a new start on life. Siana is alive for at least a while longer. You have a date with a doctor. And, well, I guess there aren't too many bright spots in all this."

Thursday morning, I once again descended into ill-humor, as gloomy as Eeyore: "Could be worse. Not sure how, but it could be." While working on a report summing up our findings for Broderick Kendall, I couldn't stop thinking about Siana and Eddie. It felt like we had let both down. She was probably already high on something and at risk for another overdose. And Eddie, well, I desperately wanted to believe Eddie was in a happy home getting the care and attention he deserved. Did he end up with a couple who had been willing to pay big bucks for a baby? Or maybe he had gone to a single male or female, a gay couple or some other deserving person who had been turned down by adoption agencies for unfair reasons.

Unfortunately, a little voice at the back of my head kept expressing doubts with these happy scenarios. Even if well-intentioned, whoever ended up with him should have been suspicious about why there was a baby for sale in the first place. No matter how strong their desire for a family, they had to realize that a black-market baby was likely part of an illegal enterprise.

On the other hand, since neither of Eddie's parents actually wanted him, any loving, stable home seemed like a good outcome. But what if …? I didn't want to close the book before reading the last chapter. There were too many possible unhappy endings to this story.

Yuri, on the other hand, was in a chuckle and trivia mood. He started by tormenting all of us with facts about "speed-dating caves for bats." At first, I thought he was making it up. But apparently there are three particular caves off the coastline of Dorset that host mating parties for bats. "They meet and mate on the wing," Yuri said. "Get it? They party until dawn when they have to leave or their Batmobile turns into a pumpkin."

Mixing fairy tales and comic book characters with a real event made his trivia rant feel almost like stand-up comedy.

"Their conversation is limited to honking, grunting, and cooing, but then you don't have time to say much on a fly by," he said. "They would mate for life, but the caves aren't lit, so it's hard to track down the father.

"Female bats give birth while hanging upside down; their pups are born in a free-fall position. They better hope their mother has a catcher's mitt on."

Grant, the father figure for our team ended Yuri's rant with a scientific statement that put to rest the quirkiness of the bat mating ritual: "Drawing on bats from as far away as forty miles ensures the genetic health of bat populations. Bat speed dating was simply an evolutionary approach to survival." No laugh lines there.

Yuri apparently couldn't think of a comeback, so that ended the rein of the speed-dating bats. Will asked if I would help him with some research he was doing, and I said yes. Unfortunately, baby Eddie was still making it difficult for me to concentrate on less urgent matters.

I was glad when Blake announced that Councilwoman Amanda Smythe was here to see Yuri and me. Yuri went out and brought her to the conference room where I was waiting.

"I have a cousin who's been living on the streets," she said without preliminaries. "I'd like to hire you to find him. His name is Luke Parker." She put a couple of photos on the table and turned them to face us. "None of the family has heard from him in almost a year, but we think he's still in the area."

"A year's a long time," Yuri said.

"It's been difficult for the family. He always refuses help. So, most of us have stopped trying." She looked down at her hands spread out in front of her on the table. From the look of them, her polished nails probably received regular manicures. "He's schizophrenic," she added. "Tends to go off his meds. When he does, he's not always rational; sometimes very emotional."

"Why are you hoping to find him now after such a long time?" I asked.

"I want to know if he's okay."

"That's it? We find him, take a few pictures to show he's alive, and walk away?"

"No, that's not what I mean. We should have looked for him when he first fell out of touch, but, as I said, he always refuses help, and the family finally gave up. He may have deliberately cut off contact and doesn't want to be found. I can't live with that. Hearing the stories about what's going on in the homeless camps—if you find him, I want to help in any way I can."

I looked at the pictures of Luke. One was a head shot of a handsome young man, clean-shaven and ruddy cheeked. In another, he was standing shoulder-to-shoulder with other people, smiling into the camera as though he hadn't a care in the world.

"Those were taken about ten years ago."

"He's been homeless for ten years? He may not look quite the same."

She nodded. "I know. The last time I saw him he had longer hair, a beard, and he was thin, really thin, like he wasn't eating regularly."

"He probably still goes by Luke," Yuri said. "That's a start. Tell us where he was living the last time you saw him."

"I brought a map," the councilwoman said. "It lists all the homeless sites in the area as of June. There may have been a few sweeps since then, but it should be fairly accurate." She spread out the map. "I've marked places we know he's stayed in the past."

Yuri and I leaned over and studied the map. I was amazed at how many encampments were listed — and how many locations Luke had frequented.

"It looks like he moved around a lot," Yuri observed. "Are there places other than homeless camps where we should look for him?"

"None that I can think of."

"Well, this gives us somewhere to start. Thanks."

"How long do you think it could take to find him?" she asked.

"If we don't get any good leads in the first couple of days, we will get in touch and see what else, if anything, you want us to try. Alright?"

After she left, we asked Adele to check out whether anyone named Luke Parker was in a local rehab center or hospital or whether he had been arrested in the last year. He could have dropped out of sight given any of those scenarios. Or he could have gone to another state, or even another country. It was thought that quite a few homeless people from the area went south and drifted across the border into Mexico for the sunny weather and cheap accommodations. Although how they supported themselves once they got there was a mystery.

Or … he could have died of either natural causes or a crime related incident and ended up as a John Doe in the morgue. Or buried in some isolated location. There were so many possibilities. None of them easy to track.

Leaving the online search to Adele, I turned to Yuri and said: "I think you need to replace those snacks you ate."

I felt lighter, almost optimistic as we picked up a couple of coffees and purchased replacement snacks; we had purpose, direction, and something to distract me from my gloomy thoughts about Eddie. But when we started really studying the map that Councilwoman Smythe had marked with places Luke had been known to hang out in the past, my optimism vanished. "We can't possibly make a dent in this list in a couple of days even if we work 24/7," I said.

"What I find amazing is the fact that this map exists. Picture some government workers identifying not only all the places where the homeless live in the Seattle area, but color coding the map to indicate the approximate numbers of people living in each location."

"I wonder if the homeless population know there's a public document like this?

"You think it's like a real estate advertisement? It's probably useful for drug dealers and people preying on the homeless too."

"I wonder if Dr. Walsh has a copy?"

"If you are going to date him, you'll have to start calling him Elliot." Yuri did his snort-laugh thing.

"Okay, so how do we narrow our search?"

"Well, we've already been to several of these sites. Not sure I want to go back again."

"I agree. It might seem strange to residents that we've been hired to find still another missing homeless person. It actually seems a bit strange to me."

"The councilwoman said his last known hangout was in Pioneer Square."

"If he truly wanted to 'disappear,' he's probably long gone."

"We don't know if he went silent, moved on, or left temporarily. But someone there might remember him, so I think that's as good a place as any to start."

"Probably best to leave No-name on the bench for this one. Easier to take the light rail without him. And, I don't think snacks will work as enticement there. There are too many places to buy or scrounge food. We will probably need cash."

"Let's stop at an ATM. We can charge it to the councilwoman if we need to use it."

The downtown homeless site where Luke had last been seen had an entirely different vibe from the park encampments. Maybe because the area was not only public but surrounded by boutique shops and galleries. The contrast made their outdoors lifestyle seem less like camping and more like down-and-out living in the midst of plenty. Rumpled clothes, unwashed hair, shopping carts filled with possessions, and people standing around or sitting on city benches looking as if they had no place to be. In contrast, men and women in suits or expensive sportswear hurried by, many staring at cell phones or talking to invisible companions through earbuds, either totally engrossed in their own busy lives or pretending not to see the homeless. It was impossible to tell for sure whether keeping their eyes focused on their cell phones or staring straight ahead was motivated by work ethic or a desire to avoid making eye contact with people who might ask them for a handout.

The location also made it more difficult for us to start conversations with people who appeared to be homeless. Making eye contact seemed to be the signal for being open to panhandling. There was no time to establish rapport or ease into a conversation. Yuri and I had agreed in advance that we weren't there to hand out cash like a couple of good Samaritans on a mission to feed the homeless. It would be like putting down a pot of honey next to a beehive. Rather, we would only offer money in exchange for information. Information first, and payment if the information seemed solid.

In trying to single out likely prospects for conversation, we encountered a fair number of aggressive panhandlers as well as several unhinged and very loud characters. No one seemed to pay any attention to the ruckus we caused, but we felt like we were center stage.

After approaching half a dozen people who lost interest in us as soon as we indicated we weren't going to simply give them money up front, we came across a woman who seemed willing to talk. She barely glanced at the picture of Luke before asking if there was a reward for information. "It depends on whether we can verify what you tell us," Yuri said.

"Not interested," she said as she backed away.

Finally though, we got lucky. A man and woman who seemed like your average city dwellers except for how they were dressed, looked at the picture. Without hesitation, the woman said, "Isn't that Luke, Dado? Remember him?"

Dado thought for a moment. "Yes," he agreed. "Though he's sporting a few extra pounds in this picture. He was pretty thin last time I saw him."

"When was that?" Yuri asked.

The man gave it some thought. "Not sure. About six months ago, maybe seven. Could even have been five … or eight." He gave us a big smile "We don't have a calendar on the wall of our tent." Then he turned serious. "I always liked car calendars. Or trains. Transportation stuff."

"What did you do before?" I asked, hoping it was okay to do so.

"I was an accountant."

"But he counted wrong," his female friend said and laughed.

"I got in a bit of trouble. But no one around here cares."

"Luke had a dog," the woman said suddenly. "Called him something odd …" She turned to Dado. "Remember? A hound of some sort, I think."

"Yes, I remember. He called him 'Grim,' cuz he looked like he was frowning."

"Any idea where he is now?"

"No, there was a sweep around then. I don't think he returned."

We thanked them, and even though they hadn't asked for anything, Yuri slipped the woman a $20.

"Hard to imagine how you go from being an accountant with a car calendar on your wall to living in a tent," I said once we were out of earshot.

"Well, the councilwoman said that Luke used to be a teacher in a community college. Hard to know how people end up on the streets."

We found a triangular spot at the end of a green space covered in tents. There were quite a few people standing around. The first group we approached was carrying on a conversation about some new tiny houses that had just become available. When we said we were looking for Luke and asked if anyone knew someone by that name, several seemed to be considering whether they did or didn't. Then when we passed Luke's picture around, someone said, "That was the guy with the dog, Grim. Nice guy." One or two others thought they remembered him too. No one claimed to have seen them lately though. We thanked them and started to leave when a man stepped out of the circle and motioned for us to stay.

"I think he hooked up with someone. Gail, from some restaurant down the street."

A woman from the group turned toward us. "I remember now. I think she had a relative who fell and couldn't get around on her own."

"That's right," the man said. "They were going to live with her while she recovered." Shaking his head, he added, "Lucky them."

Neither knew Gail's last name. Nor could they remember where she'd been waitressing. "I think it was a café between here and the water," the woman said. "Sorry, that's all I've got." The two seemed pleased when Yuri gave each of them a twenty for the information.

It only took us a couple of hours to find the café. I say "only." We were about to give up when a waitress in a tiny hole-in-the-wall eatery admitted to knowing Gail. "Why are you looking for her?" she asked.

"We're trying to locate Luke Parker for his cousin. She hasn't heard from him lately and is worried. He has a dog named Grim." I don't know why I mentioned the dog, but that seemed to break the ice.

"Grim has been staying with me," the waitress said. "Gail's aunt is allergic to dogs, so they couldn't take him with them when they moved in to take care of her." She looked us up and down, then said, "I can give you their address." She pulled out a notepad and wrote something down.

"He's a great dog," she added as Yuri took the slip of paper from her. "I was happy to take him on a temporary basis. Although after all this time, I'm not sure I want to give him up." Then she laughed. "Better not tell Luke that."

CHAPTER 22
WHEN IS A DATE NOT A DATE?

WE DROVE BY the modest two-story house, then turned around and parked half a block away with a good view of the driveway and the front door. There was the possibility that the waitress who had given us his address had already called Luke to tell him about us, so he might be in hiding or prepared to run—assuming he didn't want to be found. On the other hand, he might not mind having us give his cousin an update on his whereabouts. One way or the other, we needed to verify that he was living there before reporting back to our client.

The easiest thing to do was to simply knock on the door, and, if he answered, let him know his cousin had hired us to find him and snap a picture to prove he was alive and well. Assuming he was actually alive and well and living there, of course. Or we could pull the "wrong house" approach and surreptitiously take a picture if he was the one to answer. Instead, we decided to wait and watch and hope to get a picture from afar. Let his cousin be the one to confront him.

After about an hour, I started to get antsy. We've done lots of long surveillances, but I wasn't in the mood. Besides, all we needed was visual proof that he was there. We didn't have to catch him doing anything as was so often the case during a surveillance. "Why don't we just walk by and see what we can see? Or knock on the door and when he answers, claim we have the wrong house. That would be easier than sitting here waiting for him to put in an appearance."

Yuri didn't have to think long; he too was looking for a quick resolution. "Let's do it. Walk by first. Act as though we're looking for a particular address. Then backtrack. Pretend to consider. Then go up to the front door and say we're afraid we wrote down the wrong address and ask if the Greniers live there. Something like that."

"Are you sure we need to make it so complicated?"

"Well, if he doesn't know we're looking for him, it will only take a few minutes and we're outta here. If he's expecting us because he got a call from their friend, we can still get a picture, apologize for the subterfuge and say we wanted to give his cousin the opportunity to explain why she wanted to get in touch instead of channeling it through us."

"It still sounds unnecessarily complicated, and there's always the chance that Gail or someone else will answer the door. But I'm okay with it. I need to stretch my legs."

We walked purposely down the block, pausing to read the house numbers and then looking back at a piece of paper Yuri was pretending had more than his grocery list on it. When we reached our real destination, Yuri shook his head "no," and we walked past. Then after checking out the next house, we turned and went back to where we thought Luke might be staying.

Perhaps no one noticed our fine acting, but we did succeed overall: Luke answered the door. He was dressed casually, jeans and a T-shirt. His hair was neatly trimmed, he was clean shaven, and he looked well-fed, not at all like a homeless person.

"I think I may have written down the wrong house numbers—is this the Grenier residence?" I asked apologetically. Yuri stood a few steps behind me, off to the side, pretending to be on his phone while taking a few snapshots.

"No, no one here by that name."

"Sorry for bothering you," I said, turning away.

We headed back to my car.

"He didn't act like he was expecting us," I said. "And he looked and sounded pretty normal, not like someone off his meds."

"Then I hope he has a good reason for not contacting any of his relatives," Yuri said.

"Maybe he's been struggling to get back on his feet."

"Living off someone's elderly relative?"

"They're caregivers, not moochers."

"I bet they are mooching caregivers. Hope they're doing more caregiving than mooching."

"Well, his cousin will probably get a feel for that when she stops by to say 'hello and where have you been for a year?' Did you get a good picture?"

"Good enough to show he's clean and healthy looking."

I felt a touch of Yuri's cynicism, but wanted to believe that Luke and Gail were acting out of kindness, not greed. "Should we call the councilwoman now or wait until we get back to the office?"

"Let's ask Adele to see what she can find out about the owner of the house before giving her this location, okay? There's probably no rush. I doubt Luke and his girlfriend are leaving anytime soon. The setup is too comfy."

Yuri called Adele and told her the situation without mentioning his qualms about it. "Find out anything you can about the owner, will you?" After hanging up, he turned to me. "Maybe we should ask a few of the neighbors if they know anything about the living arrangement."

"You really have a bad feeling about this, don't you?"

"I'm not sure exactly why, but yes."

"Well, we can explain the situation to our client when we talk to her. After that, I don't see that there's much we can do. I mean, what gives us the right to talk with neighbors?"

"I agree, there's no real reason for investigating further. I'm still iffy about this, though."

"If our perspectives were reversed, you would tell me to 'let it go.'"

"And I would be right." He grinned, then got serious. "It seems like we are facing one moral dilemma after another these days. In this instance, if there's the possibility that two adults are taking advantage of a vulnerable older person, at what point does it become none of our business?"

"The question of responsibility has come full circle in my mind. I'm afraid 'you can't save everyone' has become my mantra. It's the only way I can cope. Which is pretty sad when you think about it."

"If you saw someone lying on the street in obvious distress, you wouldn't just walk by."

"We walk by homeless people asking for money all the time. What's the extent of our obligation to help?"

"That's the dilemma. When are you a bleeding heart versus when do you cross the line and become a cold-hearted bystander? Like those people in New York who listened to Kitty Genovese's screams and did nothing."

"We'd need to know more than we do to make a complaint in this instance. At least we found Luke. The burden to assess his living situation is up to his cousin."

Friday morning Adele gave us her report on Shirley Roth, the owner of the house where Luke and Gail were living as supposed caretakers. Roth was 84 years old and had no mortgage or outstanding debts. She had a son living in Montana, a deceased sister who had several children, no social media presence, and no criminal record. Her maiden name was Ames. Gail's father was Shirley's uncle. That was the connection.

"Now you know," I said to Yuri. "Gail's connection to Shirley Roth isn't bogus."

"That doesn't mean they aren't taking advantage of her."

"I agree, but I feel better about it overall. At this point, I'm willing to turn over what we know to the council-woman."

"On the other hand," Adele added, "both Luke Parker and Gail Ames have been convicted of minor drug offenses and managed to avoid jail by agreeing to drug rehab treatment. Luke on several occasions."

"Two addicts with access to an old woman's house and possibly to her bank accounts. What could be wrong with that?" Yuri said.

"Not our problem."

"I don't have to like it."

Neither do I, I said to myself. But you can't save everyone.

The rest of the day went by quickly. After we called our client and wrote up our report on the case, I caught up on my emails, asked my other colleagues if they needed help with anything—they didn't—and organized the mess on my desk.

Yuri took off to pick up the dog he'd found for the homeless man who had lost his during an encampment sweep. It was a seven-year-old terrier whose owner had died recently. Yuri had convinced the shelter volunteer where the dog was about to be euthanized to let him deliver it to a "friend" who couldn't come to the shelter himself. He didn't mention that the "friend" was homeless, and the woman he was dealing with was so glad the dog wasn't going to be put down that she gladly bent the rules.

After dropping off the dog, Yuri called me on the way back to the office. "The guy was obviously surprised that I came through. Although it's one of the most unattractive terriers I've ever seen, the guy was thrilled with him. He even liked the dog's name: Curly."

"Is Curly's disposition better than his looks?"

"He seemed like a nice dog. And the two hit it off immediately."

"Did Curly come with a large bag of dogfood and a little something for maintenance?" Knowing Yuri, I already guessed the answer, but I had to ask just to needle him a little.

"Hey, a dog's gotta eat."

"How about a blanket and a leash and a toy and …"

"Okay, so I stopped at a pet store and picked up a few items."

"Well, Curly may not have found a posh home, but he will be loved. At least he wasn't a surprise gift."

"Hey, may I remind you that Jason wanted a dog … and, yes, I should have checked with you first, but it's worked out, hasn't it?"

I couldn't argue that it hadn't 'worked out,' but there were moments—

Yuri changed the subject by suggesting some conversation topics for my "date" with Elliot. "You should ask him whether he's treated any babies at the camps since Eddie's disappearance. Another homeless person could have taken him, and the doc could have assumed the baby belonged to them. Run Luke's and Gail's names past him, just in case. Maybe show him Luke's picture."

I assured him that I would do as much probing as I could, especially since Elliot had already mentioned the homeless community as something he wanted to talk with me about, and it was the only interest I knew of that we had in common.

Wanting to avoid having Elliot pick me up and drop me off at home, I called and told him I was running late and would drive myself from work to the restaurant. That way there would be no forced small talk on the way there and, more importantly, no walk to the door at the end of the evening, wondering how it would end—a handshake, a light peck on the cheek or an awkward kiss. The last time I'd kissed someone on the front porch, my mother had turned the light on and called to us over the side of the second-floor deck. Not on purpose, but because she heard a noise, or so she said. It had made me think of my teenage years with overprotective parents. I vowed I wouldn't do that to Mara, although I knew that I would probably have the urge to keep my "baby girl" safe when she started dating.

The restaurant didn't look like much from the outside, but inside it was more upscale than I'd anticipated from Elliot's description and based on my own vision of what a restaurant where you ate with your hands should look like. I was embarrassed by my stereotyping and felt underdressed, especially when I saw that Elliot had on a jacket and tie. He was waiting for me just inside the entrance. "Cameron," he said in his best bedside manner voice, "so glad you could make it."

Well, that sounded more formal than personal, so I was probably worrying about the date thing for no reason. "Yes, good to see you, Elliot."

When we were escorted to our table, he made me uncomfortable by pulling out my chair for me. There was inevitably some adjustment needed afterwards, a subtle criticism about the help received. I wondered if the custom started at a time when women wore clothes that required careful placement when taking a seat. If so, that was a long time ago.

"What can I get you to drink?" a voice said. I hadn't heard the tall, wafer-thin waiter approach.

"Would you care for a glass of wine?" Elliot asked.

"No thank you. I'm driving. Maybe a glass of water, with lemon."

"And I'd like a cup of coffee with milk," Elliot told the waiter. To me he said, "It's been a long day."

"I would imagine that you have a lot of long days given you have a practice as well as doing all of the pro bono work with the homeless."

"You make me sound so altruistic, but I don't do it all out of the goodness of my heart—I'm researching anxiety and depression, and many of the homeless I interact with are extreme examples of both. Furthermore, they are usually more forthcoming than my paying patients, many of whom have made it a habit to hide their emotional problems."

"I can understand why they might be secretive; they probably feel they will be judged and perhaps punished professionally if they admit to any kind of mental health issues."

"Yes, sad, isn't it? It makes treatment much more difficult."

The waiter brought our drinks, and I used that opportunity to change the subject slightly. "You mentioned trying to wean Bess off drugs. Do you do a lot of that sort of thing?"

"I know it's cliché to say that they have to want to quit, but it's true. Most know they can get help. Sadly, it's an illness that's almost impossible to cure."

"That reminds me, I wanted to ask if either the name Luke Parker or Gail Ames sounds familiar to you. They had a dog named Grim." I placed the picture of Luke on the table and slipped it over to him.

He studied the picture for almost a full minute before saying, "Neither the names nor the face rings a bell. Nor does a dog named Grim. Why do you ask?"

"We were hired to find Luke. It turns out that he's living with Gail at a relative's house. I wrote the final report today. I'm just curious about how someone like him ends up living on the streets. I mean, he had a caring family, a good job and then suddenly everything changed. You must see a lot of that."

"Every homeless person has a story, some more tragic than others." He took a sip of coffee. "So, you were back at the camps and were successful in locating someone. That's not easy."

The waiter came and asked if we'd had a chance to look at the menu.

"May I order for you?" Elliot asked. "Unless you have some food allergies or preferences. Are you Vegan or vegetarian?"

"I'm open to anything you suggest. Please, order for me."

After he placed our order, I drew the conversation back to another of Yuri's suggested topics. "Yes, we've had one success and two failures recently. Not finding Eddie, the missing baby taken from the homeless woman living in her car was particularly disappointing. I can't imagine how she was coping without a place to change diapers or take a nap. I know we talked about it before, but do you come across many babies in the camps? And any in the last month or so?"

"None lately, and very seldom overall. It's not a healthy environment for a baby. I usually try to get mothers with babies to seek better accommodations. That's why I give them a list of shelters and organizations they can go to for help."

"And do most follow your advice?"

He laughed. "Hardly. But one has to try."

"Yuri and I had a long talk about that today—how much help you should feel responsible for giving someone, especially if they are not necessarily open to receiving it."

"I face that question almost daily. There are people in the camps who shun the medical attention they need. If they are in pain or need relief from some discomfort, I often end up treating symptoms instead of underlying causes. On the other hand, many are surprisingly open to being vaccinated against diseases. They understand how quickly something like measles or covid can spread through a population. I'm thankful for that at least."

"They don't want to feel sick, but they don't want to make the effort to deal with root causes, more serious health problems that would require on-going treatment, is that what you're saying?"

"You need to remember, quite a few are beyond being able to help themselves. I do what I can to ease suffering and to practice preventive care when possible."

"Some might consider you a saint," I said.

"I took an oath," he replied smoothly. "The same one all doctors take. I also receive adequate renumeration for what I do in private practice. There's ego fulfillment too. Making a difference even when patients resist treatment, for example. Last year I received an award for my work with the homeless. Peer recognition is always nice."

I found myself liking him more and more. He was self-insightful, dedicated to helping others, but realistic about needing to make a living. If only he were a few inches taller and a bit more physically appealing …

Dinner was a flavor and visual delight. The spices in the dishes were amazing. We shared several meat entrees and sides of lentils, cabbage, and cheese. After a few messy tries, I got pretty good at scooping up food with the Ethiopian equivalent of bread. By the time we reached dessert, I was stuffed. That didn't keep me from accepting the Baklava and Ethiopian coffee.

As we sipped a second cup of coffee, he asked, "So, what's next for you working with the homeless community?"

"Except for possibly having my kids help out at a food kitchen during a holiday or two, there's really nothing. We're officially through with our investigations."

"I heard the police are still looking for a witness to a kidnapping. Is that related to one of the cases you were working on?"

Several little red flags went up, although it was a reasonable question for him to ask. "Maybe that's a reference to the two men who were with Bess when she left the camp, but I don't know for sure. That case ended for us when her body was discovered. We were interviewed by the police, but we didn't have any particularly helpful information, I'm afraid. Once a case is over for us, we move on." Well, that was mostly true. I wasn't about to mention Cole to anyone.

"It's hard not knowing what happens to some people you come in contact with, isn't it?"

"Yes, but there always seems to be someone else in need of our services. I'm afraid moving on is the nature of the beast." The cliché just popped out. Did I believe that "moving on" was an inherent part of our business model, or was that wishful thinking? Both Yuri and I tended to want closure on cases. "I would think it's even more difficult for you, especially when you know they need further medical attention."

"People leave without saying anything even in my paying practice. Moving on is the only option for me, and after a while, new patients crowd out memories of former patients. Still, they remain lodged somewhere in your mental and emotional databank."

I thought that was an interesting way to describe the process. It was true of friends you no longer kept in touch with as well as former clients. It was even true of favorite characters on TV programs once the series ended. Although there were some people who were harder to forget than others.

Throughout dinner, Elliot and I both made an effort to find common interests other than our work with the homeless, but we failed miserably. I'm so focused on my job and children that I don't really do much else these days. He, too, was fixated on work in the here and now; most of the activities he mentioned were things he'd done in the past, like hiking, and bicycling and time spent in third world countries. Not only did it convince me we had no basis for a relationship, but it made me think I needed to consider pursuing some hobbies or activities outside of work and family. Otherwise, I was in danger of becoming the poster child for "all work and no play."

After we finished our meal, I thanked him for a lovely dinner. He said how pleasant it had been but didn't mention getting together again. I didn't expect that we would. Then, because I knew Yuri would ask, I went back over the evening on the drive home, sifting through our conversation to decide whether I'd been on a failed date or the object of a hidden agenda. Upon reflection, it seemed to me it had been neither. The most obvious reason for our pseudo-date was that it had been an excuse for him to have a conversation with an adult who understood a little about his work but wanted nothing from him, while feasting on food he loved. If I was right, I could chalk it up as a one-off and a truly fine meal.

CHAPTER 23
THE DIARY

SATURDAY MORNING Yuri called minutes after I finished breakfast with the kids. Mara had already headed out to spend the day with friends, and Jason was walking No-name. Mom was off having coffee with a woman she'd met in a cooking class. I'd been relishing the peace and quiet and reluctantly answered the phone.

"Nothing to report," I said.

"Like in nothing happened or nothing you are willing to share?"

"Both. I'm just sitting here enjoying my coffee while everyone is off doing their own thing."

"So, was it a date?"

"I'm still not sure what it was. But the food was great."

"Did he ply you with drinks and questions?"

"Neither of us drank any alcohol. He did ask a fair number of questions, but then, so did I, including what you wanted to know about babies in homeless encampments. None recently. Furthermore, he said it was an unsanitary environment, and he has lists of places where young mothers can go for help, but that most ignore his advice."

"That's it?"

"Pretty much. Except that he didn't recognize Luke or remember his dog."

"Too bad. So, what did he ask you?"

"All sorts of things. Nothing intrusive or … but there was one question …" I paused. "It's really nothing."

"Nothing like in …?"

"Just a feeling about one thing he asked that I keep coming back to. He wanted to know what I knew about the police looking for a witness to a kidnapping."

"And you said …?"

"That if he was referring to the two men who were with Bess when she disappeared, that case was over for us."

"We did ask around about people disappearing. He may have heard scuttlebutt about that."

"It was the use of the word witness that bothered me."

"Other than a reference to a witness, was there any indication that he knows about Cole?"

"No. And, he didn't press for more information."

"You have some doubts about the saintly doc?"

"Not really. I mean, it felt like a first date of sorts. We kept trying to find things in common to talk about. Since we failed to establish any shared interests, it wasn't surprising that our conversation kept coming back to our experiences with the homeless encampments. If he had an agenda, I can't tell you what it was. I do, however, sense that he knows more about what goes on in the camps than he lets on. If that's true, why would he hold anything back?"

"Maybe he's being protective. Officials don't have a good track record for helping the homeless. It could be that he just wanted to reassure himself that we aren't going to rock the boat in any way."

"You're probably right."

"What did he say about his research?"

"Not much. He said that there are lots of anxious and depressed people in the camps. Not surprising. He also said they are more open to preventive care, like vaccinations, than being treated for root cause illnesses. Again, not surprising given the fact that real treatment is probably cost-prohibitive and might require hospitalization. I doubt any of them have insurance."

"Depending on how long they've been homeless, the entire medical world could seem overwhelming, especially with no family support."

"I hadn't thought of it that way. You're right. Going to an emergency room is one thing; actually dealing with the medical world to get treatment requires jumping through a lot of hoops."

"By the way, I looked up some articles the saintly doc has written." He shrugged. "When I put on my 'suspicious hat,' I can't help but wonder if he's doing more than interviewing his camp patients about their anxieties and depression. Something just doesn't track for me, and I'm not sure why."

"Like what?"

"Maybe he's trying experimental drugs on them. That kind of thing has happened before with vulnerable and accessible groups."

"I can't picture him doing anything illegal. He seems to care about the people he treats."

"Sacrificing a few for the good of the many?"

"What he's doing doesn't have to be sinister—he could be experimenting with legal drugs."

"That's possible. But whatever kind of research and experimenting he's doing, I bet he is tracking results, successes, and failures. That's what researchers do."

"Wait a minute—you're not thinking what I think you're thinking."

"Don't worry. I'm not going to involve you."

"Because I have kids."

"I was hoping that maybe Gary would help. If you asked him."

"Just so I'm clear about what I'm thinking you're thinking—you want Gary to help you break into Elliot's office so you can look for notes on his research."

"Well, he certainly wouldn't admit he was doing something illegal if we simply asked, would he? Taking a look for ourselves would be one way to find out, don't you think?"

"You can't seriously believe he's in some way connected with homeless people disappearing, can you?"

"Maybe some experiments fail. I don't know, but my gut says we need to see what we can find. What do you say?"

"It's risky. It probably doesn't have anything to do with any of the issues we've stumbled across. But … he does seem obsessive and a bit secretive." I paused. "Okay, count me in."

"No, just Gary and me."

"Sorry, it's non-negotiable."

"Well, we could probably use a look-out."

I thought of Mara and Jason … and Mom. "I might be willing to do that." With Gary involved, I had confidence they would come up with a plan that worked. And as the driver, I could serve a function while not leaving any fingerprints behind or screwing up the job. B&E wasn't one of my core strengths.

"Okay, then let's call him."

"Before I do, explain to me one more time exactly why we are doing this?"

"There are a lot of shady things going on in the camps. You think the doctor knows more than he's saying. And, he admitted to using the homeless in his research."

"I'm still not sure that justifies breaking into his office."

"Doesn't it depend on what we find? We can't connect any dots if we don't know what dots we're trying to connect."

I knew that Yuri hadn't trusted the doctor from the beginning. He would undoubtedly proceed with the plan whether I approved or not. So, I called Gary, and he answered right away. Before I could explain the reason for my call, however, he said: "Cole just gave me something we need to take a look at—Bess's diary."

"She kept a diary? And he's had it all this time?"

"She gave it to him for safekeeping and told him not to read it. Being the honorable kid he is, he didn't. Until I told him about her death, he didn't think it was important."

"You told him."

"Last night. He said he wasn't surprised—it was what he'd feared."

"Have you looked at the diary?"

"No, I got home late, and by the time I talked with Cole, I was wiped out. Thought I would sit down with it over coffee this morning."

"Well, don't get too comfortable. Unless you think you need to stay with Cole, Yuri and I have a proposition."

After I explained what Yuri wanted to do and why, Gary immediately said he was in. If the doctor was taking advantage of homeless people, he wanted to help expose him. If he wasn't, no one had to know we suspected him of anything. From Gary's point of view, the break-in was a no-brainer.

"I'm pretty sure Cole will tell me it's okay if I leave, but I'll check with him to make sure. Unless you hear otherwise, I'll be there this evening to work on the details."

As I hung up the phone, I heard Jason come back from walking No-name. Before I could say anything, he had already disappeared into his room to play video games.

I really wished he would spend more time outside instead of at his computer. On the other hand, since I felt like climbing into a hole and spacing out, how could I criticize him for escaping into game land? Even No-name seemed to want some down time. He climbed up on the couch and promptly fell asleep. I joined him on the couch to read a cozy in which the protagonist ran an ice cream shop and came up with what I considered odd combinations for ice cream. After falling asleep myself, I woke up somewhat refreshed—and hungry for ice cream.

We didn't have any, so I fixed Jason and me a snack with what we had on hand and went back to my book. By the time Mom and Mara returned, I was ready to face the world again. I also had a hankering for "Peach Basil Bliss Sorbet." I wondered if that was something you could actually buy or existed only in the author's imagination.

We met at Yuri's condo that evening as planned. It's the end unit of five connected, three-story structures, each painted brown with a different accent color for gables, window trim and front doors. Yuri's accent color was bright green, almost chartreuse, making his unit easy to spot. Inside it's a comfortable space with masculine brown leather furniture decorated with brass upholstery tacks, the effect softened by the artwork on the walls. I have always been surprised by how neat he keeps his place given how sloppy he is at the office.

Gary accepted a whiskey neat, and I was given a glass of red wine, a very smooth Malbec. Yuri knows my preferences. Then, we all got down to business.

"Before we start talking about checking out the doc's office, I have some news," Gary said. "About the diary."

"You've read it?"

"Perused parts, but read and re-read the stuff about her sister."

"Elinor?"

"Yeah, the evil twin."

"Evil?"

"Bess was convinced Elinor hated her since they were kids. At one point she mentioned that Elinor didn't like sharing and always wanted to be the center of attention. Apparently, it got even worse when they went away to different colleges. Bess thought the separation would help, but it didn't. It's about then that Bess started taking drugs. According to her diary, she thought that at first, Elinor was pleased; it made her feel superior. Then Elinor began to resent the fact that everyone expected her to help Bess, to 'save' her. Here, read this passage."

He handed me the diary and Yuri leaned over to read the tagged section with me. It was dated three weeks before the two men came for Bess.

> *Elinor came by today. She called me horrible names and said I was a disgrace. She said people blamed her for my problems. As my twin, they feel she has an obligation to take care of me. Then she warned me that she wasn't going to lift a finger to help me, ever again. That she hoped I died so she wouldn't have to continue being embarrassed by me. On and on. It was awful. When she left, she threw some twenty-dollar bills at me and said, "Here, have an overdose on me."*

"You don't think Elinor hired those two men and then murdered her own sister, do you?" I asked, horrified by the thought.

"It makes sense," Yuri said. "If it had been a random hate crime against a homeless woman, I doubt they would have hired someone to kidnap her and then try to hide the body after beating her to death. The same is true if it was about drugs. They could have murdered her in her tent." He looked at Gary for confirmation, and Gary nodded.

"We have to tell Connolly," I said.

"What about Cole?" Yuri said. "We can't tell Connolly where we got this."

"We can say someone else found the diary and gave it to us."

"He'll want to talk with them," Gary said. "I think you are going to have to be truthful. Tell him you won't reveal your source. Say they are afraid and made you promise you wouldn't identify them. And assure him that there is nothing else they can add."

"How did they get it?" Yuri asked, getting into the growing scenario.

"They searched her tent after she went missing. That wouldn't be unusual. And it's another reason they wouldn't want anyone to know how they came across it."

"And they just happened to find it when I already told Connolly that we searched her tent."

"Stranger things have happened."

"What about the fact that Elinor was our client?"

"The operative word is 'was.' And we didn't have this in our possession when we were working for her."

"He's going to push hard for a name," I said.

"Then you will have to be both strong … and charming," Yuri said.

"And lie with a poker face," Gary added.

CHAPTER 24
CALL ME CONOR

"I HATE TO CALL you on a Sunday," I said. I'd been hoping Connolly didn't answer and I could leave a message, but no such luck. "But I have something I need to hand over to you, a piece of evidence in Bess's murder. Her diary." I spit it all out at once before I could change my mind.

"You have her diary?" He sounded shocked.

"Yes. Do you want me to drop it off at your office?" I had to fight to keep my voice matter of fact. I could have been offering to drop off his laundry.

After the briefest of hesitations, he said, "Why don't we meet for coffee?"

We agreed on a time and place. Since Mom had taken the kids out for brunch, the only one I needed to say goodbye to was No-name. When I didn't get his leash, he realized he was being left behind and immediately picked up what was left of his African wild dog and started chewing on it. I really did need to replace it soon, just not today.

The drive didn't take long, and I got to the tiny French cafe ahead of Connolly. I bought us both coffee and a couple of Madeleines, found an empty table in a corner and set the diary on the table in front of the chair across from mine. The stage was set.

"Thanks," he said, glancing at the coffee and cookies before sitting down, his eyes flicking across the diary before staring intently at me, obviously waiting for an explanation.

"In some ways I wish I'd never read any of it. It's depressing, really depressing." I flipped it open to the tagged page. "Read that," I said.

"No, small talk, right down to business?"

"After you read it, you'll understand."

He quickly scanned the page. "That's your client she's talking about, right?"

"Former client. Unfortunately, we didn't suspect a thing when she hired us. Now it's clear that she was using us to cover up the animosity between them and perhaps to keep tabs on the investigation into her sister's disappearance. Yuri and I hope this is enough for you to get a warrant to look at her financial records. See if she withdrew a sizeable amount to pay the two guys who kidnapped her sister. There might even be other clues in here. I haven't read it."

He perused a few more pages before asking the question I'd been dreading. "Where did you get this?"

I had my script memorized but seeing him there across the table with his intense blue eyes and beautifully shaped chin, I hesitated. "I can't tell you who gave it to me."

"Because …?"

"I want to tell you the truth …"

"But …?"

"It will put someone at risk."

"It would be helpful to know the circumstances." He locked eyes with me and asked, "Was it that 13-year-old that you stashed somewhere to keep him safe from the two guys we picked up?"

Connolly already knew too much about the situation with Cole, so I went off-script. "Bess gave it to him for safekeeping. She made him promise he wouldn't read it, and he didn't. That's the kind of kid he is—trustworthy and loyal. We didn't tell him right away that Bess had been murdered. When we did, that's when he gave us the diary. He thought someone should take a look in case there was information in it that was helpful in solving her murder. And, as you've just read, there's enough there to suggest her sister should be considered a suspect."

"I'd still like to talk to him."

"I understand why, but in your professional role, if we turn him over to you for questioning, you will feel that it's your duty to return him to foster care. Believe me, that would be a mistake. He's had some really bad experiences with it, and he would just run away again."

Connolly sat there studying me. "Do you believe there is absolutely nothing more that this young boy could contribute to our investigation?"

"Absolutely."

He chewed on a bite of Madeleine, probably not tasting it. "So … I received this diary from an anonymous source."

"Anyone from the camp could have found it and turned it over to you anonymously."

He washed down the Madeleine with a sip of coffee. "That's plausible."

"Can I tell you something off the record?"

"If it doesn't involve anything illegal."

"Something can be illegal if it's not 'sanctioned by official rules.' That's a bit vague."

Connolly laughed. "If you're reading definitions of what's legal and what's illegal, you must be walking a fine line."

"Sometimes rules can be rigid and actually work against their intended purpose."

"I trust that you are trying to do what's right for your client."

"Speaking hypothetically, if I came across someone like the boy I mentioned, I would leave him in a safe place while working on a long-term solution."

"DSHS does a good job 95 percent of the time. I could—hypothetically—refer someone to an individual they could trust."

"Could you hold that thought for now?"

He took a deep breath before saying "Yes." Then, "On a different note, have I told you that I have a son?"

"No. I didn't even know your first name until the other day."

He laughed. "My full name is Cormac Conor Connolly. I usually introduce myself to strangers as Cormac Connolly. At work everyone calls me Connolly. My friends call me Conor."

"So, what do I call you?" I hoped I didn't sound coquettish. That wasn't my intent.

"Detective Connolly," he said with a smile. "Or perhaps under the circumstances, 'Conor' will do."

"Well, Conor, about your son. How old, and what's his name?"

"Liam Cormac Connolly. 'Cormac' was my grandfather's name. He's seventeen."

"Yuri thought your first name might be Liam."

He raised his eyebrows in question.

"I admit it, we've talked about you. In so many ways Yuri and I feel like we know you, but only professionally."

"Well, here's another fact. I'm divorced. It's been three years. Three rather tough years sharing parenting responsibilities. My work schedule makes me a bit undesirable as a father."

"I hope I didn't take you away from your son today."

"No, he's spending the day with his mother and her fiancé."

"In some ways, maybe it was easier for me with my husband dying like he did." Conor raised his eyebrows in question again. "Oh, did that sound cold?"

"No, perhaps a bit cynical. But, I don't know much about you beyond having met your gutsy mother and your two irrepressible kids."

"I'll have to think about those descriptors."

"And your crazy dog that you refuse to name. He bite anyone lately?"

"That really was a one-off. He's a good dog, if a bit irritating at times."

Conor flashed another smile before saying, "I hope we can continue this conversation sometime soon. Like over dinner?"

"I would like that." My heart did a little pitter-pat.

"But first, I have to get on with my investigation." He picked up the diary. "This will help. And for now, I'll say that someone from the encampment turned it in and leave it at that. But my offer to help with DSHS stands."

"Thank you."

He stood to leave. "I assume you are no longer investigating Bess's death."

"No, all of our cases related to the homeless are closed. After finding Bess, we tracked down another homeless man we'd been hired to find—he was alive, fortunately. And we have been forced to give up looking for a missing baby. Not finding the baby makes me feel awful, but we ran out of leads."

"A missing baby? Recently? I don't remember hearing anything about that."

It hadn't occurred to me that no one had reported Eddie's disappearance. I assumed that, as usual with missing persons cases, we were a last resort.

"The mother lives in her car and has a bad drug habit," I said. "She didn't even realize her baby was gone at first. The father doesn't want to be involved, but he did hire us to find the boy. We assumed one or both of them reported him missing."

"You'd better verify that. If no one else has reported the baby missing, then you should."

That seemed so obvious when he said it that I couldn't believe we hadn't already done so. Looking back, it was likely that Broderick Kendall hired us in lieu of going to the police, so he could avoid having his wife find out. And Siana might also have avoided an official inquiry, but for different reasons. "I'll do that right away."

Then Connolly gave me still another smile, a wide, warm one. "I'll give you a call," he said. "Two calls—one to let you know what we learn about the 'evil twin,' and another to make arrangements to get together."

I involuntarily found myself smiling back at him. "That sounds good." I wouldn't hear the end of it from Yuri, but I had a feeling it might be worth the teasing.

He stood there for another few seconds before saying, "Take care, Cameron." Then he left. I finished off my coffee and ate the rest of my cookie before calling Yuri.

"The deed is done."

"Is that code for 'things went well'?"

"You might say that."

"Oh, oh, do I detect a slight whiff of romance in the air?"

"All I can say is that I know his full name and his son's name."

"Oh, he has a son."

"Yes … and that's all I'm saying for now."

CHAPTER 25
THE BREAK-IN

Yuri had some things to do to prepare for our break-in, and I didn't think it was necessary for him to be with me when I asked Siana if she had reported Eddie missing. I wasn't sure what state I would find her in—assuming I could find her—but I was hoping she was coherent enough to realize that if she hadn't done it already, as a mother, she had both a moral and a legal obligation to report her son missing. It crossed my mind that if Eddie turned up—either dead or alive—and she hadn't reported his disappearance, the police might conclude she was in some way involved. It was undoubtedly in her best interest to turn in a report, even if she wasn't that invested in locating him.

My best guess was that she'd be back living in her car, and I was counting on it being parked in or near the same place where we found it before. But it wasn't. I drove up one street and down the next, covering all of the nearby territory, but was unable to find it.

While waiting for a coffee at a drive-thru window at a corner stand, I called Broderick Kendall and got his voicemail. I said I had a quick question and asked him to call me back. So far, my simple task wasn't turning out to be at all simple. If I didn't get one of the two parents to report their son missing, then I would have to do it myself.

When the barista handed me my coffee, I squeezed a little too hard and some dark liquid slipped out and ran down the sides of the cup. I cursed the coffee gods before securing the lid, wiping up the excess, and driving off. After several sips of my double expresso, I was sufficiently fueled to continue my search for Siana's car. I wanted to think that she had moved on for a good reason, like for getting help with her addiction or maybe to return to her hometown, but my gut said she had simply gone some place in search of drugs. Eventually, I had to call it a day.

Mara was helping me make spaghetti for an early dinner when Gary called to bring me up to speed on the plan. I left her stirring the sauce and went into the other room to talk. Gary said that he had driven by Walsh's home and office building several times late Saturday evening and early morning. "Walsh worked late; didn't go home until midnight," he said. "I checked out the building after he left, looking for cameras, security alarms and types of locks. Then I had Yuri do some camera reconnaissance in the daylight before we mapped it all out. Unless we've missed something, I can easily take out the critical ones."

"How about security?"

"They obviously aren't too concerned; they have a basic system. I can bypass it temporarily, and no one will be the wiser."

"What's my job?"

"As we agreed, you're our driver and our lookout. We'll need you to keep an eye out and warn us if someone comes. Be prepared to whisk us away when the deed is done."

"What if a police car shows up?"

"If you see one coming, drive away. Nice and slow. Just let us know as quickly as possible. If necessary, we can leave on foot. I've scouted the area and have a couple of getaway routes in mind."

"Will you have a weapon?" I was almost afraid to ask.

"I always carry a legal handgun, but I don't plan on shooting anyone." I could almost hear him grin. "This is a simple break-in, not an undercover op."

"There are probably street cameras too."

"There always are these days. As well as the official ones, everyone seems to have a private camera or two. Yuri and I will stay out of sight in the car on the way there. After we're done, we plan on leaving everything the way we found it, so no one should know there's been a break-in. If they don't know, they won't go looking at camera footage."

"You can do that? Put everything back the way you found it?"

"Yes."

"But what if they get a picture of me driving your rental car? Or you getting out of it?"

Gary grinned. "You'll be wearing a wig and a cap that I have for you. You can ditch them afterwards. Yuri and I will try not to pose for any pictures. And … the rental car isn't in my name."

Of course it wasn't.

"Yuri will pick you up in the alley behind your house so you can leave your car out front. Just in case anyone in the neighborhood is asked about it, but that shouldn't happen."

"Got it."

"Now tell me how it went with Connolly."

"Relatively smoothly. He's okay with not having a name for the person who took the diary. And, he will follow up on the relationship between Elinor and her sister and track any money trails that may exist."

"Good. Then we're making progress. All systems 'go.' See you at Yuri's around 11:00. You might take a nap before then."

"You forget, I have a family."

"Speaking of families, did Connolly tell you he was divorced?"

"Yes, why?"

"Just curious."

"He is, isn't he?"

"Yeah. That's part of his profile."

"You checked him out?"

"I like to know who I'm dealing with."

"And did he pass your test?"

"Yeah, he did. You have my permission to have a fling with him. Or even to get serious."

"Your 'permission'?"

"You need to have a little fun, Cameron."

I didn't know how to respond. "Well, thanks for the advice." I knew I shouldn't resent both the fact that he had looked Connolly up and that he was telling me to have fun, but it made me feel like a stick-in-the-mud, which I probably was in many ways.

After dinner I told Mom I was going on a stakeout later with Yuri. She knew I did that occasionally and only asked about timing, not about where I would be or who we were watching. I said I would be there for breakfast Monday morning, hoping that was true. Things could always go sideways.

When I arrived at Yuri's, Gary gave me a blond, shoulder-length wig and a baseball cap with an "OL REIGN" logo. I had no idea what that referred to, not that I was going to admit it.

Yuri laughed. He can sometimes read my mind. "It's a professional women's soccer team based here."

"Attending sporting events can be fun," Gary said. "Maybe Connolly is a fan." Gary and Yuri exchanged a knowing look.

I didn't respond but put on the wig and the cap and instantly felt like a different person—like someone who would wear a wig and a cap.

Next, Gary instructed us on how to use our earpieces. "They have a range of a mile and can be heard through walls."

"Thanks, Q," Yuri said.

"And don't lose them."

"Pricey?" I asked.

"And worth every penny when you need them."

Yuri went outside, and I went upstairs. "Come in, James Bond," I said.

"007 here. Is this Moneypenny?"

Gary broke in. "Maybe she's a 'Bond girl.'"

"They never gained womanhood status, did they?"

"Some were more than eye candy though," Gary said.

"More than, yes, but always eye candy," Yuri chimed in.

After the communications test, Gary went over the plan one more time. I got the impression that Yuri wanted to play a bigger role, but he knew Gary was more experienced than he at this kind of thing and didn't push it. Maybe he hoped to surreptitiously learn a few tricks of the trade.

Gary had two small packs with the tools they would need. "There are some duplicates in this one," he said as he handed one of the packs to Yuri. "And a few things I don't think we'll need, but it's nice to have them, just in case. One last thing—" He looked at Yuri, then me, then back to Yuri, like a lawyer about to make a closing argument. "If for any reason we have to make a break for it, I'll say 'homeward bound,' and you both know what to do, right?"

"Homeward bound?" Yuri said.

"You prefer 'flamingo'? Or, 'Graceland'?"

"I get it;" I said. "The code needs to be something that we won't mistake for conversation, right?"

"Oh." Yuri sounded embarrassed.

"So, if I say 'homeward bound,' you know what to do."

"I've memorized the getaway route," Yuri said.

"And I will drive slowly away."

"Okay, let's go see if the saintly Dr. Walsh has gone home for the evening."

We didn't drive past his house to check whether he was there or not. Instead, I drove to a nearby strip mall and parked on a side street while Gary went on foot to see if his car was in the driveway. Saturday night he hadn't put it in the garage, but that was a contingency Gary was prepared to investigate if necessary. But it wasn't. The car was right where we were hoping it would be.

"All clear," he said as he got in the back seat. Let's do it."

Gary and Yuri crouched down out of sight while I drove to a narrow alley used for deliveries and garbage pick-up for the row of buildings where Walsh's office was located. "After we get out, drive to the end of the alley and wait a few minutes before pulling around front. Then park where I suggested and stay alert." Gary was starting to sound like someone in charge of an op, but I wasn't complaining. I was thankful for his specific instructions. "If we see anything that doesn't feel right, I'll let you know."

As instructed, I waited a few minutes before driving around the block and parked across the street with a view of the front of the building and the alley. That way I was poised to drive around back when they were ready to leave or away from the action if they were hotfooting it out of there.

There were quite a few cars parked on either side of the street, but the only person I saw was a janitor silhouetted on the third floor in the newer glass-sided structure next to Walsh's older building. Walsh's building had only a handful of lights on and no one moving around inside that I could see. The exterior walls surrounding its large windows provided a modicum of privacy to occupants and prevented people on the street from viewing everything that went on inside. Some of the windows were covered with blinds. It made me wonder where the owners of all the cars were. I started worrying about cleaners and security guards. Surely Gary would have considered the possibility of night-shift employees.

The best-case scenario was that they would find the information we were looking for without getting caught in the process and have plenty of time to return things to their original state. How they reconnected disabled alarms and "unpicked" locks was above my pay grade. My biggest fear was what happened if they were forced to leave in a hurry and it became obvious there had been a break-in. Was there a chance Elliot would name Yuri and me as possible suspects? I was too nervous to let my mind go there.

"We're in the building," Yuri said in my ear. It seemed like forever until he added, "We're in the office." We'd agreed to keep communication to a minimum, but I'd asked if they would at least give me periodic updates.

Sitting out there, waiting in the dark—literally and figuratively, was one of the more painful things I'd done in a while. The minutes ticked by so slowly that if I hadn't had a second hand on my watch, I would have thought it had stopped. It was barely ten minutes later when I was sorely tempted to ask how things were going, but I managed to convince myself everything was okay—otherwise I would have been given the code to leave. No mention of "homeward bound" meant that things were going as planned.

Then I saw someone enter the lobby from the back of the building. He was wearing a uniform and pushing a cleaning cart toward the elevator.

"Janitor at 1st floor elevator," I said, my tone deliberately flat and unemotional, although inside I was panicking. I got out the binoculars Gary had left with me and tried to see the elevator floor indicator, but the angle was wrong. When the janitor disappeared inside, I found myself holding my breath.

"Got it." Yuri's voice in my ear was reassuring, although my senses remained on high alert.

Waiting for a report as to what was happening was torture. I kept expecting to hear a hasty "homeward bound" warning me to take off and pictured the two of them racing out the back entrance while sirens pierced the nighttime silence. What if I was stopped while slowly driving away and they noticed I was wearing a wig or asked to see my ID? My cover if caught was that I was a PI doing surveillance for a case I preferred not to comment on. Gary had assured me that there was no way they could connect me to a break-in, unless the entire operation went belly-up.

It was almost forty minutes later—thirty-nine minutes and twelve seconds to be exact—that Yuri said, "We're on our way." I took a deep breath. That was my cue to start the car and head to our rendezvous spot. Between the time they'd gone in and now, only a handful of cars had driven by. I'd written down their license plate numbers, more out of boredom than anything at first, but after the janitor went into the building, more out of fear. Fear of what I wasn't sure. None of the cars appeared to have more than a single person in them, a driver focused on the road ahead. No one had so much as glanced my way as they passed. All indications from the outside were that nothing was amiss, but I knew things could change at any minute.

Even though I'd been anxiously awaiting their return, I was startled when two men appeared out of the shadows, got in and immediately dropped down out of sight. "Remember, drive around the block and take the main street back, like you aren't trying to be secretive."

"Got it."

When no one said anything about the job, the relief I'd felt when they called to let me know they were ready to leave turned into anxiety. What didn't they want to tell me? I didn't want to be pushy if for some reason they weren't ready to talk about something that happened, but their silence pressed in on me until I thought I would burst with curiosity. "So, how did it go? Did you find anything?"

The two men started laughing. "I win," Yuri said.

"He said it would take you less than a minute to ask, and it took exactly 44 seconds."

"That isn't funny." They had just committed a criminal act that could have ended badly, and they were joking around—making fun of me. "How could I not ask when I sat out there for almost an hour worrying about whether the building would suddenly be surrounded by a swat team?"

"Well, there are two pieces of good news then. First, no swat team. Second, we found his little notebook that he takes with him on trips to the various encampments. We also found some 'results' summaries. Good news for us, perhaps not such good news for him."

"All in his safe," Yuri added, sounding impressed. "You ever want a safe cracked, this is your man."

"It wasn't anything special," Gary said. "This guy thinks no one is onto him."

"And you took pictures of everything?"

"Between the two of us, that went pretty fast," Yuri said.

"What about the janitor?" I asked.

"He started on the floor above us," Yuri said. "Given the position of Walsh's office, Gary figured we had enough time. We did."

"Is there a calculation per room for cleaning?"

"Ideally, you should check that out in advance. This building wasn't very security conscious, so it wasn't as critical. What I didn't know was whether they would have someone come in on the weekends, and if so, whether they would start on the ground floor or on the top floor. Either way, being in the middle was an advantage for a short job."

He talked about it like it was all in a day's—or night's—work. No big deal.

"And as planned, I reactivated the alarm system and turned the cameras back on when we left. Unless someone checks the time stamps, it's doubtful anyone will know there was a coverage gap. Your tax dollars at work," he added.

"What do you mean?

"Where do you think I learned how to do all this?"

"I've assumed you were an independent, ah, contractor," I said.

"I am. But I got my training from the government, and I still mainly work for them. There are a lot of things they can't do in-house. Don't repeat any of this. If you do, I'll be forced to turn you in for this little heist that I had absolutely nothing to do with."

"Very funny," was the only clever thing I could think of to say.

When we got back to Yuri's without being stopped, I finally started breathing normally. I've bent the rules upon occasion, sometimes at a pretty sharp angle, even operating in a distinctly gray area, but I wasn't cut out for such blatantly illegal activities. My kids need their mother, and I don't look that good in orange.

Yuri printed what they had copied, and we spread everything out on his dining room table. We each took a section and started reading and highlighting important items. None of the "participants" was identified by name. Instead, he used some kind of code to refer to individuals and locations. We decided it didn't matter at this point, but I'd been hoping to see if there were any references to Bess or Siana. Maybe I could figure out something later by looking at entries for dates around the time Bess was taken or when baby Eddie went missing. Not that I thought the doc was linked to Bess's death or Eddie's abduction, but I was curious about whether either woman was involved in what was looking more and more like illegal research.

"I think I'm getting the gist of most of these entries," Yuri said. "It's too bad none of this can be legally used in court."

"Maybe if they get a warrant and find his original records—"

"Yeah," said Gary. "It definitely looks like the sainted doctor is doing research on unsuspecting subjects. His notes clearly show that he is administering a variety of different drugs and tracking their effectiveness, adjusting their composition and amounts based on what he finds. It would be hard to prove what he's been doing is illegal without names and more information. Maybe blood tests on some of the subjects would do it."

"Based on some of his shorthand comments, it also looks like some of his patients don't make it," Yuri said. "If I'm reading correctly between the lines."

"They may not have been all that healthy to begin with," I said. "I mean, I'm not condoning what he's doing, but from these records, it looks like he's trying to find treatment for some very common medical problems, including addiction."

"There's such a thing as legitimate clinical trials," Yuri said. "Where participants volunteer or get paid to participate. This smacks of quackery and malpractice to me. Although I see what you mean. Undoubtedly, it takes forever to get permission for this kind of research; there are probably a ton of legal hoops to jump through given the nature of what he seems to be doing. Still, if he makes a breakthrough, then what? He can't admit how he figured anything out."

"It might speed up the whole process for him though, from application to approval. I mean, if you know what the pitfalls are in advance, that has to make things easier, doesn't it? Especially if it helps you avoid negative side effects or deaths. Even one death would probably require delays and lots of re-testing."

"There's a reference here to some animal testing," Gary said. "Maybe he has that already in progress. Legally, I mean."

"And maybe he got impatient. Couldn't wait to find out if lab rats and the homeless respond similarly." Yuri obviously wasn't convinced that what the doctor was doing was in any way justifiable.

After the initial look at the information, Yuri made a pot of coffee, and we went back over the highlights and discussed next steps. "We obviously have to expose what he's doing," he said.

"I wonder what happened to the people who died?" I asked.

Gary and Yuri both turned to me. "Seriously?" Yuri said.

"I mean, he can't be burying them in the woods or tossing them overboard from a boat … can he?"

"He's a doctor," Yuri said. "And he visits the encampments on a regular basis. He just needs to be the one to identify cause of death and make sure there is nothing to set off red flags to friends or relatives about their passing." He turned toward Gary. "Am I right?"

"That's what I would do. After all, it doesn't look like too many of his subjects actually died. Assuming we're reading these codes correctly. There don't seem to be any listed as cured either, unless there's something in his coding that we're missing. Given more time to analyze these results, we might discover he's making progress, at least with some things. In a way, it's a shame to call this to a halt."

"We can't let him get away with this," Yuri said firmly.

"So, what do we do?" I asked.

"Think Connolly would suspect you two if we anonymously sent significant pieces of this to an investigative reporter?" Gary asked.

Yuri and I looked at each other. "We haven't talked much about the good doctor with Connolly, have we?" Yuri said.

"No, but the timing is a bit coincidental."

"Could you tell him a convincing lie if necessary?" Gary asked, looking at me.

"Given what's at stake, yes, I believe I could."

"Maybe there's some medical board we should be reporting him to," Yuri said.

"Too slow. And, they would want more evidence."

"It all depends on what our goal is, doesn't it?" Gary said. "If we want to stop him immediately, we need to get at least a few facts about what he's doing out there quickly. But if we want the State to press criminal charges, that will take longer."

"Once you start pulling one thread it will eventually unravel the whole ball of wax," Yuri said.

"Balls of wax don't unravel, you unwrap them," I said.

"Hey, a mixed metaphor, but I get it," Gary said. "He votes for whatever is fastest."

"Me too. He needs to be stopped," I said. "Still, I can't help but feel some regret. He's done a lot of good with his volunteer work at the encampments, and I suspect the same is true for his time spent in other countries. Even with this research, his goal is to ease suffering and help people."

"You're not suggesting we give him a free pass, are you?" Gary asked.

"No, I agree that he has no moral or legal right to experiment on people without their permission. I just wish he wasn't misusing his talents like this."

"Once we expose what he's doing, it's up to the medical board and the courts to decide his ultimate fate," Yuri said.

"The press then?" Gary looked from me to Yuri.

Yuri waved his hand at the pile of papers. "I believe I can put this together in a provocative package to attract the right reporter."

"Know one?" I asked. Yuri knew a lot of journalists, mostly attractive females, but that didn't mean one of them was the right choice.

"Not off the top of my head; I need to think about it, maybe ask around."

"Your usual sources?" I said, teasing him in part for tricking me earlier.

"I have male sources too."

Gary laughed. "I sense some history here."

"How about the councilwoman?" I asked. "She has a personal interest and lots of connections."

"She would definitely suspect it came from us."

"She'll probably figure it out anyway, no matter who breaks the story."

"But I don't think she will out us. I see her as being on our side."

"You mean the side of truth and right."

"Something like that."

Gary was smiling at our exchange. "You two sound a bit like you're reading from a whistleblower movie script." He added, "I'm not defending what he's doing, but I do understand his motivation. Given all of the time he spends at the encampments, I can see how he rationalizes it. In some ways, he's giving them the only chance at a normal life that they will ever get. The problem, of course, is that he's making their decisions for them, and some die without ever knowing they were at risk."

CHAPTER 26
CONFRONTATION

MONDAY MORNING, I parked in my usual spot near one of the mall's side doors that opened into a narrow corridor lined with tiny specialty shops: herbal medicine, felt hats, stickers and stamps, unpainted ceramics, that sort of thing. There were always parking spaces there when I arrived, and it was closer to the office than going in through one of the main entrances. I pulled in next to a blue Prius. There were several other cars nearby, but I didn't see anyone around.

I got out and walked to the other side of my car to get my purse and briefcase. When I opened the door and started to reach in, I sensed rather than heard someone behind me. Whirling about, I found myself just inches away from Elinor. "You startled me," I said, feeling both startled and somewhat frightened.

"Get back in your car," she said, sounding like Betty Davis in a classic horror movie, crazed and terrifying.

"We can go inside if you want to talk," I said, trying to hide my distress and sound reasonable.

"Don't make this hard, just get in the passenger seat, and I'll go around to the other side. This won't take long."

What wouldn't take long? Was she going to shoot me? What if I got in and locked the door? I could call Yuri. But he wasn't faster than a speeding bullet, so that probably wasn't a good idea.

"Elinor, I don't know what's going on, but you're making me uncomfortable."

"Are you getting in the car? I've asked you nicely ..."

I sensed an ultimatum in the unfinished part of the sentence. I wanted to scream that I was a single mom and my kids depended on me for their livelihood. Maybe I should grab my briefcase and hit her with it, then make a run for the mall. Why did I always arrive early? Another half hour and there would be lots of people milling about.

"I'd rather not," I said as firmly as I could manage. Once inside the car, my options were limited. Where were all the seniors who jogged around the mall before the shops opened?

She took a step back. "I just want to know what you told the police."

"About what?"

She scowled and leaned toward me, her voice harsh and menacing. She really did do a good Bette Davis imitation. "Don't play the fool with me. I know you're the one who found the diary."

"What diary?" I felt like I did a good job of sounding truly puzzled. When your life might depend on your acting ability, you give it all you've got.

She stood there, as still as death, her eyes black holes waiting to decide whether to suck me in. "If you found Bess's diary, why didn't you give it to me?"

"Because we didn't find a diary. If we had, we would have given it to you." I took a quick breath and added, "Did someone find a diary?"

"Didn't you tell me you'd searched her tent?"

"Yes, quite thoroughly, actually. If there had been a diary, I'm sure I would have found it. Unless … unless she didn't keep it in her tent."

"Where else would she have kept it?" Elinor's eyes had become narrow slits of doubt.

"I don't know. Maybe she had a hiding place for when she left to go to the grocery or out to buy drugs, whatever."

Elinor took a step back. "The police haven't talked to you about the diary?"

"Why would they?"

"Don't you have a cop friend?"

Connolly wouldn't like being called my "cop friend," and I couldn't remember telling her about him anyway. "Elinor, we do try to work with the police when they request it, but they don't consider us partners in any way. We only learn things on a 'need to know' basis, and once our involvement in a case is over, we move on. If you have questions about a diary the police have that you think belonged to Bess, I'd be happy to call Detective Connolly on your behalf."

She still looked dubious, but she was no longer ordering me to get back in my car. That was progress.

Suddenly, Yuri pulled into the space next to mine, parking slightly askew, but I was so glad to see him, I wouldn't have cared if he'd bashed the side of my car in. Well, maybe a little.

"Cameron, Elinor," he said as he got out of the car. "Am I late for a meeting?"

Elinor took a few more steps back.

"Elinor had some questions for me. It seems the police found a diary they think belongs to Bess."

"Really? Anything interesting in it?" Yuri sounded so relaxed and genuine that for a moment even I believed him.

Elinor stared at him a moment, then said, "Just the ramblings of a junkie." She turned to me: "It was nice running into you, Cameron."

"Yes, nice to see you, Elinor," I manage to say without sounding too relieved.

"Take care, Elinor," Yuri called after her. Then we headed toward the entrance to the mall. "What was that about?"

"She wanted to know why we gave the diary to the police."

"She knows that we gave it to the police? How is that possible?"

"It isn't, but a damn good guess. She referred to Connolly as my 'cop friend.'"

"Did we mention him to her?"

"I don't remember, but it's possible."

"Well, it's obvious that Connolly either questioned her or is about to."

"I think I'll park someplace else tomorrow."

The rest of the week was filled with anxious anticipation of worst-case scenarios. Fear that Elinor would return and force me at gunpoint to go with her somewhere, hopefully not to a school yard. Concern that Connolly would come by with photos of me in my blond wig and cap and ask me what I was doing in disguise driving a rental car around the block twice near a building where a break-in occurred, and dread that Dr. Walsh would somehow find out what we had done. I kept seeing him in a lab coat with a syringe in his hand, laughing maniacally.

Fortunately, Elinor did not reappear, there was no call or knock on the door from a member of the police force, and I didn't run into or hear from Elliot. Furthermore, there wasn't a whisper in the news about any downtown break-ins. By Thursday, I started to relax.

On the way to work, I picked up a local paper and saw the headline front page center: "Doctor Using Homeless for Experimental Treatments." I had known it was coming. Yuri had found a reporter who was thrilled to get the notebook and promised to keep him as her source a secret. The article showed a picture of Elliot taken in one of the encampments. He was giving an older man a shot. It didn't say when the picture had been taken or whether the man knew what kind of shot he was being given. It could have been for Covid or the flu. Basically, the picture was misleading, but it was a real eye-catcher in conjunction with the headline.

The story contained excerpts from the doctor's notes and commented on some of the articles he had published in medical journals. At one point they referred to "much needed research," but pointed out there were legal avenues for pursuing it. The reporter said that Dr. Walsh had no comment when asked about the facts in the story.

By noon, he had made the local news on TV. I saw him being confronted by a TV team with cameras, a pushy blond reporter thrusting a microphone at him while demanding to know why he was running illegal experiments on members of the homeless population. He looked deflated and a bit confused by what was happening. I felt sorry for him and a tad sorry for the role I'd played in his downfall. Maybe I would take him cookies and books if he ended up in jail. Or if he went to prison in another state, I could mail cookies and books to him.

My guilt and retribution dissipated somewhat when his offenses were outlined in detail in the morning's newspaper. He had clearly violated the rights of the individuals he had treated. Thinking of the homeless people we had met during our investigations, my sympathy for Dr. Walsh ebbed quickly. They were people down on their luck, but the majority would have been perfectly capable of deciding for themselves whether to participate in a legitimate clinical trial. Given his popularity among the homeless, the doctor could most likely have recruited volunteers if he had set up a legal process. It was his bad, not mine.

The most problematic part of the local news coverage from my point of view was the reference to the anonymous source who had given the reporter the hand-written records that opened the door to the investigation. Although we were fairly certain the reporter would not reveal her source, it was probably clear to anyone who gave it any thought at all that copies of the notes had not been obtained legally. It was highly unlikely that the doctor had left any records lying around for anyone to find.

Connolly called within hours of the television coverage: "We need to talk" was his opening line.

"About what?" I thought I managed just the right neutral and oblivious tone.

"This is serious, Cameron."

"What is?" I'd assured Gary I could lie to Connolly, but hearing his voice at the other end of the call made me realize just how difficult it was going to be. I was glad this wasn't a face-to-face conversation. I might have succumbed to his blue-eyed interrogation.

"If that's the way you want to play it, we'll leave this discussion for later, but don't think I'm not going to investigate this 'anonymous source' referred to in the press."

After he hung up, I thought about his response. Of course he was angry. He would have immediately suspected that the reporter was hiding her source for a reason. One likely reason was that the information had been obtained illegally. And, if I were Connolly, I would have considered Yuri and me as possible sources. It was even more likely that he would suspect Gary's involvement. For everyone's sake, I was somehow going to control any and all urges to confess. Connolly might like me, but he would definitely not condone or forgive what we had done.

When I arrived home that evening, I heard Mom in my kitchen talking to someone. A woman. The voice sounded familiar.

CHAPTER 27
SURPRISE VISIT

"CAMERON, IN HERE," Mom called. She never yelled from one room to the next; she considered it impolite.

"Be right there. I have to change shoes," I yelled back. I always wear comfortable shoes—it's one of P.W.'s "be prepared" rules. Mom knew I never changed shoes when I got home, unless I took them off altogether.

I rushed to check on the kids. If I was right, and the voice I'd heard was Elinor's, I needed to know where the kids were. Hopefully, they were not in the kitchen with Mom and Elinor.

Mara was on the phone. I motioned for her to pause and whispered to stay in her room and lock the door until I came for her. She didn't panic, but I could tell she got the message. "And go tell your brother to do the same, okay?" She nodded and told the person on the other end of the line that she would call her back. Before she could ask anything, I punched in Yuri's number and signaled her to go.

"Cameron, what's up? Didn't I just say goodbye to you?"

"I'm pretty sure Elinor's here," I said. "In my kitchen, talking with Mom."

"Be right there," he said.

At the last minute I slipped off my shoes, remembering that I'd said I was changing them. Then, I joined Mom and Elinor, feigning surprise to see Elinor having a cup of tea with my mother. Mom asked if I wanted some, and I said that I did. Elinor sat there watching the exchange, smiling as though we were all old friends.

"I didn't know you were coming by," I said.

"I thought I would pop in and surprise you."

You did achieve that, I shouted in my head, struggling to remain calm. Mom handed me a cuppa as I joined them at the table. "We were talking about the challenges of juggling work and family," Mom said.

"Yes," Elinor agreed. "Being a single mom with two children must be challenging."

"It is." I took a sip of tea. Had that been an implicit threat? "It's been helpful having my mother here though." I took another sip. "This needs some sugar," I said, standing up. I never take sugar in my tea, so when Mom didn't comment, I knew for sure that she knew that I got her message. Hopefully, she would also have guessed that I had checked on the kids and called for backup. Although I wasn't sure what had made her leery of Elinor in the first place. Instinct? Something Elinor had said? Or simply the fact that a former client had dropped in unannounced.

"Sit down, Cameron, I'll get it for you. Sorry I didn't ask, Elinor, do you take anything in your tea?"

"I'm fine, thanks."

How about a pinch of arsenic, I said to myself. I wasn't sure if making small talk was smarter than getting to the point. On the other hand, polite conversation put off any potential showdown, giving Yuri time to get there. If Elinor still thought it possible that I wasn't the one who had discovered her sister's diary, I'd have no reason to suspect her of anything, and therefore, I wouldn't have any reason to find her visit disturbing. Unusual, yes. Disturbing, no. "You must have a reason for dropping by," I said to Elinor as neutrally as I could manage.

"Oh, I mainly wanted to give you an update on what's been happening."

"About the diary?" Wasn't that what I would ask if I knew nothing about it? I prayed I was right.

"Yes, the police wanted verification that it was Bess's handwriting. Apparently, there were no names mentioned anywhere. Some initials, but no way to identify who they referred to. So, I took them some letters she'd written to me, and it turns out, it wasn't hers."

"Is that good news or bad news?"

My mother's cell phone rang. It was on the counter. She went over, glanced at it and said, "Sorry, I have to take this" and quickly disappeared.

"Your mother is nice. I've enjoyed chatting with her."

I was tempted to mention her pink Glock but didn't. "You were telling me about the diary," I said instead.

"In some ways I'm disappointed that I won't find out what Bess was thinking and feeling since I last saw her, but in a way, I'm relieved. It felt a bit like a voice from the grave. Unsettling."

"Best to move on," I agreed.

"That's what I think. Better for everyone."

Again, it sounded like an implicit warning. "I agree. Although that's one of the things I don't like about my job, having to move on without closure. But at this point, it's something I accept." Hint, hint.

"Well," Elinor said. "I just wanted to update you so you could put thoughts of the diary aside. Now I'd better get going."

"It was nice of you to drop by with the information." If that's all you wanted, you could have called, I thought. Unless you were here to judge my reaction to the information. If so, hopefully I passed the test.

"Next time I hope to meet your children." Her lips smiled, but her eyes didn't.

Were we really having two conversations at once? I couldn't tell for sure, and I certainly wasn't going to admit that I was even remotely considering the possibility. "You know teenagers, they never want to be around a parent or a parent's guests." That was probably a somewhat strange thing to say under the circumstances, but I didn't know what Mom had said about whether the kids were home or not.

At the front door, Elinor wished me a pleasant evening and departed, like she had been an invited guest who really did come over simply to update me on a trivial matter and have a cuppa. I closed the door and locked it. Mom immediately appeared at the top of the stairs. "Did she leave?"

"Yes, it's okay to come down." I half expected to see her standing there with her Glock in her hand.

Mara, Jason and No-name also came out of their rooms and wanted to know what was going on. Well, No-name didn't actually ask, but he picked up on the fact that everyone was anxious about something and added his voice to the mele.

"Everyone calm down," I said. "I'll explain, but I have to call Yuri first."

"I already talked with him," Mom said. "I expect he'll arrive any minute."

"Well, I'd better let him know she's gone so he can quit worrying."

He picked up on the third ring. I could hear an engine in the background. "I'm following her," he said.

"What?"

"You mother said things were under control and that Elinor was leaving just as I was arriving, so I decided to see where she goes. It may be a stupid move, but when I saw her get in her car, I thought, why not?"

"Thanks for responding so quicky. Let me know if you find anything interesting, okay? Or, you can come back here and have dinner. We owe you for being there for us."

"I'll see where she goes and get back to you."

I was glad when he hung up; driving while not being on the phone was challenging enough for him.

The kids and Mom were waiting for me in the kitchen, anxiously awaiting an explanation.

"I wish I could tell you what that was all about," I said. "But I'm not sure that I know. We suspect she either murdered her sister or hired it done, but it isn't our job to prove that; it's up to the police. Maybe she thinks she told us something incriminating or is worried we know something that could help convict her."

"But you don't?"

"No. Once we found her sister's body, our part was done."

"But what about the diary she mentioned?" Mom asked.

"It looked like a good lead, but sounds like it wasn't after all." I hated lying to my family even more than lying to Connolly. But I didn't think it was a good idea for them to know about the diary and Cole's connection to it. Not until the police arrested Elinor. As long as she was free, she was a danger to all of us. The less they knew, the more innocent they could sound if she approached them. I was going to do everything in my power to make sure that didn't happen.

"There's something off about her," Mom said. "I couldn't quite put my finger on it though. Just the fact that she came by unannounced was strange."

"Very."

"That's why I warned you."

"How did she warn you?" Jason asked.

"She did some things she normally doesn't do, like yelling at me from the kitchen and offering to get me sugar for my tea. Subtle but clearly unusual."

"That was smart, Grandma." Jason looked impressed.

"What makes you think she killed her sister?" Mara asked.

"Well, we can't prove it, but there's some evidence that suggests she hated her sister. That asking us to find her was a ruse."

"That's sick," Mara said. "I mean, my kid brother is a pest, but I don't hate him." She rolled her eyes at Jason.

"If you really hate someone," Mom said, "why not just stay away from them? That's what I don't get."

"Elinor claims that having a drug addict sister reflected badly on her, and she was tired of bailing her out."

"I can understand that," Mara said. "But murdering her? That seems a bit extreme."

"Well, hopefully the police find sufficient evidence to prove she did it, or the whole mess simply fades way," Mom said. "I don't relish more visits from her."

Yuri didn't call until dinner was almost ready to serve. "You're going to miss dinner," I said before he had a chance to speak. "But we can warm up a plate for you."

"You won't believe where she is."

"Where?"

"The airport. She had a bag in her car."

"She's running away." I shouldn't have been surprised, but I was.

"That's my impression. I called Connolly and told him. He asked me to stay on her until someone from the department can get here. They apparently aren't prepared to arrest her yet, but he said they are getting close. They can't stop her from leaving, but they can ask where she's going and how to get in touch if they have further questions."

"Sounds pretty weak to me."

"We'll at least know where she's headed."

"But we won't know if she's going to stay there. Any flight could be an interim stop. She's a cagey woman. And a scary one, I might add."

"If she's determined to skip out, that could be good for us and for Cole."

"I'd rather see her behind bars."

"My first choice too. Well, I'd better get going. She's on the move."

"Don't let her see you," I warned. "And let me know what happens."

Yuri called back fifteen minutes later. "Do you know which countries we don't have extradition agreements with?"

"Oh, oh. Why do you ask?"

"She just got on a flight to Cambodia, and I seem to remember there was some other person about to be indicted for fraud who fled there a few years back."

I was quickly Googling the question. "Well, that looks like an admission of guilt to me."

"That's what I'm thinking. The police haven't shown up yet. They're boarding first class, and it looks like she is about to slip away."

"I've read that Cambodia is a cheap place for Westerners to live, but not terribly safe."

"Probably safer than life in prison."

"The beaches are supposed to be lovely."

"That sounds like a mixed review."

"Better than some of the other non-extradition countries on the list I've found: China, Russia, Cuba, Laos, Indonesia. It's actually quite a long list, although it's a bit unclear about whether some of these countries make exceptions for certain crimes. Personally, I would have considered the Maldives."

"She didn't have a lot of time to plan. Maybe she picked the country based on timing and direct flights."

"And, as I said, she can always go somewhere else after her first stop."

"Oops, gotta go, the police are here."

The next time Yuri called it was to tell me that the police never got a chance to talk to Elinor and that she was on her way to Cambodia. He was going home to have a drink and call it a day. I thanked him again and called Gary to report.

"Next time I'm in Cambodia, I'll look her up," he said.

After a brief hesitation, I asked: “You’re serious, aren’t you?”

“It wouldn’t hurt to make it clear to her that the smart thing to do would be to leave the past in the past. Because if anyone stateside was harmed, I would find her. I can be very convincing.”

I had no doubt about that. “What if she moves on?”

“I’ll find her.”

Somehow, I had no doubt about that either. I wondered how often he went to Cambodia.

CHAPTER 28
CASE CLOSED

FRIDAY MORNING, Yuri and I met with P.W. She was stunning in a black and white dress that looked like something a model would wear in a trendy fashion show. It had an uneven hemline that was about six inches longer on one side and it included a cape-like throw over one shoulder. If any clients came in today, they would definitely be impressed. I wondered if she had plans for after work.

Although I had dressed carefully in anticipation of a debrief about what had been happening and a possible visit from Connolly, I felt frumpy by comparison to my classy boss. You have to be careful who you compare yourself with. There's always someone smarter, better dressed, with more money and a body a Bond girl would envy. At least that's how it always feels to me.

Blake brought us coffee, not the usual office fare, but Starbucks. Was this a debrief celebration for doing at least a few things right? Either that, or a way to console us for failing to apprehend a murderer?

"You two have been busy." P.W.'s understated compliment made me feel a flicker of pride that Yuri quickly extinguished.

"Busy, but not entirely successful," he said.

"Well, all three clients you've had of late paid their bills, that's something."

"Elinor paid for our services before she skipped town?" I was surprised.

"Yes, in full, as did Councilwoman Smythe and Broderick Kendall. The councilwoman seemed pleased that you located her cousin. She said their reconciliation went well and to make sure I thanked you. Kendall, on the other hand—he just wanted to make sure his name remained our little secret."

"We will never know how he would have responded if we'd found his baby," I said. "I would like to think he would have told his wife the truth and adopted Eddie."

"Dream on," Yuri said.

"Nor will we know what happens to Siana. I couldn't find her to see if she ever reported Eddie missing, so I turned in a missing person's report yesterday, although they told me I didn't have standing to do so. I said that I was acting on behalf of Eddie's mother who was homeless. I didn't mention our client's name—I couldn't see how that was helpful."

"Well, you tried," P.W. said.

We were all silent for a moment before Yuri said, "So, from the Penny-wise perspective, we successfully closed out our investigations."

"Yes," P.W. said. "I know that's not how you feel at this point. That's why I wanted to have this conversation." She picked up her unlit Kazbek Papirosi and tapped it gently on her desk. "Let's consider what you managed to accomplish. First, you saved a young boy's life, in several ways, I understand. Second, you identified a murderer and gave the police a good lead. They may not be able to make an arrest, but you never know. Finally, you stopped an unethical doctor from performing experiments on unsuspecting homeless people. I'd say you've managed several impressive achievements in a very short time."

Yuri and I looked at each other for confirmation, even though I wasn't feeling that great about how the last few assignments had turned out.

"Don't dwell on the downside," P.W. continued, sensing our resistance to emphasizing accomplishments over failures.

"But—" I started to say.

"Let's talk it through, then move on, okay?"

Yuri and I nodded.

"What's the thing that bothers you most?" P.W. asked.

"A murderer getting away with it," Yuri said.

"Getting away with the brutal murder of her own twin sister," I added.

"I know you realize that statistically, only half of all murders in the U.S. are solved. You managed to succeed where most don't."

We nodded again. In my mind "solved" was a long way from getting "justice" for the victim.

"And although she isn't in prison, she had to leave her job, her home, and her roots and start anew in a foreign country."

"Which some people might consider an adventure," Yuri said.

"And with fake ID, she might still slip back into the country."

"I know some people in Cambodia. I'll make sure they keep an eye on her."

I wanted to say, you know some people in Cambodia? but that was part of her mysterious past that we didn't question, at least not directly. "And Gary told me he is going to pay her a visit the next time he's in Cambodia," I said.

P.W. smiled. "I would like to be there for that." Then she asked, "So, what else is bothering you?"

"Not finding Eddie. Thoughts of where he might have ended up haunt me."

"I know it doesn't help to try to convince yourself he's in a loving home and will be raised as if he was a blood relative, because doubts always pop up when you try to envision a bright future for someone without anything to back it up. Unfortunately, there are lots of Eddies out there. I console myself by knowing I occasionally do something that makes a positive difference in someone's life. As you have for Cole."

P.W. raised her eyebrows in question. "Anything else?"

"I'm almost embarrassed to admit that I feel sorry for Dr. Walsh," I said. "His heart was in the right place even though his approach was unethical, immoral and illegal."

"To him, the ends justified the means," Yuri said. "And even though I know that's wrong, sometimes that approach seems to benefit more people than following the rules."

"I've struggled with that in the past," P.W. admitted. Her comment made me wonder about the nature of those struggles during her life before Penny-wise. "But in the end, the law is the law."

"That reminds me of the Auden poem, Law Like Love," I said.

"I believe the last line is 'like love we seldom keep.'" P.W. smiled.

"Want to explain?" Yuri asked.

I turned to him and said, "The poem is about the complexity of striving for one perfect standard, but laws are created by flawed humans and there is a constant struggle between objectivity and self-interest. There's more to it, but that's the essence."

"Someone was paying attention in class," P.W. quipped.

"I just hope that his research won't fall through the cracks, illegal or not," I said.

After a slight pause to acknowledge my concern, she asked, "Any loose ends that we should and can follow up on?"

"Quite a few, actually," Yuri said. "I always knew that crime stalked the homeless, but after what we've learned, I'm appalled by what goes on and how ill-equipped we are to deal with all of their issues and problems. I want to find some way I can help."

P.W.'s cigarette tapping increased in speed. "It's hard to know which humanitarian issues to devote time and energy to; there are so many."

"Is that why you keep advising me to remember you can't save everyone?" I asked.

"It's sometimes difficult to accept your limitations. As a responsible member of society, you have to keep trying to make a difference where you can." She put down her cigarette. "And that's what I believe you two have been doing the last few weeks. With considerable success. I'm proud of you."

We left the meeting feeling buoyed by her praise. Still, I hated the lack of closure on so many fronts. I prefer my life tidy. Although realistically, I knew I'd made a bad job choice if that was something I needed from a profession. I would have to learn to reconcile the push and pull of my day-to-day existence with an interesting and sometimes exciting job, because it was clear that I couldn't have the latter without occasionally encroaching on the former.

When we got the invitation from Jenny to spend a day at her farm, my kids were thrilled. The last time they were there they'd had a great time. The same wasn't true of No-name. He'd been intimidated by the farm animals, including an aggressive rooster. He's a city dog at heart. Fortunately, he didn't know what was causing all the excitement, so as we were making plans for our excursion, he pranced around as if he was about to receive a year's supply of dog treats all at once.

My mother and Yuri were also included in the invitation. All of us were looking forward to seeing Cole and hearing about what island life was like for him. I was hoping he was as settled in and as happy as Gary had said so we could all move on—at least for now.

The morning of the event, we crammed ourselves into my car and took off amidst lively chatter and anticipation. No-name was pleased to be included in a family outing, moving from lap to lap, and sticking his head out the window from time to time to enjoy the wind and aromas of the outdoors. He remained energetic and excited as a kid the night before Christmas … until we reached our destination, and he leapt out of the car and suddenly realized where he was. He immediately became glued to my right leg, his head swiveling this way and that, apparently on the lookout for aggressive farm animals.

Bandit, Gary, and Cole were already there and rushed to welcome us to the farm. As I later discovered, they'd arrived the night before. The rest of the day was filled with activity and merriment. I did occasionally experience a pang or two of envy seeing how much Gary and Jenny enjoyed each other, but I told myself to "get over it." Especially since I felt like Yuri was keeping an eye on me keeping an eye on them.

As for Cole, he talked enthusiastically about his new "family" and thanked Yuri and me for making it happen. It was clear from watching them together that Cole and Gary had bonded. Maybe the arrangement was good for both of them. Although it certainly didn't fit my image of Gary as a loner with a secret life.

I hadn't been sure Mom would enjoy herself, but she seemed to fit right in. Maybe I needed to ask more about her "hippie" days. People do experience different stages in their lives, but the thought of her with long hair, wearing a dashiki and short shorts, and high on something just wasn't the mother I grew up with. She even seemed to enjoy being around Bandit. Although maybe it was simply a question of not having to worry about him shedding in her home.

The only one who didn't have a great time was No-name. Even when inside where he didn't have to confront farm animals, he didn't seem to be a happy camper. He was used to being the only dog child and appeared to be put off by how much fuss everyone made over Bandit. When Bandit tried to be friendly, he pouted a while before finally accepting Bandit's attempts to socialize.

The entire day had a "happy ending" feel, and I was starting to think that this was the closure I'd been waiting for. Yesterday's news coverage had hinted at Dr. Walsh's imminent arrest, so that was another wrap-up, but no word on Eddie. Elinor was probably on one of those lovely beaches Gary had referred to. After today, I promised myself I would put thoughts of Eddie and Elinor on a back burner.

Just before we were about to have dinner, I had a call from Detective Connolly. I stepped outside to take it.

"Have I caught you at a good time?" he asked.

"Actually, I'm with my family at Jenny's, and we're about to sit down to dinner."

"Oh, well, what if I call you back tomorrow?"

"Nothing urgent then?"

"I just wanted to see if we could find a time to have dinner … assuming you would like to have dinner with me." Was that a touch of uncertainty in his voice?

"I would love to have dinner with you," I said truthfully.

"Good. I'll call tomorrow then." I was pleased that he sounded pleased. Maybe he no longer suspected me of having something to do with Dr. Walsh's downfall. Or maybe he did but had decided to let it go.

Mom would also be pleased. I just hoped she didn't get too obsessed with the idea of me getting into a serious relationship with Conor. From my point of view our family arrangement had become quite comfortable. Mom was no longer leaving messages on my refrigerator about the diminishing prospect for marriage as one aged or critical about my single-parenting lifestyle. In addition, we seemed to be coping with the dangerous aspects of my job that occasionally spilled over into my personal life. I was reluctant to risk destroying our domestic bliss for the sake of a few dates with someone she would consider potential marriage material. On the other hand, the idea of spending some time getting to know Conor was very appealing.

When I went back inside, Yuri asked me what Connolly wanted. "Just some follow-up," I said, narrowing my eyes in warning. For once he took the hint and kept his teasing and opinions in check.

Jenny took me aside and looked around to make sure no one was listening. Given the impish grin and secrecy, for a moment I thought she was going to tell me that Gary was moving in with her. But I was way off.

"I've been dying to tell you what Cole asked me," she said. "He wanted to know if he could have one of our Sherlock bear mascots … for Bandit. It was all I could do to keep a straight face."

"For Bandit? But you think—"

"Well, let's put it this way. He told me he wanted to give it to Bandit after they got home. I loved the fact that he referred to the island as home. Then, when he thought I wasn't looking, I saw him wrap the bear in a towel and carefully stow it in his pack. So like a teenage boy, afraid to be seen as too soft or sentimental. You want to place bets on whether he gives Bandit the bear or it ends up on a shelf in the room he shares with his new bro?"

"Maybe in spite of all he's gone through he has a few years left to enjoy being a kid." I found myself smiling along with Jenny. Cole had a home and a future. That was something to celebrate.

After dinner, Gary and I were in the kitchen doing some clean-up. I decided it was a good time to ask him a few questions that had been on my mind. I started with the one I was most curious about. "Do you often have work in Cambodia?"

"Work and or play. It's a beautiful country."

Not exactly the answer I'd been looking for, so I asked a different question. "P.W. mentioned having contacts in Cambodia. You two ever cross paths there?"

Gary had been about to put some dishes away. He set them down and turned to look at me. "Like on the beach? Or in a bar?"

"I know it's a big country, but to be honest, I've wondered if she wasn't in your line of work at some point."

"My line of work?"

"Okay, so I don't really know what you do exactly. But I don't know what she did before Penny-wise either. Two mysterious people, one country—just thought I'd ask."

Gary chuckled. "Maybe you should ask her about time spent in Cambodia." He turned away and continued what he'd been doing, putting dishes away. He seemed to know where they belonged.

"That means you aren't going to tell me anything … but you either have direct knowledge or suspicions."

"No comment."

"I know the government has been trying to improve relations with Cambodia, so there are probably a lot of projects she could have been involved with focusing on education, health, economic assistance, environmental issues—"

"Unexploded ordnance and landmines," Gary added playfully.

"You really aren't going to give me any hints, are you?"

"If she wants to tell you about her past, she will. It's not my call. Sorry."

My big mistake wasn't in asking Gary about Cambodia but in later on sharing our conversation with Yuri. He became convinced that this was the clue he'd been waiting for. This was the clue that would lead him to P.W.'s secret life before Penny-wise.

EPILOGUE

MY DINNER WITH Conor was a bit awkward at first. It was clear that we were both aware of crossing the line from professional to personal, and neither of us seemed to know how to best handle the situation. What continuing to see each other outside of work would look like depended on so many unknowns. I kept thinking about the good working relationship we had and wondering what would happen if our personal relationship either didn't materialize or worse, went sour. How hard would it be to go back to some semblance of how it had been before trying to date?

When I'd been forced to tell Mom about having dinner with Conor, I tried to play down its significance by emphasizing that it was an opportunity to improve our working relationship. Mom nodded as if she understood but had a hard time hiding how pleased she was, not that she made much effort to do so. Mara's response surprised me a bit: "It's about time, Mom." Jason was more specific: "You mean you're going out with a police detective?" I wasn't sure from his tone if that was a plus or a minus. No-name didn't comment, but he checked Conor out carefully when he came to pick me up.

"What have you got there?" Conor had asked, trying to make friends with the family dog. No-name snatched his latest toy away from Conor's extended hand—a North Atlantic Right Whale made out of some very tough rubber—and took off. I wanted to apologize for his manners, but instead I laughed at the look on Conor's face. "Dogs usually like me," he said.

"He's protective about his endangered species toys. I'll explain over dinner."

Once we were settled in at the restaurant, things slowly got more comfortable. We had a quiet table in a corner at a local seafood eatery with a view of the water. By the end of the main course, we'd found several things in common other than work to talk about: an interest in local politics, adventure movies, the British series Task Master, and a dislike of gardening and housework. We also both had teenage children; that produced an instant bond of pride and shared frustrations.

When the evening came to an end and he walked me down the shadowy path to the carriage house, I didn't know what to expect. Mom had promised she wouldn't come out onto her balcony and ask who was there as she had done the last time I'd gone out on a date. That had been my fault for not telling her about the date in advance. This time she knew, but I was apprehensive for other reasons.

As we approached the house, I noted that there was no porch light on. It was supposed to switch on automatically in the evening.

After such a pleasant evening, it seemed inevitable and natural to engage in a goodnight kiss. Although I confess that as our lips touched, thoughts of my comment to

Yuri about "sizzle" took some of the spontaneity out of the moment. What on earth was wrong with me? Conor was a handsome, intelligent man with a pleasant disposition, and I'd fantasized about a romantic conclusion to the evening. Was I afraid to let myself feel again? Had Dan ruined not only my memories of our marriage but dealt a deathblow to my ability to trust someone enough to take a risk? If only my late husband hadn't been so convincing as a paragon of virtue while at the same time suffering from a gambling addition that wiped out all of our money before he died of an unexpected heart attack.

As our lips unlocked, Conor asked, "Was the 'no porch light' your idea?"

"I'd bet money on the kids, but I wish it had been me."

"They want to see you in a relationship?"

"They want me to be happy."

"How about Yuri?"

"The same. Although we don't really talk about it."

"Here's to happiness." He gave me a short but warm kiss, and I felt a little sizzle. Not a heart-stopping electrical shock, but a sizzle nonetheless. Then he added, "I sincerely hope this is the start of a long and happy friendship." He touched my lips with two fingers and left me standing there stung by the word "friendship." I didn't need any more friends. I wanted more sizzle!

Monday morning Yuri brought donuts. "Sweets for the sweet," he said.

"Trite."

"Does that mean you don't want any?" He picked up the box and held it in the air out of my reach.

"I didn't say anything about not liking trite."

"So, the date didn't go well?"

I was stunned. "How did you …"

"Aha, I guessed right."

"You tricked me."

"Well, you lied to me. I didn't think Connolly would call you for follow-up that didn't include me."

"Okay, give me a donut and I'll confess."

"You have first choice. Then I'll pass these around and join you in the small conference room for your full confession and absolution."

By the time he got to the conference room, I was ready for a second donut. He'd brought what remained with him. "You look like a woman who needs all the sugar she can get this morning."

I grabbed a chocolate covered donut and took a big bite.

"No sizzle?" he asked.

"I don't know yet," I said. "He used the word 'friendship' to describe our relationship."

"Ouch. Before or after physical contact?"

"I have a family, remember? A kiss at the door is about it."

"So, before or after?"

"After."

"Sorry."

"So, you agree? It means the relationship will not be a romantic one?"

"Well, maybe it just means taking it slow. That's not so bad. And, look on the bright side—in our profession, having a detective as a friend is a good thing."

"Thanks for cheering me up."

"Well, I do have one thing that might cheer you up."

"And that is?"

Yuri pulled out a blurry copy of a picture from a newspaper. It showed a group of people posing together on a sandy beach in front of a row of round huts on a dock that reached out over the water. He covered the names of the people in the picture with his hand. "See anyone you recognize?"

I leaned closer to the clipping and studied each face in turn. "It's hard to tell. It's not a good photo." But there was one tall, dark-haired women in the back row who looked vaguely familiar. "Where was this taken?"

"Preah Sihanouk in Cambodia. It's an international port with lots of ties to China."

"Noooo."

"The face you keep coming back to looks like a younger version of P.W. to me too." He removed his hand so I could read the names at the bottom of the picture. When I came to "Penelope Watson," I said, "You're convinced that's her?"

"The initials are right. When undercover, keep it simple."

"What's the group?"

"Supposedly a team of medical professionals organizing a new hospital and a couple of clinics."

"I have two issues with what you just said. First—supposedly? How do you know that's not exactly who they were? And second, P.W. isn't a medical professional."

"But she could pose as one, couldn't she?"

"Like a fake TV doctor?" I shook my head. "How did you find this?"

"I picked a ten-year time period that made sense given her age and when she moved here. Then I researched government projects happening over that decade and googled the name Penelope. At one point I thought that might be her name, so it seemed worth a try. I pulled up as many archived project websites as I could find. There were lots of pictures, so I started going through them, and behold—a plausible possibility."

"You're thinking some sort of covert op? Something to do with China and their link to the Cambodians?"

"Well, think about what Gary told you. That makes sense, doesn't it?"

"I also remember him saying that I ought to respect her privacy. Have you told any of this to the others?"

"Not yet. But with their help, we may be able to find out a lot more."

"To what end?"

"To satisfy our curiosity?"

"It wasn't that long ago you were convinced she was a Russian sleeper."

"I'm starting to think I was wrong about that. She cares too much about people. Maybe she had an affair with a Russian as part of some operation."

"Your imagination really has taken a flight into the ether." I was fearful that he was perhaps too close to the truth, a truth that might be better kept secret.

"You have to admit, she sees a lot of gray in terms of what's legal and what you should and shouldn't do to help the good guys."

"So do I, and I'm not a government spy."

"Prove it," Yuri said, laughing.

I rolled my eyes.

"You have a great cover if you are," he went on.

"Well, you may be onto something, but I say we drop this line of inquiry. It could be bad for P.W. and for you. Think of her like the unicorn that doesn't want you to touch its horn. If you don't respect her wishes, you may face some very bad consequences."

"A strange but apt analogy. P.W. as a unicorn. Mysterious and elusive." He considered my advice, then folded up the picture and put it back in his pocket. "You're probably right. I admire P.W. and love my job. I don't want anything to endanger either." He tapped his pocket with two fingers. "Okay, I'll add this to my box of clues and move on." He grinned. "But I'm loving the idea of it."

I hated to admit it, but I did too. The image of P.W. as a magical woman of mystery was appealing. Righting wrongs and saving our democracy from the bad guys. Unfortunately, my view of the fanciful unicorn had become tainted. I now also considered their dark side and the fact that in some stories they were harbingers of death. I sincerely hoped neither P.W. nor Gary had a past littered with dark secrets. But if they did, they were making up for it now. Unicorns can be deadly, but they are also symbols of hope.

ACKNOWLEDGMENTS

HOMELESSNESS in the Seattle area has been a big problem for a number of years. As a consultant, I worked with a consortium of concerned groups and companies on strategic planning to improve ways to provide resources and housing to the homeless. I also created a training program for food bank volunteers. Having an opportunity to learn about the complexities involved rather than simply seeing the tent camps and panhandlers at traffic stops changed my views on what we should be doing both short-term and long-term to balance community preferences with the needs of the homeless. At the time, I was living within walking distance of one of the largest encampments in the area and frequently walked a trail that was also used by those heading for the encampment. Although I could empathize with the complaints of the homeowners in the area, I also understood why the locale was so appealing to the homeless.

Do I have definitive answers for solving the problems associated with homelessness? No. I wish I did. It's a societal conundrum that requires addressing a multitude of issues as well as financial support for solutions.

As Franklin D. Roosevelt said, "The test of our progress is not whether we add more to the abundance of those who have much; it is whether we provide enough for those who have too little."

This is the fifth book in the Discount Detective series. I continue to be grateful to Kristina Makansi, Laura Robinson, and Lisa Miller of Amphorae Publishing Group for making this series possible. With a special "thank you" to Lisa for her editing.

Most of all, I want to thank you for reading *Unicorns Can Be Deadly*. Please take a few minutes to write a short review. Just a sentence or two will do. Ratings and reviews are every author's best friend.

ABOUT THE AUTHOR

IN A WORLD FILLED with uncertainty and too little chocolate, Charlotte Stuart has always anchored herself in writing. As an academic with a Ph.D. in communications, she wrote serious articles on obscure topics. As a commercial fisher in Alaska, she turned to writing humorous articles on boating and fishing. Long days on the ocean fighting seasickness required a little humor. Even as a management consultant, she gave presentations with a playful spin: Stress—Clutter and Cortisol or Leadership—Super Glue, Duct Tape and Velcro. Her current passion is for writing humorous, character-driven mysteries with twisty plots.

Books in her Discount Detective Mysteries have won a number of awards including a Pinnacle Book Achievement Award, a Firebird Award for humor, Global eBook gold, and placed 2nd in Incipere and Pacific Book Award competition and 1st in the Chanticleer International Mystery & Mayhem Series competition. Charlotte lives and writes on Vashon Island in the Pacific Northwest and is the past president of the Puget Sound Sisters in Crime.

OTHER BOOKS IN THE SERIES INCLUDE:

Survival Can Be Deadly
(A Discount Detective Mystery Book 1)
Campaigning Can Be Deadly
(A Discount Detective Mystery Book 2)
Shopping Can Be Deadly
(A Discount Detective Mystery Book 3)
Moonlight Can Be Deadly
(A Discount Detective Mystery Book 4)

You can visit my website at www.charlottestuart.com, or contact me on social media:

X (Twitter):
https://twitter.com/quirkymysteries
Facebook:
https://www.facebook.com/charlotte.stuart.mysterywriter
Goodreads:
https://www.goodreads.com/author/show/19305587.Charlotte_Stuart
Instagram:
https://www.instagram.com/cstuartauthor/
BookBub:
https://www.bookbub.com/authors/charlotte-stuart